Praise for

"I find Jessica Eissfeldt's books sweet and gentle and often wonderfully atmospheric, too. They tell stories I can enjoy and relax with and lose myself in, a special gift during times of stress, whether personal or collective."

—Mary Balogh, *New York Times* bestselling author

"Jessica Eissfeldt's talent for combining compelling characters, unique stories and charming settings guarantees I'll be reading far into the night."

—Karyn Good, romantic suspense author

"Jessica Eissfeldt writes with heart. A reader can get lost between the pages of history and then come back to today with her contemporary stories. Whether you're wanting to escape for a brief time or a long time, these novellas and novels are fun to read. You have so many choices."

—Annette Bower, award-winning author

FOR A LIMITED TIME
GET YOUR FREE SWEET ROMANCE HERE!

Get your free copy of the sweet romance *Beside A Moonlit Shore*. Normally, it's $2.99, but this GIFT is yours FREE when you sign up to hear from author Jessica Eissfeldt.

When you sign up, not only will you get this FREE GIFT, but you'll also receive sneak peaks of Jessica's upcoming stories, have the opportunity to win prizes, get exclusive subscriber-only content...and more!

After her sea captain husband dies, schoolteacher Anna Hampton wonders if she'll find the courage to love again...beside a moonlit shore.

Go here to get started:
www.jessicaeissfeldt.com/yourfreegift

FOR A LIMITED TIME

At last
it's true love

At last
it's true love

A Novel

Book 3 in the Prince Edward Island
Love Letters & Legends Trilogy

JESSICA EISSFELDT

At Last It's True Love: A novel
Jessica Eissfeldt

Print Edition
ISBN: 978-1-989290-31-6

ALSO BY JESSICA EISSFELDT

Sweet Historical Romance:

Sweethearts & Jazz Nights
Dialing Dreams
Shattered Melodies
Fancy Footwork
Unspoken Lyrics
The Sweethearts & Jazz Nights Boxed Set: The
Complete Collection

Love By Moonlight
Beneath A Venetian Moon
Beside A Moonlit Shore
The Love By Moonlight Boxed Set: The Complete
Collection

Sweet Contemporary Romance:

Prince Edward Island Love Letters & Legends
This Time It's Forever
Now It's For Always
At Last It's True Love
The Prince Edward Island Love Letters & Legends
Boxed Set: The Complete Collection

Collections
Love & Lattes: A Sweet Romance Short Story
Collection
Pieces of Me: A Poetry & Lyrics Collection

Chick Lit
Love, Your Fangirl

To Prince Edward Island—
thank you for the inspiration.

Chapter One

ICKY STENDAHL'S EYES drifted to the worn and crumpled envelope with its faded, spidery handwriting and vintage stamp.

A few lines from the antique love letter inside echoed through her mind. *I feel that the only thing keeping me sane is thinking of you. Of us. Of being together again. Of kissing in dimly lit hallways with flickering bulbs, closed canteens, and the sounds of swing music floating in from the street while laughter dances in your eyes...*

She picked up the envelope and ran a fingertip across the surface. Inside, she knew, was an antique love letter written from what had been Nazi Germany. She'd found it last summer when she'd flown out to Prince Edward Island for her friend Maggie's wedding.

The ink on the postmark had smeared badly. But she could just make out the word Berlin and the date: March 8, 1948.

The handwritten New York address on the front had been crossed out and a forwarding address had been neatly typed.

```
Vivian Robinson-Leard
General Delivery
Victoria, Prince Edward Island
Canada
```

She frowned. No return address. Odd for a love letter. Even stranger, the letter's postmark was five years after the letter itself was dated.

Nicky reached into the envelope and was about to pull out the pale blue, tissue-thin sheaf of paper when her phone's alarm buzzed.

She glanced at her watch. Crap. It was ten after. Already late. Maggie didn't like to be kept waiting. She grabbed her purse off the shelf by the door and shrugged into her vintage, plum-colored wool jacket.

Nicky opened her apartment door and rushed out. But as she pulled the door shut behind her, she almost ran into a rail thin balding man.

"Hi Reg," Nicky said, even as her fingers tightened on the doorknob.

"Nicky," he said as he shoved his glasses up on his nose. "Do you know what day it is?"

Nicky chewed the inside of her lip. "Tuesday?"

Reg cleared his throat and crossed his arms across his chest. "That's right."

Nicky said nothing. Maybe he'd forget that it was now October.

But Reg tapped his foot and just looked at her.

"Can I have a few more days? It's only the fifth. I'm still waiting on *Ivory* magazine to send me a payment. They said they'd pay me forty-five days after I submitted, but I still haven't seen the check. I've tried calling and emailing and haven't gotten an answer. But that'll give me what I need to pay you the rent."

Nicky's landlord studied her a minute. She saw sympathy and frustration war on his face.

Nicky held her breath.

He rubbed his jaw and studied the green swirl-patterned hall carpet, then looked back up at her. "All right," he said. "But only because you've never been late on the rent before. I'm giving you fourteen days. By Tuesday the 19th at 9:00 a.m., you'll need to give me the rent money you owe for this month. Otherwise, I'm sorry, but I'll have to give you an eviction notice."

Nicky sighed in relief, then took a breath to speak.

"You're welcome," Reg cut her off. "This is your first warning." He walked away.

"Thank you," Nicky called out, but he'd already disappeared.

She jiggled the doorknob to make sure it was locked, then dashed down the stairs to the subway stop around the corner from her building.

She threaded her way through pedestrians and withheld another sigh. It seemed New York just kept getting more crowded.

With one eye on the busy sidewalk, she got out her phone. Yep, still battery left—it'd been acting up lately and sometimes died. She pulled up her email.

Maybe one of the small magazines or blogs had accepted her pitch? She hoped so.

That was the risk of being a freelancer. But she came by it honestly. Both her parents, now retired, had worked for themselves. They were basically living on Social Security now. No other safety net. Still, she believed the risk was worth it.

She ran down to the platform and darted onto the train car. Out of breath, she squeezed into the last available seat and scanned her inbox. Several new messages.

From: editor@womanslife.com
To: nicky.stendahl@gmail.com
Sent: Oct 5, 7:13 a.m.

Dear Ms. Stendahl,

Thank you for your article pitch about Vivian Robinson. At this time, we are not accepting any new story ideas on women during WWII, as our usual stable of freelancers has filled our needs.

Best wishes,
The editorial team at Woman's Life

Nicky gritted her teeth and opened the second.

From: tina@vintage40sgalblog.com
To: nicky.stendahl@gmail.com
Sent: Oct 4, 5:53 p.m.

Nicky,

Great blog idea about this Vivian woman, but I've already assigned the next few months' guest posts. Sorry about that. Better luck next time!

Tina

Nicky opened the rest of the new messages. All rejections. She propped her chin in her hands and sighed as she fiddled with the ends of her over-long bangs. She needed to trim them.

Now what? She had to pay the rent somehow. She worried her bottom lip between her teeth. But she couldn't just sit here and mope.

She lifted her head. She would keep going. Stay determined. After all, that's how anyone who had gotten anywhere had succeeded.

Yes. She wasn't going to give up. Someone out there had to like her story idea about Vivian enough to run it...

She reached into her purse. Under the World War II spy thriller she'd just finished, she fished out her copy of *Between Silk and Cyanide*, pulled out her bookmark, and started to read.

Twenty minutes later, she squeezed out of the subway car and up onto the busy Manhattan sidewalk near her favorite corner Starbucks. She glanced around for Maggie. No sign of her friend and former boss, a successful jewelry designer.

She chewed on a cuticle as she headed inside.

Nicky saw Maggie wave from a corner

table across the crowded coffee shop. She waved back and made her way over to the tiny bistro table.

"Hey! Sorry I'm late. Got waylaid by my landlord." Nicky shrugged out of her coat and draped it across the back of the chair.

"I only just got here, so no problem. Wow, gorgeous jacket. I just love that deep, rich shade. Really sets off your strawberry-blonde hair."

"Thanks! It's vintage forties. Couldn't resist when I saw it in Charlottetown at Linda's Closet on Queen Street. I'm just gonna grab something. You good?" Nicky asked.

Maggie nodded and held up what looked like a mocha latte.

Nicky returned a few minutes later, chai tea in hand.

"So," Maggie said, "I haven't seen you since—"

"—your wedding on P.E.I.," Nicky finished for her. "I bet things are a bit quieter for you and Zak now that you two have figured out the whole mystery behind the legendary ghost ship of the Northumberland Strait."

Maggie grinned. "Yeah. Zak and I had a great time solving those riddles. Funny to think it all started with that gold dou-bloon…" She took a sip of her latte. "It's good to be back in the city for awhile."

"New York's great." Nicky paused. "I don't mean to complain, but to be honest, I'm getting a bit tired of the wall-to-wall people and all the car fumes."

"Really?"

"Yep. Maybe someday I'll move some-where quieter." Nicky took another sip of her drink.

"Aww, I can understand that. I've missed all the hustle and bustle. But only a little. Prince Edward Island is definitely where my heart is."

"I can tell," Nicky said. "So you got it finished?"

"I did. I told Zak I was coming here to tie up a few loose ends. Including this." She tapped a small white jewelry box on the tabletop. "Wasn't too hard to resize. Here, take a look." She slid the box across the table to Nicky.

Nicky lifted the lid and peered inside.

QUINTEN LEARD RAN a fingertip across the gold lettering of the words *Princess Royal* written on the front of the antique upright piano. Grandma Viv had always said this one was special.

He started to slide the newly polished cover over the piano's keys. But as he did so, the mechanism stuck slightly.

Quinten frowned. Hadn't he oiled everything and double-checked it all? Apparently, when he'd put things back together, something had shaken loose. He reversed the lid's direction and that's when he saw it.

A small, now crumpled piece of paper.

He plucked it from its sticking place between the edge of the keyboard and the outer edge of the cover.

His brow furrowed. The yellowish-brown tinge of the faded paper made him think it had to be antique.

It was blank, though.

He moved to throw it into the waste basket near his workbench when he reflexively flipped over the small square.

He cocked his head. Five letters were written across it.

B I O P W

Hmm. Why did that handwriting look kind of familiar?

"Hey Quinten, where are you?" His

cousin, Elliot MacEwen, called out from the front of the shop.

On impulse, Quinten shoved the small piece of paper into his faded jeans pocket.

He glanced at his Apple watch.

Damn. He was going to be late for that call with the accountant he'd just hired to straighten out the books. The accounts had gotten pretty mixed up last year in the chaos of Grandma Viv's worsening illness and death. If he didn't get going—

"Quinten?" Elliot called again.

"Be there in a sec. I'm just finishing up in the back here," Quinten called as he put his piano tuning tools down on the workbench nearby and headed to the doorway that divided the private work-space from the public storefront of Leard's Piano Tuning & Restoration.

Elliot had one hand in the pocket of his neatly pressed navy blue chinos while he drummed the fingers of his other hand on the counter. The same counter that their grandmother had sat behind for nearly fifty years. And the counter that Quinten himself had worked behind for the last twelve years.

Quinten stepped out into the storefront space.

"Hiya, Quinten!" A four-year-old girl

with blonde curls waved as she leaned against Elliot's leg.

Quinten smiled and crouched down. "Hi there, Rosie. Did you get to go to the chocolate shop today?"

The little girl beamed. "Daddy had chocolate waffles and I got to pick out my favorite jelly beans."

Quinten chuckled. "I'm glad to hear it. My favorite are the yellow ones."

Rose's eyes widened. "Me too."

Quinten straightened back up. "What can I help you with, Elliot?"

"When's my piano going to be finished?"

Quinten resisted the urge to cross his arms. "Well, today's Tuesday... It's nearly done. I just have a couple more adjustments to make."

Quinten held back a sigh of impatience. Elliot had always been a bit pushy. Ever since their grade school days. As a kid, he'd always tried to curry favor with Grandma Viv. She'd never played favorites between the two cousins—Quinten's father and Elliot's mother were brother and sister—but somehow Elliot felt Quinten had gotten the better deal. He'd held a grudge because of it.

In the years since Rose's birth and with

Grandma Viv's worsening health, Elliot's sense of entitlement had intensified. Probably because the man felt he needed to secure a bit of family legacy from Grandma Viv.

Elliot glanced around the room. "I see you haven't changed the place much in the three months since she died."

"I like to preserve the character atmosphere for the customers."

Elliot shrugged. "I'm not a fan of quaint and down home. Sleek, modern and trendy is the look I've achieved for all the businesses I own. And acquiring more of those businesses, er, assets is always beneficial. Though I prefer to spend my time golfing, not behind a desk." He fiddled with some change in his pocket. "I'm glad to hear you're making progress on the piano—but I guess when it's something you love, you don't procrastinate much, do you? It needs to be done for my wife's birthday next Tuesday. We're settling into our new house at Dunrovin Estates across the way this week so the piano movers can come by and pick it up next Monday."

Quinten shifted his weight and shoved his hands into his own pockets. Even though this Princess Royal, made in

Amherst, Nova Scotia, had been a copy of the one that the princesses had at Buckingham Palace in the 1930s, it hadn't been easy to refurbish.

But that's what his cousin had wanted done. And Quinten was the only piano tuner and restorationist on this side of Prince Edward Island. He'd loved the challenge. Had a chance to put all his music certifications to work.

So he'd done it for Elliot—at half his usual rate. Quinten tightened his jaw. He couldn't really afford to do that, but family was family. He couldn't let them down, even if it meant the business that his grandmother had started might take a hit.

"It tuned up really well," Quinten said.

Elliot smacked a palm against the wooden countertop. "That's great."

Quinten started to head toward the computer. "I'll just print out your invoice now."

Elliot took Rose by the hand and glanced at his watch. "Don't want to keep the boys at the country club waiting, so we'll settle up soon, yeah?" He headed for the door.

Before Quinten could reply, his phone started to buzz. He fished it out of his back jeans pocket. But before he could answer it, Elliot turned in the doorway of the shop. "Don't forgot our lawyer meeting on Thursday."

Quinten nodded. He wasn't planning on forgetting to attend that particular meeting about the family business.

After Grandma Viv's death, no will had been found. So, due to succession law, the company was, for the moment, equally divided between the two cousins, since they were the only surviving kin. But Elliot had been making noise about getting full control of the company ever since Grandma Viv's death. Quinten's phone buzzed again.

Elliot paused in the doorway. "Don't worry, Quinten, after Thursday's meeting, you'll be able to give me advice on how to run the place once things are sorted out and I take over." His Rolex flashed in the sunlight as he waved and stepped out onto Victoria's main street.

If only there'd been a will...

Quinten took a couple of deep, calming breaths before he pressed the answer button on his phone.

"Quinten. Hope you're good. Listen, you've been doing a great job running the shop since Vivian passed," his accountant said.

"Thanks. I appreciate that."

"So I've begun to straighten things out. From what I've gone through so far, the earnings at the beginning of last year aren't great. We'll get through the rest of the paperwork backlog by the end of this month. But Quinten—"

Quinten's stomach knotted at the grim tone of his accountant's voice.

"—as you know," the other man sighed, "your grandmother's health went downhill over the past five years, especially the last year of her life. I'd be prepared for the possibility that the profits the rest of that year would be dangerously low, if not negative numbers. Now, I have more calculations to do to determine the extent of things, but obviously, if things are in the red, it would have serious repercussions for the business."

Quinten winced. "So you're saying I could be going bankrupt?"

"I can't say that for sure as I haven't done all the math, but things aren't looking good."

Quinten swallowed. He should probably mention this to Elliot. Then again, it would give the man more reason to push for full control. Better to not say anything til things are more clearly sorted out.

"A three-generation business like this doesn't come around every day. But," the accountant sighed again, "they don't always survive the third generation, either."

Quinten's fingers tightened on his phone. His family had lived here for two hundred years. In fact, his branch of the Leards had been one of the first families to settle in Victoria when it was founded in 1819.

"I'm not going to let that happen. I was born and raised here. I'm practically the last piano tuner on the whole island. I'm going to make this work. I won't just let this piece of island history—my family's heritage—slip away without a trace."

"IT'S ALL ORIGINAL to the Middle Ages, you know," Maggie said. "Where did you say you got it?"

Nicky reached into the box and carefully held up the ring. The piece of moss-green amber was set in delicately wrought sterling silver with a pattern of vines and leaves that held the large stone in place.

"At a flea market in Nobo. For five bucks." Nicky said. "I just liked it because I

16

thought it looked neat. And it would go well with my fall wardrobe. The old woman I bought it from said she'd gotten it in an auction lot of assorted World War II stuff from an estate sale up the coast."

"Well, you got really lucky. From the research I did online," Maggie said, "that specific design of leaves and vines is actually Polish."

"Wow," Nicky said. She slipped the ring on her finger. "It fits perfectly now, too."

"I was really careful to make sure the integrity of the piece was maintained. Could be worth a lot. Maybe you could do some research on it. Find out a bit more about it."

Nicky slipped the ring off her finger and put it back into the box. "Good idea. Now I'm kind of nervous to wear it."

"I wouldn't worry about that. 'Cause if you don't wear it, it's just going to sit there in that box collecting dust. Which would be a shame."

"You're right," Nicky said and tucked the box into her purse.

"So how's your venture as a freelancer?" Maggie said as she took a sip of her coffee.

"I'm not sure that things are really

17

going all that well."

"Oh?"

"Well, you know that after I, uh, stopped working for you, I thought I'd have loads of time to pursue my writing. And I did. But—not to complain here—it took more time and effort than I thought to build up a contact list of editors and magazines who wanted my work, who liked my voice. But I did it."

"Yeah, I remember," Maggie said. "Especially when you got that really great little piece in the *Historical Woman* magazine."

"I know. That was amazing. Especially because they're like the *National Geographic* of women's history." Nicky laughed. "They even paid me a dollar a word."

"Hey," Maggie snapped her fingers. "Have you thought of pitching to them again?"

Nicky straightened. "I didn't even think of that! In fact, that'd be the perfect place to pitch the letter..."

"Letter?"

"Yeah," Nicky said and reached into her jacket pocket. She carefully pulled out the yellowed envelope. "I know, I know. I shouldn't be carrying around an antique letter in my pocket but somehow, it doesn't feel right not to have it together with this jacket."

Nicky eased the tissue-thin sheaf of paper out from the envelope and handed it to Maggie.

June 7, 1943

My dearest Viv,

Funny how war makes you remember the best times and the worst times of your life simultaneously. I can't imagine what would've happened if the canteen had been open that night and we hadn't met. Would we have never climbed up to the roof, a little drunk, with the summer wind in our hair and shared secrets in our eyes?

And I would've never taken up the cause, never learned what it meant to truly fight for what is right, what is good, in this world, in the face of such darkness. Sometimes I think that you are all that's left of that world I once knew. But if Churchill has anything to do with it, that world will exist when this damn war is over.

They've been quite inquisitive. But I shall withstand as I've been trained to do. They cannot know what is in my heart, and they cannot destroy my soul, though undoubtedly, they shall try. Even if my background puts me at greater risk, I am grateful. Grateful that I have a cause to fight for.

I feel that the only thing keeping me sane is thinking of you. Of us. Of being together again. Of kissing in dimly lit hallways with flickering bulbs, closed canteens, and the sounds of swing music floating in from the street while laughter dances in your eyes.

I will think of those times and remember. Remember the future. Remember the past. Remember us.

My heart is with you always,
—A

"Ooo," Maggie handed the page back to Nicky. "A love letter."

"Yep." Nicky grinned.

Maggie's eyes widened. "So where did you find it?"

"In a hidden inside pocket of this jacket, actually. Along with a tiny little key. I think Viv probably owned the coat and kept the letter there."

"Interesting theory." Maggie leaned forward. "Who do you think was writing to her?"

"I'm not sure. I've only just started

doing a bit of research about this Viv woman."

"So you're gonna write an article about her?"

"At first it was idle curiosity, you know? I wanted to find out who this was. But then as I started to do the research, I realized she could be a great candidate for a history piece. Lots of people know about the female codebreakers who worked at Bletchley Park during WWII. Next to no one's heard about other women like Viv who worked with codes, ciphers, and decryption but didn't actually break enemy ones."

"Very cool. I can see why you'd want to write about that." Maggie sipped her drink.

"Right now, I'm just waiting to hear back about an additional records request I made on her work during the war. I'm hoping the record's been declassified." She fiddled with a few strands of her hair. "But I can't figure out who this 'A' is."

"Sounds pretty mysteriously romantic to me." Maggie grinned.

"And tragic," Nicky said. "I think he was captured or something..." Goosebumps rose on her arms and she rubbed them.

"Who knows, it might lead you in a

direction you never even imagined."

Nicky laughed. "Maybe so. If I can find the right angle to pitch my idea about Vivian to the *Historical Woman* magazine... They always have such interesting articles about pioneering women doing things in history."

"Like what?" Maggie took a sip of her coffee.

"Well, they did a piece last year on Hedy Lamarr."

"She was that forties actress, right?"

"Yep," Nicky said, "but she was also a brilliant scientist responsible for essentially creating Wi-Fi." Nicky waved her hand. "In simplistic terms."

"Yeah, you should definitely aim high. Pitch it to that magazine."

"You think?" Nicky said.

"Definitely." Her phone buzzed and she glanced at it. "I should run. I'm Skyping Zak for our lunch date together."

"He can't stay away from you a moment longer than he has to, can he?" Nicky teased.

Maggie laughed, a sparkle in her eye. "Nope. Well," she said, and stood up, "it's been great to see you. Come up to the island and visit us sometime. We'd love to show you our new beach cottage. It's up near North Cape."

"That'd be fabulous, Maggie." Nicky hugged the other woman.

"Anytime," Maggie said, and waved goodbye, a spring in her step.

Nicky waved back. But as she turned to gather up her empty coffee cup and her jacket, her smile faded.

If only she could be as lucky in love as Maggie had been with Zak.

Nicky withheld a sigh and pushed down a dart of irritation at herself for feeling the tiniest bit jealous of Maggie's happiness.

Sure, she'd loved the men she'd been with. Enjoyed their company. Enjoyed their attention. The time spent together. But there'd always been something missing... She'd never been in love. Not truly. Nicky pursed her lips.

She was wasting her time feeling like this. She had no man in her life at the moment and there was no point moping about it.

She was better off single anyway. All relationships did was stir up your issues. Then you became so busy fending off the demons in your head you couldn't enjoy the man you were with.

That's what'd happened between her

and Ben. He'd been her first long-term relationship. They were together nearly four years. That first year had been great. He was kind, attentive—everything she could've hoped for, and more...

She'd been a romantic, once. Read lots of romance novels. Believed them all.

But when she'd asked him to move in with her the second year they'd been dating, things changed.

He was never a big sharer. At first, she'd liked that. The whole strong and silent thing. But then it had begun to frustrate her. She'd felt shut out, which made her worry about why he wasn't opening up to her more.

So she'd thought moving in together would fix things, and he'd come to live at her apartment; but it didn't last long. There were still a few of his things around she hadn't gotten a chance to give away. Like his second-best microscope set. The man had loved science. She loved writing, history, and being creative...

She'd felt, in a way, that he'd never really taken the time to know who she was. He was more by-the-book; she was more willing to take chances.

He was a nice guy. But he just lost interest in her. Lost interest in wanting to be in the relationship.

And he lied to her about it by staying in the relationship when he really wanted to leave. Always covered up his feelings. Never told her what he'd really been thinking...

She'd tried to ask him about it. Shared her own vulnerabilities in the hopes he'd reciprocate. But that's when he'd really started to pull away—which caused her to hold back; she'd never let him in fully because she'd never felt secure in his love for her. She'd been afraid to open her heart that much, the way that she really wanted to.

Sure, he'd agreed to couples counseling. But that only created more tension than good between them. The relationship had ended not long after that.

It seemed as if everything had been off-kilter between them. The timing. The feelings.

Nicky brushed away a single tear and pushed open the door of Starbucks and headed to the subway stop.

The October air lifted the white silk scarf she'd tied loosely around her neck. She was thirty-one. She wasn't going to drown in all her old issues, her old fears, her old loves.

It was time for something new.

MAGGIE WAS RIGHT, Nicky realized, as she headed up the steps to her apartment and unlocked the door. She needed to aim higher. What would it hurt? What was that quote about shooting for the moon...?

Nicky rolled her eyes at herself as she sat down at her computer desk. It wasn't like she had delusions of grandeur.

But the more she discovered about Vivian, the more she realized that Vivian's story, well, it deserved to be told. Readers would be interested.

She just wanted Vivian's voice to be heard. Okay, maybe not just that. She wasn't that altruistic. She wanted her own voice to be heard too.

Nicky drummed her fingernails on the desktop, then straightened up. Yes. Why not?

From: nicky.stendahl@gmail.com
To: susanolmsted@historicalwoman.com

Hi Susan,

You might remember last year that I wrote a 100-word article for you about Amelia Earhart when you did that aviation edition.

Well, I have an idea for another piece that I think might fit well with your publication.

I came across a letter from the 1940s—World War II, actually—that was written to a woman whom I've begun to do a little research on.

She apparently worked for an organization called the SOE—the Special Operations Executive, headquartered on Baker Street in London—that sent secret agents to occupied Europe. But she wasn't a spy. At least, not from the declassified records I've started to look through. She worked in the codes department.

If you'd be interested in publishing the article, I'd expect it to be between 1,500 to 2,500 words, perhaps for your upcoming spring issue on pioneering 20th century women in the math and sciences fields.

Thanks so much!

Regards,
Nicky S.

Nicky hit the send button and grinned. If the editor accepted her pitch, since this publication paid very well, she'd be able to put aside money for future rent.

Hmmm. This magazine had also run one of the photos she'd taken for that Earhart article. Which reminded her...she had to empty her photo card so she'd have enough room on it for this new assignment. She didn't want to splurge on a new, bigger card while her rent debt loomed.

So she logged onto Shutterstock then grabbed her Nikon. She hooked up the USB cable to her laptop to upload the latest batch of shots she'd taken over the past month.

Every extra penny of royalties counted. Like last summer when she'd made enough to buy herself that vintage jacket.

Even if sometimes her pictures had nothing to do with the articles she'd written in the past, she just loved taking photos. And apparently, sometimes people actually wanted to buy them.

She checked her royalties tab. Empty today. Well, maybe tomorrow...

"I'M SORRY, QUINTEN, dear, but Al just sold

our piano. You know what the economy's been like lately. Down the drain, if you ask me, which you didn't. But believe me, if we still had it, I'd ask you to tune it up good for us right away—this afternoon, even."

Quinten could hear the older woman tsk on the other end of the line. He forced away the sinking feeling in the pit of his stomach. "Okay, well, thank you anyway, Mrs. MacPhail."

"Well, now, don't hang up yet. Let me just get my glasses..."

He heard the sound of the phone being put down and papers being rustled.

"Here we are," Mrs. MacPhail said. "Try Mabel. I heard her playing the piano just yesterday evening."

"Thanks a lot, Mrs. MacPhail. I'll give her a try."

"And from what I hear," the older woman chuckled, "her new next-door neighbor is quite pretty. And around your age, too. You and Sarah broke up, didn't you now? Yes," she continued without waiting for Quinten's reply, "last September, I believe. How long had you two been dating?"

He winced. He'd always been a bit shy around women he found attractive. But he'd also spent too much of his twenties getting an education to have had much time for a love life.

First, he earned an undergrad and then a graduate degree in music at UPEI. But by the time he finished his graduate work, he realized he loved to work on pianos more than play them.

For twelve years, he had worked in the shop. He'd started when he decided to work with Grandma Viv part time while he went back to school again for piano tuning and restoration certification and an apprenticeship.

Then he spent his early thirties working in the piano shop full time as Grandma Viv's health started to go downhill. What with taking care of her as well as running the store for the past five years, he hadn't had too much time to be in any sort of relationship.

As a result, at thirty-five, Sarah had been his first, and only—so far—real relationship. It had failed miserably.

As Mrs. MacPhail chatted on about her new neighbor, Quinten's mind drifted back over the past.

Dating. He withheld a sigh. It was easier being single. No complications. No drama. No demands for professions of love that he couldn't quite make.

His and Sarah's last big fight had been about that, in fact. Just because he never said "I love you" to her during their entire relationship, she'd seemed to think he hadn't loved her. Even though he had. She'd accused him of being too guarded, too closed off from his emotions.

But he'd felt love for her. And he thought he had shown his love for her in his actions toward her. But he never said "I love you" outright. And that hadn't been enough for Sarah. Maybe she'd been right about his guardedness?

But Quinten wanted to consider things before he spoke, and take the time to know he truly meant them, before he said them out loud. Granted, "I love you" was a pretty big one...

Because Sarah *had* been right. He'd been afraid to say those three little words. Afraid of what might happen if he said how much she'd affected him... Afraid she'd reject him. Like his father had. He much preferred the privacy of his own thoughts.

He made the mistake of sharing his thoughts too many times with his dad growing up, thinking his dad would accept him instead of judge him. Safer to stay quiet. Easier to just say yes and agree with others' opinions instead of stating his own.

Less risk of being hurt, blamed, or criticized.

Quinten cleared his throat and opened his mouth, but Mrs. MacPhail spoke first.

"Sorry, sorry, dear. Can't help myself these days. Al canceled our Netflix subscription to save on our oil heat bill for this winter, so now the next best thing to Netflix is being a nosy neighbor."

"Appreciate your suggestion, Mrs. MacPhail. Thanks again."

"Good luck, Quinten. If I hear of anyone needing their piano fixed, I'll let you know."

Quinten hung up the phone. Now what? He'd gone through almost his whole list of contacts and everyone had given some version of the same answer...

He rubbed the back of his neck. Maybe it was time to give up his half of the business? Elliot wanted it, after all. He could get a job at Long & McQuade in Charlottetown and—

Quinten shoved his hands into his pockets. No.

He wasn't going to just roll over and play dead. There was still life in this business, there was still hope; and he wasn't going to let Grandma Viv down...

"How you doing, Grandma?" Quinten said softly as he knocked on the door of her room at Whisperwood Villa in Charlottetown. "I brought you something." He held out a crossword puzzle book and a bouquet of lupins. He put the flowers in a vase by the nightstand. "Your favorite."

She sat on the neatly made bed, her snow-white hair freshly combed, her hands folded in her lap. A box of photos sat beside her on the bed, the lid askew.

"Thank you."

Quinten fought back a sinking feeling at her blank look.

"Do you have time to look at some pictures, young man?"

Quinten eased into the overstuffed chair across from her bed. "Yes, Grandma."

As she handed him a photo, he couldn't help but notice the way the liver spots on the back of her hand stood out against the golden evening sun that streamed through the sheer organza curtains.

Quinten's brow furrowed as he studied the photo. He'd never seen it before in his life.

But even in the black and white of the picture's depths, he saw the sparkle in his grandmother's eyes as she grinned at the camera, the dimple in her left cheek apparent.

She was standing in a busy train station, suitcase in hand, other people in dark coats only blurs in the background. Her figure, in sharp focus, was outlined in bright morning light. Her Victory roll and lipstick were perfectly in place.

"I was very good at crosswords," she said.

He looked up at her. Her voice conveyed confidence, but her face showed only confusion.

He forced himself to swallow the lump in his throat. He had to be stoic. He couldn't show his emotions. That was something she'd taught him.

Must be her British heritage. Or perhaps a product of her times. Or something. But for whatever reason, he'd learned from her that it was best to have a calm exterior. It made things much easier.

He glanced at her. For a moment, a flicker of recognition lit her expression, but it left as suddenly as it had come.

He looked back down at the photo, sudden moisture in his eyes. He blinked hard and flipped the picture over. Pencilled on the top left-hand corner in her neat handwriting were the words "Last day at the Office."

He frowned and murmured, "Was this when you'd been a file clerk in London before you got married?"

She'd married his grandfather right after the war ended. In fact, she'd come to Prince Edward Island as a war bride when she'd met Colonel Wallace Leard in London in the last days of the war. It had been, from all accounts, a whirlwind romance.

"Quinten." His grandmother's voice brought him sharply back to the present.

She'd stretched out a hand as he started to give back the photograph but she batted it away. A steady look came into her eyes and Quinten felt the hairs on the back of his neck stand up.

Never breaking his gaze, she said in a calm, clear tone, "Remember...Amber. You must. Remember. Amber."

AT TEN O'CLOCK that evening, Nicky wrapped her cashmere robe around herself and sank onto the couch in her living room, a mug of steaming vanilla rooibos tea in her hand.

She inhaled the flowery scent and her shoulders relaxed. It always tasted best when it was as hot as possible. She gently blew on the steaming contents and gingerly took a sip. Perfect.

She'd made some progress today. Sent

out ten more queries. That article was going to get published if she had anything to say about it.

Her mind drifted back to the conversation she'd had in Starbucks with Maggie. She glanced at the coffee table where the small white ring box sat, the ring itself resting on top.

Too tired to get up off the couch properly, she stretched out a hand and managed to snag the ring with the fingertips of her free hand.

But as she started to lean back, the steaming tea sloshed over the rim and hot rooibos spilled onto her hand.

"Ouch!"

She jumped up off the couch. Reflexively, she dropped the mug and the ring; the tea sloshed out when the mug shattered.

She ran to the sink to run cold water and then rub apple cider vinegar over the burn.

She dabbed it dry with a paper towel, then got the broom and dustpan to sweep up the broken mug. After she tossed the shards in the trash, she went to change her robe and pajamas.

She came back out into the living room, carefully poured herself another, somewhat cooler mug, and sat on the other side of the couch.

She took a sip and felt herself relax again. She closed her eyes. But then they snapped open again. The ring.

It had bounced when it hit the hardwood floor and now lay under the edge of the couch. Swinging her feet carefully back down onto the floor, she leaned down to pick up the ring.

But as she did so, she noticed that the stone was now at a strange angle.

It must have shifted and loosened as it fell. Nicky winced. Maggie wouldn't like that, especially given how old it was.

But as she brought it up to her lap to examine the extent of the damage, the stone fell out.

Nicky swore under her breath. Maggie *really* wouldn't like that.

Nicky picked up the stone to try to wedge it back into place but noticed a slender piece of...what was that...wedged between the prongs that held the stone in place?

How had Maggie missed this? Nicky frowned. She'd resized it. But she probably hadn't had to do anything like remove the stone, as she'd said there hadn't been much resizing needed, just a little tweak.

Using her thumb and forefinger, Nicky plucked the item from its resting place.

Paper, she realized.

She examined it and saw only a single tiny black dot on the small piece of paper. The dot was the same size as the period at the end of a sentence, maybe a little bigger.

Nicky frowned and held up the small slip of paper to the light. Why would anyone conceal that under a stone? She turned the paper side to side.

She squinted at the tiny dot again. It couldn't be, could it? She'd been reading one too many spy thrillers.

It looked almost like...

She laughed at herself at the thought—a microdot?

Well, she wasn't going to get any sleep unless she found out.

She got up and rummaged around in her junk drawer until her fingers closed around the hard black plastic of the microscope set Ben had left.

She picked it up, shut the drawer, and returned to the couch.

She held her breath as she examined the microdot on the tiny piece of paper. Several lines of type came into view as she peered through the high-powered lens.

```
The secretary marches
To a tune unplayed
But the pianist's journey
Mirrors a plan well-laid
```

Nicky caught her breath. Was this some sort of...riddle? Now she really had been reading too many spy thrillers.

Or had she?

Chapter Two

QUINTEN SHOOK OFF the memory as he headed into the workshop. There was no one named Amber. Just another one of Grandma Viv's lapses. Like the time she'd insisted on mailing all her valuable jewelry to the Salvation Army. He shoved his hands in his pockets.

Who had Grandma Viv been, really? Maybe in order to find that out, he should go through all her things. He really needed to sort through it thoroughly. It'd been three months already. But somehow, doing that task felt monumental. Overwhelming. It would mean she was really gone. So he'd put it off. He rubbed the back of his neck as his thoughts returned to her life.

Grandma Viv was his dad's mother but she'd always had a side of herself that Quinten had never really known... even though, growing up, Grandma Viv had been more a mother to Quinten than his own. *She'd* left when he was a toddler.

In fact, he'd spent most of his growing-up years with Grandma Viv, since he and his father hadn't had the best relationship. She'd taught him piano; encouraged his music career choices.

But she'd always refused to talk about her time during the war, or much of her past, actually. If he'd tried to ask, she'd pretend she hadn't heard him, or tell him to take the pie out of the oven. She'd believed in him, though, and listened to him. He should've done more for her in the end. Been there with her more often.

He'd done all he could, he reminded himself, what with running the shop with Grandma Viv part time before she'd gotten dementia, and then full time after. He was an only child. Elliot hadn't helped out. Grandpa Wallace had already passed away.

And after Quinten's dad's death five years ago, Quinten began to notice worrying little signs...Grandma Viv would forget a friend's name. Or go to the hair salon even though she'd just had a trim.

At first, he'd been able to look after her. But he couldn't take care of her twenty-four hours a day when her dementia had worsened. She'd needed professionals for that. So he'd put her in one of the best care homes on the island and had regretted every second of it.

But he'd visited her every day and done everything in his power to make her life there as comfortable as possible.

If he was honest with himself, in some ways he'd been trying to heal his relationship with his father through taking care of his grandmother.

Maybe if he'd shown her more love in all the ways that his dad hadn't shown him love growing up, he would've been able to really know his grandmother, and by extension, connect with his father?

But mulling this over wasn't going to get Mabel's piano tuned. He picked up his tool bag and headed to the door. Most of Grandma Viv's things, he mused, were still all packed away, aside from that box he'd let Mabel have.

Quinten walked across his lawn and then headed across the paved main street. It wasn't far to Mabel's house on Nelson Street.

Autumn sunshine backlit the red maples and yellow oaks as their branches swayed in the light sea-scented breeze.

Leaves in shades of crimson, gold, scarlet, and russet carpeted the road.

Some tourists chatted, and Quinten

caught a few words of Japanese. One headed across the street in front of him and took a seat at one of the bistro tables arranged alongside the wrought-iron lampposts in front of the Victoria Playhouse, which was, when originally constructed, the local community hall.

Well, he conceded with a grin, the place *was* pretty cute. A fair number of the heritage homes in the village had been turned into profitable businesses.

He took a right on Howard Street and headed over to Nelson Street.

The scent of seafood chowder and the sound of laughter drifted past him as he walked by the Landmark Oyster House. Its white-shuttered windows were wide open and its flower-filled deck overflowed with happy visitors and even happier locals who traded stories and gossip over glasses of wine and appetizers.

He walked on and waved a hello to the owner as he strode past The Studio Gallery and neared the corner of Nelson and Howard.

The shrieks and giggles of kids playing in the empty green space across the way made him remember the previous summer when that same green space had served as the croquet pitch for Victoria's annual croquet tournament.

He and his teammate Grant had won that year. They'd even had their victory photo taken nearby, next to the rickety old rowboat that served as a gathering spot for bonfires, potlucks, and tournaments.

Quinten headed up the street to a grand old dove-gray Edwardian with a second-floor sunroom. Its wide front porch had a cane-back rocking chair and pots of bright pink geraniums.

A long-haired fluffy gray cat sat on the edge of the porch.

"Hi there, Rainy," he murmured to the cat as he paused to stroke its head. Its rumbling purr vibrated against his fingers.

He continued to the front door.

A woman with short blonde hair, dressed in a rose-pink hoodie and a pair of jeans, answered before he'd even had a chance to knock.

"Quinten!" she said, "Haven't seen you in awhile. And by awhile, I mean since last weekend. How the heck are ya?"

"Doing pretty well, Anna," he said. "How's the food drive going?"

"It's going great. Got lots of donations this week."

"That's good to hear."

"Mom said you might be coming over

to take a look at her piano. She loves that thing. Even though she's nearly ninety-eight, she plays it every day—thinks she's younger than I am. Had it for at least sixty-five years, long before I was even thought of." Anna laughed. "It needs tuned up pretty badly. I'm just about to head over to Crapaud to pick up a few groceries from Harvey's, but you know you don't need an invitation. Hang around as long as you need to get that piano back into shape."

"Thanks, Anna."

"Any time, Quinten. Any time."

She made her way out the door.

Quinten stepped out of his shoes and headed to the old upright in the far corner of the living room.

He ran a hand across its slightly warped surface and smiled. He'd come over here so many times growing up.

Anna was practically an aunt; the Leards and the Hendrickses had known each other for generations. Ever since the village was founded, in fact.

He raised the piano top and got to work.

"You know, your grandma had her first piano lessons on that very one."

Mabel's quiet voice made Quinten jump. Not sure what to say, he didn't reply.

But she continued as if he'd encouraged her. "We were fast friends, your grandma and I. But you already knew that."

Quinten did, but he knew she liked to tell the story, so he just nodded and let her talk as he continued to work.

"Met right after she came to town when the war ended. My, that seems like only yesterday." The old woman chuckled. "None of us islanders quite knew what to think of her at first." She clucked her tongue. "But soon enough, she made her way into the hearts of pretty much everyone in this community. I think it helped that her Wallace was from Victoria here, o' course."

"Mmm-hmmm," Quinten murmured as he made some adjustments.

"Viv was whip-smart, too," she continued. "Not like some of these flighty young girls these days. No siree." She rapped her cane against the polished hardwood.

"Uh-huh." He continued with his adjustments and paused to test a few keys. Almost right.

"You know they had U-boats around the island here during the war. All the way up to North Cape lighthouse."

"Oh?" Quinten paused in his work and glanced over his shoulder at Mabel. He hadn't heard anything about that...

"Yes." Mabel paused and inhaled a long breath. She sat on the vast leather sofa, her neatly pressed, pale green cardigan wrapped around her thin shoulders and her glasses perched on top of her head.

"The CBC would make special broadcasts. Tell fishermen to keep a watch out for them. Turn in those Nazi bastards." Mabel chuckled and adjusted the collar of her cardigan. She leaned forward on her cane and narrowed her eyes as she held Quinten's gaze.

"There were strange doings, though, back in '43. Supposed to have been some sort of prison breakout in New Brunswick. A U-boat was gonna try to sneak the German POWs aboard and skedaddle back to the Third Reich. Some even say that U-boat came with a whole hoard of treasure in tow. Hitler's gold and diamonds."

She drew in a breath. "Heard tell it's still out there, in some old rusting trunk, sunk somewhere at the bottom of the St. Lawrence Seaway. But one thing's sure—your grandma musta known something because she was in love with one of them Nazis."

NICKY YAWNED AND stretched and glanced at the clock. Six o'clock on Wednesday morning. She'd been awake, the yellow cotton of her nightgown tangled around her, for what seemed like hours. Unable to think of anything else but that microdot and its contents.

But she'd better start thinking of something else or she'd never get the rent paid on time.

She heaved herself out of bed and into an almost-too-hot shower—the better to wake up with.

She towelled off and pulled on a pair of faded blue yoga pants and a lime-green halter top. Then she made herself some toast in the toaster oven that doubled as a real oven in her tiny suite. Once, she'd crammed half a chicken into it and roasted it. She'd been so proud of herself.

She slathered raspberry jam onto two pieces of Texas toast and took a big bite.

Then she headed over to her laptop and logged onto her email. One new message was waiting.

From: susanolmsted@historicalwoman.com
To: nicky.stendahl@gmail.com
Sent: Tues, October 5, 7:45 p.m.

Dear Nicky,

I remember you! I think your pitch is great. I think it'll fit really well in our spring issue, as you've suggested.

I'd like it to be 3,000 words. Unfortunately, with the publishing business being what it is now, we can only offer you 50 cents/word. If that's acceptable, please let me know by 5:00 p.m. today. We have a few other story slots that need to get filled as soon as possible, and yours might fall by the wayside if you don't reply today.

To formalize everything and make it official, I've attached a copy of your work-for-hire contract. Just email it back to me with your electronic signature and things will be good to go.

—S

Nicky scrolled through the contract. Always good to know what you're signing.

Huh. That was interesting. The *Histori-*

cal Woman was owned by the same parent company as *Ivory* magazine—the one that was late on its payment to her. Well, the world of magazine publishing was small, and conglomerates were big. So it made sense.

But Nicky's heart sank a little as she reread the email. Work-for-hire contracts meant that you actually didn't own your words. They paid you a flat fee, and you gave away all your rights to the work, forever.

What was worse, if your article, for whatever reason, came under scrutiny, or you got slapped with a libel case, you had to fork over the lawyer fees. For something you didn't even own the rights to anymore.

But Nicky signed the document electronically anyway.

Even if she didn't agree with it, this was the usual type of contract these days for freelancers.

She hit reply and let her now-boss know that her contract was signed and attached.

Hmm. Sometime she should probably shell out some cash for liability insurance. She gnawed the inside of her lower lip for a moment.

It was so expensive, she couldn't really

afford it. Besides, the work-for-hire contracts were totally normal.

Her mind strayed back to the piece of paper she'd found inside the ring. She typed *microdot* into the search bar.

Hmmm.

Nicky's heart beat a little faster as she read the first result. They'd come into use during the Franco-Prussian War and then had been used during World War I and World War II to communicate vital information between clandestine operatives. They were also used during the Cold War and even into the present day.

She shook her head.

She couldn't get carried away and just jump on conjecture and assumptions. She'd learned that much from the journalism certificate she'd earned a few summers ago.

She'd always loved reading and writing.

She remembered how she wrote stories in grade school. It'd been so much fun to interview her classmates.

But then when it came time to pick a college and get a degree, she'd chickened out of applying to journalism schools on the East Coast. Instead, she'd listened to the voice in her head that said business admin close to home was the better way to go.

She'd gone with a generic business admin diploma at a local community college in Michigan not far from her home town and then worked for five years at a law firm in her home state.

It had paid well and had been stable, but she'd hated it. That's where she'd met Ben, actually. They'd dated for such a long time and she'd always hoped he'd ask her to marry him. Settle down together.

But he never had. And she never asked him about that.

And that had been that.

She sighed. She wouldn't make that same mistake again. The next man she fell for, she was *not* going to spend her time guessing what he was thinking or bending over backwards figuring out what he meant. If he couldn't tell her outright, she wasn't going to waste her time with him. She was going to take charge and take her destiny into her own hands.

NICKY TAPPED A fingernail against her stack of research books on the polished oak surface of the table in the New York City Public Library.

She could've just used her own laptop

at home. But sometimes she found it useful to get out of the house and go to a place that felt smart and was quiet.

A public space like a library created a certain anonymity that had always felt safe and good to her. A trusted silence was like a trusted friend. Or something like that.

Nicky glanced back through the pages of notes she'd made since her editor had given her the green light for the article.

What, exactly, did she know about Vivian Robinson?

Well, thanks to the SOE file she had received the other day from the National Archives in Kew, England, she knew a bit more about Viv.

It had been useful. The declassified part, at least. She'd put in that request for the additional information, but the other parts of her file were, frustratingly, still classified.

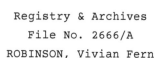

Registry & Archives
File No. 2666/A
ROBINSON, Vivian Fern

21.8.40

DF/OR/5234

Dear Miss Fordham,

I have interviewed Miss Vivian Fern Robinson. I am inclined to believe that her previous experience with mathematics and music makes her quite suitable for a vacancy in our cipher department.

I would, to that end, be grateful to your agreement of my employment of her.

Yours,

(Miss) T. WILLIAMS

Miss Fordham
Ministry of Labour & National Service
Lion House
Red Lion Street, W.C.

Vassar College

August 14, 1940

Dear Madam,

With reference to your letter of the 9th of August, I am pleased to provide the following reference for Miss Vivian Fern Robinson. She graduated magna cum laude from this post-secondary institution on December 15, 1939.

Her work during her student years here was exemplary. She has, from my observation, the utmost ability to apply diligence and reliability in any task she performs. I recommend her very highly.

Sincerely,

J. Smith

Dean, Department of Mathematics

Miss T. Williams
Inter-Services Research Bureau
64 Baker Street
W.1.

DF/OR/5234

22nd August, 1940

Dear Miss Robinson,

I am delighted to confirm that your application for a post in this Department has now been approved.

Would you be so good as to report for duty at 9.15 a.m. on September 2nd? In the meantime, if you receive any communications from the Ministry of Labour, please do get in touch with me before making any response.

Yours truly,
(Miss) T. WILLIAMS

Miss V.F.Robinson
Meadows Hotel
Bridge St., W.1.

F O R M C.R.1.

DATE: 8.1.40   INTERVIEWED BY:(Miss)
T. Williams

Surname (in block capitals): *ROBINSON*

Christian names: *Vivian Fern*

Rank or title:

Decorations:

1. <u>FORMER NAMES(IF ANY)</u>

2. <u>PERMANENT ADDRESS</u> *89 Chestnut Lane,*
Manhattan, New York
     <u>TEL. NO.</u> *Endicott4 8907*

3. <u>IF SERVING</u> (Regiment)

4. <u>DATE & PLACE OF BIRTH</u> *May 28, 1919, New*
York, New York, United States

5. <u>NATIONALITY</u> At birth *American*
     At present *American*

6. <u>EDUCATION</u>
     (a) Schools attended *New York City*
     Public High School

(b) Universities *Vassar College*
Degrees taken *mathematics education, music education*

7. <u>MARRIED OR SINGLE</u>? *single*

9. <u>RELIGION</u> *Methodist*

10. <u>PEACE TIME OCCUPATION</u> *student; part-time piano tutor*

12. <u>OCCUPATION SINCE 3.9.39</u> *piano tutor*

13. <u>LANGUAGES</u>
What languages do you speak and how fluently? *French – fluent German – fluent*

14. <u>WHAT COUNTRIES HAVE YOU VISITED?</u>
(other than in passage) *Austria, Germany, Switzerland*

16. <u>HAVE YOU MADE A WILL?</u> *No*

17. <u>NEXT OF KIN</u>
(a) Name *Lyle Robinson*
(b) Address *22 Ford St., Manhattan, New York*
(c) Relationship *father*

18. <u>APPEARANCE</u>

    (a) Height *5' 4"*

    (b) Weight *120 pounds*

    (c) Colour hair *black*

    (d) Colour of eyes *hazel*

    (e) Complexion *medium*

    (f) Distinguishing Marks *dimple in left cheek*

F O R M C.R.2.

<u>Office Use Only.</u>

                  (TOP SECRET)

<u>Former occupation:</u> Student

<u>Current cover occupation:</u> File clerk for Inter-Services Research Bureau (ISRB)

<u>Real occupation:</u> Process agent traffic, codes department, SOE

<u>Employment start date:</u> September 2, 1940

<u>Employment end date:</u> December 31, 1945

<u>Agents assigned to:</u> Oak, Ash, Maple

<u>Country sections assigned:</u> X, F, N

<u>Duties:</u> Decipher incoming coded

messages from SOE agents in the field

Notes: Highly intelligent; excellent with crosswords and puzzles; very chatty and chipper; friendly & helpful to the other girls; works well with other codes department girls to decipher indecipherables as they come in (due to Morse mutilation, language mistakes, transposition errors, etc.)

Recruitment: While on holiday after graduation in the spring of 1940, she was seen to be completing a crossword puzzle at a corner table of a pub; she was interviewed by Miss W and accepted the position promptly thereafter; the matter of her citizenship was overlooked, as her skills with both math and music overcame such details.

Nicky pursed her lips. Math and music? Math, she could see. But music—why would that be important? Then again, music had patterns, and if Vivian was deciphering codes, looking for patterns would be an asset.

Nicky drummed her fingers on the

tabletop. If Vivian had worked for the U.S. instead of the U.K. during the war, this might be a little easier to research.

Nicky had just finished a great book called *Code Girls* by Liza Mundy, which told all about American women breaking Japanese and German codes during WWII.

That had been a pretty fascinating read, actually. Apparently, the U.S. women had sometimes been recruited by secret letter, which asked them just two questions: did they like crossword puzzles and were they engaged to be married.

A whole ton had been written about the female U.K. codebreakers at Bletchley Park. There had also been a bunch written about the SOE's secret agents and even their female spies.

But only a little bit had been written about women working at the SOE headquarters. And that didn't really mention women in the signals, also known as codes, department.

Then again, the women in the codes department at the SOE weren't breaking Axis codes and ciphers...they were deciphering the incoming enciphered traffic from SOE agents sent into occupied Europe.

Sometimes articles and books lumped

together the women codebreakers at Bletchley with the women working at the SOE who deciphered agents' traffic.

Nicky sighed and rubbed her temples. Maybe this wasn't worth her time. Maybe she should just write about something easier. Less complicated to research...?

She laughed softly to herself. Less complicated? That would make it far less interesting. Just because there were a few snarls, a few plot twists, a bit of missing information, didn't mean it was time to quit.

"Far better to roll up your sleeves than wring your hands," Nicky murmured under her breath.

Nicky picked up her pencil and returned her eyes to the screen.

```
Agents  assigned  to:  Oak,  Ash,
Maple
```

Wait a minute. Ash? Nicky cocked her head. The letter had been signed A. Interesting. Could that mean Ash and the A of the letter were the same person? Hmmm. Probably.

But her story was about Vivian, not whoever wrote to her. She turned her attention back to her pages of notes. What had Vivian been like? She wanted to bring her to life, flesh out the bare facts, find out more about the person behind the file. There had to be a way to figure out more...

Was Vivian still alive? Nicky straightened up. It *was* possible...

If that were the case, Nicky would have all her questions answered from the woman herself.

Hmmm. She pulled up ancestry.com.

After about three hours and lots of help from a research librarian, as well as Facebook, Nicky found a few more records for the correct Vivian Robinson.

She scanned the screen.

Apparently, she'd immigrated to Canada as a war bride when she married Wallace Leard from Prince Edward Island. But he was definitely not the A of that love letter...

Nicky's heart sank. Looked like Vivian had passed away three months ago at a care home in Charlottetown, Prince Edward Island. She and her husband had owned and operated a business called Leard's Piano Tuning & Restoration in Victoria, P.E.I.

Hmmm. Maybe that was something to go on? Nicky made a few keystrokes and sat back.

Yes. Nicky grinned. It was still in business.

Question was, had it been sold or was it still in the family? Because if it was still operated by family, chances were, the relatives would know something about Vivian and maybe could answer some of Nicky's questions.

She brought up the search engine and typed in the company name.

It looked like—Nicky leaned forward in her seat—the company was still in the family.

Perfect. She'd no doubt have all her questions answered in no time. She sent an email off to her editor.

AT HOME THAT night, Nicky's phone buzzed and chirped. She glanced at it. A new email from Susan. She opened the message.

From: susanolmsted@historicalwoman.com
To: nicky.stendahl@gmail.com
Sent: Wed Oct 6, 11:58 p.m.

Nicky,
Thank you for sending your contract.

Payment will be made to you 45 days after the story has been submitted.

According to the email you just sent me, this Vivian woman ended up living in Canada—Prince Edward Island, I think you said.

Since this is our cover story, if you could go up there and find out more about her, that would really add perspective to the piece. It'd help our readers get a sense of place as well as person, especially since you'll be taking all the photos accompanying this feature, too.

Talk to whatever relatives you can. Get as much in-depth information as possible. I need the completed story by October 19, two weeks from now. Plenty of time to cover it.

Let me know if you need any research assistance.

—S

Nicky brushed her bangs out of her eyes and sat back against the couch. Three thousand words in two weeks? She swallowed. She'd never had to write a cover story before. Never something quite that long, either.

They'd always been short 100-word blog articles, or at the most, 250 words...

The online readerships she'd written for usually didn't have long enough attention spans to warrant quite such long pieces. But print was different. A feature story was different.

Could she actually do it? Would she be able to find out enough information? Would anyone want to read the article when she was done?

She shook off her swirling doubts and focused on the facts. Susan had been willing to take a chance on her. So Nicky needed to believe in her own abilities.

She couldn't let her editor down. She couldn't let the readers down. And she couldn't let herself down. This would be a big step up in her freelance career.

She winced. The plane ticket purchase would pretty much drain the last of her savings... But it would definitely be worth it once the article was published.

She pulled up the Expedia app on her phone and bought a ticket for the next flight to Prince Edward Island.

EARLY THURSDAY MORNING, Quinten glanced at his watch. If he didn't stay too long, he had just enough time to grab an espresso and a couple of chocolates before he headed into Charlottetown for the lawyer meeting.

He walked over to Island Chocolates.

"Hi Quinten. Your usual?" Gemma called out from behind the long wooden counter as Quinten stepped into the heritage space.

"Yeah." He pulled out his wallet to pay. "Thanks. How're the house renos going?" The scents of chocolate and freshly roasted coffee intermingled with the sounds of locals chatting at tables and the excited murmur of tourists examining the bags of brightly colored candy and fresh chocolates on the shelves of the former general store.

"Good, good," Gemma said as she rang up the sale. "Todd really appreciated you loaning him your cordless drill."

"Glad to help you and your boyfriend."

"He's almost done with it, so we'll get it back to you next week."

"Sure, no problem. What are neighbors for?"

Quinten put away his wallet and glanced around. Pretty packed in here this morning. Just one table left—his favorite—near the big picture window by the door.

Quinten took the two chocolates he'd selected and then sat down at the small forest-green metal table and looked out the big picture window.

A wedding party walked by. The bride held the skirt of her billowing white dress in one hand as she laughed at something her new husband said, his slightly lopsided bow tie matching the lopsided grin he gave his bride.

A swell of sadness filled Quinten as he looked at the happy couple. Would he ever have that?

Chapter Three

THE SCENT OF woodsmoke lingered in the cool autumn air as Nicky got out of her rental car in Victoria mid-morning Thursday.

Nicky noticed the tiny shingled visitors' center as she walked from the parking lot by the wharf up to Main Street. Might as well look around a bit to get a feel for the place before she got to work. She slung her Nikon around her neck.

A stray crimson maple leaf drifted down from the branches of the nearby tree. Nicky snapped a few shots.

Such a quaint place—straight out of a picture book. A lot more charming than the small Michigan town she'd grown up in. She smiled and shook her head.

Bright orangey yellow leaves crunched under her feet on the paved road.

She passed a blue character house called Ewe and Dye Weavery & Shop.

Cute. She'd have to stop in there later.

As she walked just a bit farther, she noticed a cream-colored clapboard building on her left. The gold-lettered sign above its green antique double doors read Island Chocolates.

"HERE YOU GO, Quinten." Gemma set the steaming cup down in front of him.

"Thanks."

Definitely a gorgeous fall day for photographs—a bright blue sky and a hint of a breeze, Quinten noted. He picked up his cup and saw the bride kiss her new husband as the photographer snapped away in front of the chocolate shop's steps.

All through the summer and fall, wedding parties were a regular sight around here as they posed for photos on the picturesque streets or by the waterfront and its red-and-white lighthouse.

His thoughts circled back to his love life. Would he ever get married? His heart squeezed. Thirty-five was practically forty. And if he was so afraid to open up and share his vulnerabilities to the point that he couldn't give someone what she wanted by telling her how he really felt, things would never work out. A longing filled him. He *wanted* things to work out.

He took a sip of the espresso but it scalded his tongue, so he put the cup down quickly. He tapped his fingers on the table as he waited for it to cool and tried to ignore the lingering wedding party.

Lots of couples did that. Came here to get married. In fact, the old Presbyterian church on the edge of the village had been converted into a full-service wedding venue called the Grand Victorian.

Practically half the locals in the village worked the big weddings there; he'd done it himself more than once. He loved helping out there and enjoyed the feeling of community and togetherness it brought. The place had been doing well these past couple of years, with P.E.I. becoming a haven for destination weddings...

The wedding party started to move on, and Quinten resisted the urge to circle back to thoughts of his nonexistent love life.

He looked at his watch. He should get going soon.

He glanced out the window and noticed a woman with strawberry-blonde hair walk up the steps and open the door of the shop. Must be another tourist.

Right behind her was Mrs. MacPhail.

NICKY CAUGHT THE scent of chocolate as she stepped inside. The uneven floorboards creaked under her as the low sounds of light jazz floated across the cheerful murmur of the customers seated at round tables that dotted the space.

"Hi there!" A young woman with bangs, light brown hair pulled into a ponytail, and a friendly smile addressed Nicky from behind the long wooden counter.

"Hey," Nicky replied. She eyed the ornate glass case filled with neat piles of handmade chocolates. Colorful, hand-chalked signs declared flavors like Peppy Peppermint and Salted Caramel. Her mouth watered.

"I'll take one salted caramel chocolate and..." Nicky scanned the drink list overhead. "...a hot chocolate, please. No whipped cream though."

"Got it." The girl grinned as she handed Nicky the single chocolate on a small green porcelain saucer. "This is my favorite flavor."

Nicky paid for the drink and the chocolate.

"Your hot chocolate'll just be a sec. I'll bring it out to you. Have a seat anywhere."

Nicky glanced around. It looked like all the tables in the small space were taken.

The woman who'd come in right behind Nicky caught her glance and smiled as she said, "We're not above sharing tables with strangers here. That's how people make new friends."

Nicky's eyes drifted to a man who was seated right by the big storefront window near the door. The chair across from him was the only empty one in the place.

He was looking out the window at a bridal party.

She took the few steps toward the table. "Hey, do you mind if I sit here? I just ordered a hot chocolate and—"

The man turned his head and looked up at her. The beams of bright gold sunlight streaked through his sandy blond hair. Nicky caught her breath as he caught her gaze.

Something in the way the sun streamed through the glass and into his blue-gray eyes made him look both vulnerable and guarded at the same time.

She felt a tug at her heart. Because behind the guardedness, something in his posture and body language conveyed a quiet strength. He reminded her of one of the trees she'd seen along the street outside: standing firm with deep roots and strong, solid branches.

He simply nodded once in response to her question and then carefully studied his coffee.

Her heart pounded beneath her ruffled chiffon blouse as she cleared her throat and sat down. "Thanks."

QUINTEN PRETENDED TO study the dregs of coffee in his cup as he studied the woman sitting across from him in his peripheral vision.

Her shoulder-length, strawberry-blonde hair and wispy bangs framed her heart-shaped face. And the ruffled emerald blouse she wore, paired with light-blue ripped jeans, complimented her creamy complexion and hazel eyes.

But it was more than her looks that made Quinten's heart beat faster. She had something about her that was decisive. Certain. She brought to mind a river winding through a canyon. As if she knew exactly where she was going and exactly how to get there.

He swallowed. He hadn't known what to say when she'd approached him. He hoped the nod he gave her didn't come across as rude, but damn if he couldn't talk very well to women he found attractive. Probably because he was afraid of being rejected.

His fingers tightened on the handle of the cup.

"Can I get you a refill, Quinten?" Gemma came up to the table with a coffee pot and a single hot chocolate on her tray.

"Uh, sure, Gemma. Thanks. But just half, please." He avoided looking over at the woman across from him.

Gemma filled his cup halfway and gave the woman her hot chocolate. "Enjoy."

"I'm being rude," the woman across from him said as Gemma left. "I'm Nicky." She stuck out a hand.

"Quinten," he said, as he shook it.

"Hello, dear," Mrs. MacPhail called over to Quinten and waggled her fingers in his direction.

He raised a hand in response.

Maybe Mrs. MacPhail would just go get her tea like she usually did and—

No such luck. She made a beeline for his table. "How are you?" She raised her eyebrows at Quinten and glanced at Nicky across from him. "Don't you two look cozy. I'm glad to see that you're feeling like...entertaining."

Quinten felt heat creep up the back of his neck.

"Hello there, dear. I'm Zella MacPhail." She extended a hand in Nicky's direction.

"I'm Nicky Stendahl."

"Fabulous," Mrs. MacPhail said. "Here for a little holiday? Most people are. Except the locals."

"I'm actually here to cover a story. I'm a freelancer writer."

"And a photographer too, I see." Mrs. MacPhail glanced at the Nikon case on the floor beside Nicky's chair.

How had he missed that detail?

Probably because he was too busy feeling awkward and being worried about what to say to her. He took a breath.

He was perfectly capable of talking with women. He talked with Gemma, with Mrs. MacPhail, with female customers just fine. But this was different.

He glanced at his watch again and ate the second chocolate on his saucer.

"—going to be here for the next five nights, 'til Tuesday. I've booked a room at the Orient Hotel," Nicky finished.

What was it about Mrs. MacPhail that

made everyone want to tell her all their secrets? Or at least, all their business. Quinten shook his head and smiled. That was P.E.I. for you. No other place quite like it.

He took the last sips of his coffee. He needed to get to Charlottetown.

She was going to stay here for a few days? He glanced at her again as she took a sip of hot chocolate.

He could deal with this. With her. He just had to think of the right thing to say to her. The perfect thing to say. That way, she wouldn't reject him.

No. He had to think more positively than that. Had to be more confident than that. Victoria was tiny, even with the tourists. He wasn't going to hide from her.

"Quinten here runs a lovely music shop and piano restoration business you have to visit. It's actually on the first floor of his house."

Nope. He'd treat her like he would a customer. Be polite. Professional.

"I love music. Played the flute all through high school and college. Or, uh, university, as you say here, don't you?"

"That's right," Mrs. MacPhail said. "But we knew what you meant, didn't we, Quinten?"

Quinten just nodded. Best to say as little as possible when she was like this.

"And you know, if there's anything I can do for you, please let me know. I consider myself the village ambassador."

"Thanks so much. Actually..." Nicky hesitated and glanced over at Quinten. "I'm looking for information about Vivian Robinson-Leard."

"Well, you're right in luck, you know. Her grandson's sitting across from you."

Quinten shifted in his seat.

Mrs. MacPhail leaned toward Nicky and said in a stage whisper, "Last closest living relative of Viv's, don'tchya know? Well, besides that Elliot MacEwen. But they're only cousins."

"Really? This is great," Nicky said, and sat up a little straighter as she pulled a small notebook and pen from her purse.

Mrs. MacPhail's phone buzzed. "Oh!" She glanced at it. "I really have to run. Minutes to type up and email out to all the board members. By the way, Quinten, thanks so much for helping Al with uploading that video to his crowdfunding page last week. He surely couldn't've done that techy stuff with my knowledge of computers."

"Happy to help," Quinten said.

"Just a second, Mrs. MacPhail," Nicky said. "Do you know anyone else in town here who was close to Vivian?"

Mrs. MacPhail paused a second and tapped a finger against her chin. "Mabel Hendricks," she said in a brisk tone. "One of her closest friends. And Quinten? Don't forget the village council meeting at the end of the month."

"Mmm-hmm."

"Good. I'll see you there, if not before. Nice to meet you, Nicky," she added as she left.

"You too," Nicky replied as she scribbled down the name and then turned her attention back to Quinten. "I'm so glad that we ran into each other like this. But in such a small place, nothing is really coincidence, is it?" She grinned and Quinten could see a dimple in her left cheek.

Like his grandma. A pang filled his heart for a second. But he forced it away.

Quinten shook his head. "Unfortunately, no."

Nicky laughed even though Quinten hadn't intended his comment to be funny.

"Well, this was easy," she continued. "Maybe you have a minute right now?" She handed him her card. "And then we can set up a time to—"

"No." Quinten winced and took a deep breath. That sounded rude. "I'm sorry but I have to go." He pushed back his chair.

Nicky sat back in her chair and he saw her shoulders droop a little.

He cleared his throat and wiped his mouth with his napkin. His heart sank. He'd handled that badly. But what was he supposed to say to her? He stood and glanced at his watch again. He had a lawyer meeting to get to.

"Why not?" Nicky said. "I want to write an article about Vivian. I've been doing a lot of research on her—"

His shoulders tensed and he said simply, "I have other things to do. Now, if you'll excuse me, I have to be somewhere."

He picked up his dirty dishes and headed over to drop them off at the counter.

His jaw tightened. Nosy journalists. Sure, Grandma Viv had worked during the war—but so had everyone else in that time period.

Then again, there were those two reporters who'd showed up at Whisperwood Villa a few months before Grandma Viv's death. They wouldn't stop asking her questions about her time during the war. Had upset her so much she'd begun to shake.

He'd been angry at himself for days afterward because he hadn't taken better care to prevent that. But then why had those journalists come around if Grandma Viv was *just* a file clerk...?

Mabel's words ran through his head. *She was in love with a Nazi...* That just couldn't be true.

He frowned. It was far better to just stay away from drama, from this woman, and move through his life as quietly as possible. Grandma Viv's life was nothing to over-glorify or make a big deal about.

He hated people making big deals about things that actually weren't as significant as they claimed.

His ex-girlfriend had always done that—made a big deal about the tiniest things. Which caused him to retreat even further...

He didn't want attention called to himself, or to his family. Especially not now with all this uncertainty about the business.

He handed his dishes back to Gemma, who was wiping down the counter.

"Have a good morning, Quinten," she said.

"Thanks. You too," he said as he headed out the door.

Nicky walked down the steps of the chocolate shop and headed up the street in the direction of the Orient Hotel. May as well try to start a draft of the article, just to get something down on paper.

She'd be typing it up on her laptop, actually, though she liked to keep a pen and notebook in her purse all the time just in case some great idea occurred to her.

The breeze buffeted a strand of her hair and she tucked it behind her ear.

Nicky's mind drifted back to the chocolate shop. That guy—Quinten Leard—he'd seemed...distant? Preoccupied?

Yet something about him, as he'd sat across from her and had carefully studied his coffee, had made a thread of longing pass through her.

What was she thinking? The man had barely said two words to her. A pretty clear brush-off. She clenched her jaw. If he didn't talk to her about Vivian, who else besides Mabel was she going to interview?

For half a second, she wondered what he'd thought of her and her project. No. Why was she even thinking that? He was a stranger. And she was here in a professional capacity. She wasn't interested in him. She was only here for her story.

But she hadn't really had a chance to fully explain to Quinten what she wanted to do. Was that because someone else had tried to talk to him before about Vivian, and caused some sort of issue?

She needed to interview him; but she hated to bother him again to try and persuade him to tell her what he knew about his grandmother.

She chewed on a hangnail. Quinten was the perfect source. Trouble was, she wasn't a hardened journalist. She wrote for magazines and blogs, for heaven's sake. She recalled that look of vulnerability and guardedness that had flitted across his face.

She didn't have the guts—well, the callousness—of investigative journalists. Some of them would do anything, including make people cry, just to get to the truth for their stories.

Nicky rolled her eyes. She couldn't help but feel that wasn't the point. She believed in the truth, yes. She believed people's voices needed to be heard. But not at the expense of undue pain and unnecessary suffering on the part of the source.

That seemed, in spite of a journalistic

code of ethics, well, pretty unethical.

Despite herself, her mind wandered back to Quinten. His eyes were an unusual shade of blue. Didn't that hint of gray in them give him a—

She had no business wondering if his eye color defined his character. Besides, that wasn't even really possible. Another thing you only ever saw in books.

She shoved her hands deeper into the pockets of her jeans and kept walking up the street.

At the corner of—she glanced at the street sign—Howard and Main, she noticed on her left a two-story pale blue clapboard house with white trim.

It sat comfortably on its corner lot, surrounded by a white picket fence, shaded by a large tree. It had a wide porch with pots of bright yellow marigolds on either side of the door. A blue-and-gold hand-lettered wooden sign read Leard's Piano Tuning & Restoration.

Her heart beat a little faster.

She'd have to go in. Maybe if Quinten wouldn't talk, one of the employees would be able to tell her something about Vivian. Or at least, the history of the area so she could get some context for her story.

She paused mid stride. Wait a minute.

The visitors' center down on the water-front might know something about Viv. At least about the village. It was worth a shot. And would allow her to avoid bothering Quinten for a little longer.

She turned around and walked back down the way she came. She passed Island Chocolates again. She couldn't help a glance at the big picture window. An East Indian couple sat inside with their little girl who had chocolate all over her face.

Nicky walked on. She noticed a bright orange house with paler orange trim on her left. Then she passed a few more wooden clapboard homes with woodpiles and white picket fences and big hardwood trees on their lawns.

The seagulls wheeled overhead. The scent of saltwater told her she was getting close to the waterfront. She passed Richard's Fresh Seafood on the corner across from the pier.

She'd heard that place had pretty good fish and chips. She'd have to go there for lunch or maybe dinner.

She took a left and went diagonally through the lot where she'd parked her rental car. She headed over to the small single story one-room building with gray-shingled siding that stood to one side of the lot. A heavy rope fence surrounded the small building.

To her right was a sandy pathway that led down to a small strip of beach beside the wharf.

She passed a bike rack with several bikes. One was a cherry-red retro Schwinn with a woven wicker bike basket. She couldn't help but grin as she pulled out her camera to take a few shots of it. Everywhere you turned, this place had picture-postcard photo ops.

Pots of bright orange and yellow flowers stood on either side of the doorway to the little building.

She went inside.

"Hi there, can I help you?" A woman in a black T-shirt and black jeans, with chin-length, gray-and-white-streaked hair, greeted her. A pair of reading glasses dangled on a chain around her neck.

"Actually, yes. I'm looking for some information about one of the village residents. Vivian Robinson. She married a Leard."

"You're not a relative, are you." The woman's bright blue eyes didn't seem to miss a detail.

Nicky drew out her pen and notepad. "I'm writing an in-depth article about her, actually."

"That's great. I'm working on a book, myself. I have several friends who are Leards. Well, I can tell you that she was from away. Came to Victoria in late fall of '46, I think. She was a war bride and married a successful local man, Wallace Leard. They met in London. He'd been in the air force and flew a Tiger Moth. Got promoted to colonel. Have you talked with Quinten Leard? He would be your best bet. He's her grandson and would know the most about her."

Nicky bit her lip and felt a blush come to her cheeks. "I just met him at the chocolate shop. He seemed...busy, and I was hoping to get several viewpoints, actually, for the story. I want to give it as much scope as possible."

"Well..." The woman looked speculative for a second. "Elliot MacEwen's her grandson too, but let's just say Elliot's not exactly interested in history. He wouldn't know what I imagine you're needing to find out." She tapped a finger against her chin. "But Mabel Hendricks'll help you out if you talk with her."

"Thanks so much," Nicky said. She couldn't help the smile that came to her lips. People in small towns everywhere, it seemed, liked to share what they knew.

"Oh, and miss?" The woman held Nicky's gaze for another moment. Nicky shifted her weight.

"Don't judge Quinten too harshly. He might be stoic but he has a good heart. Been going through a bit of a rough time lately trying to save the family business, what with his cousin Elliot having designs on it and all."

ALONG SYDNEY STREET in downtown Charlottetown, Quinten opened the brass-handled wooden door of the low red brick building. Originally it had been a warehouse back in the 1800s but now it contained converted office suites.

He headed up the stairs to his lawyer's third-floor office.

He nodded a polite hello to the receptionist. "Just head on back to the conference room, Quinten," she said. "Elliot's already in there."

Elliot, who had taken a seat at the big old oak conference table, watched a video on his phone. It appeared to be about how to improve your golf swing.

Quinten fought an unsettled feeling that only grew in the pit of his stomach as he sat on the hard, oak chair and rested his forearms on the table.

The lawyer walked in a few minutes later with a glass of water. He cleared his throat. "Thank you for coming in, gentlemen. As you know, this meeting is in regards to Vivian Fern Robinson-Leard's business."

The lawyer sat down and pushed his black-framed glasses up on his nose. "Vivian's business was a sole proprietorship. That sole proprietorship ceased upon the owner's, in this case Vivian's, death. After which, the assets went into the estate to be divided evenly between surviving kin."

"Which has already been done via probate," Elliot reminded him. "Quinten and I each own fifty percent of her business now."

Quinten clenched his jaw. "But we both want different things for the business."

"Yes. Therein lies the problem." The lawyer rubbed his temples. "I've seen this before with family businesses. People can take things personally. Egos can get in the way. As things stand now, well, basically either of you could do anything. And with that kind of equal distribution of power between you both, it can lead to feuding, poor business decisions, bad results and, ultimately, failure of the business."

A muscle in Quinten's jaw ticked as he glanced at Elliot. "Isn't there a way to...fix this?"

"Well," the lawyer pushed up his glasses again, "someone needs to be assigned as the sole heir in order for the business to be run smoothly. Otherwise, well, I hope I won't see the two of you in court."

The lawyer glanced from Elliot to Quinten and shuffled papers.

"Quinten could decide to keep on with the sole proprietorship but that would only happen if he was the only heir. The same goes for you, Elliot," the lawyer said.

"But Quinten isn't the sole heir, because there's no will," Elliot countered.

"No, not at the moment," the lawyer agreed. "Your grandmother never gave me any documentation. And as I've said, because of that, there was no article, no item that said or clearly indicated, or directly established, who received ownership of Leard's Piano Tuning & Restoration. Sometimes people get so caught up in the daily running of their business that they don't remember to designate a successor. Or write a will."

"So that means I could buy out Quinten's half, now that the probate's gone through," Elliot said.

The lawyer took a sip of water. "At the moment, the business belongs fifty percent to each of you, which is in accordance with intestate succession law. So yes, Elliot, since the probate's gone through, you could buy out Quinten's half."

"But if a will was found and it said I was the heir," Quinten managed to force the words through the tightness in his chest, "then I wouldn't have to sell to Elliot?"

"If a will is found," the lawyer said, "and if it specifically named one of you, then yes, the company would belong to whomever that was, as per the will."

"So then," Quinten said, "that would settle, once and for all, who has the company, legally?"

"Yes," the lawyer said.

Quinten shifted in his seat.

Elliot crossed his arms over his chest.

"Listen, gentlemen, I understand that you may have...differences of opinion about the business. Regardless, in order for this whole mess to be sorted out, a sole successor needs to be designated as quickly as possible." He looked from one man to the other. "This current arrangement isn't doing either of you any favors."

"What do you suggest?" Quinten asked.

"I would advise that the two of you come to some sort of agreement right now."

"On?" Elliot raised his brows.

"On what you both want to do. It looks to me that Quinten, you want some time to look more thoroughly for a will. But Elliot, you want to buy out his half right now. I would propose a compromise."

Elliot shot the lawyer a sidelong glance. "What do you mean?"

"Set a deadline to look for inheritance documentation."

"Fine, fine." Elliot waved a hand.

Quinten's jaw tightened. He should've sorted through his grandmother's papers in detail sometime in the past three months. But somehow, between arranging the memorial service, running the shop, worrying about the financial state of the business, and feuding with Elliot, he'd only had time for a cursory search and had come up empty-handed. But regretting what he couldn't undo wasn't productive. He could only go forward. "That sounds fair."

"Good. I'll get my assistant to draw up some papers for you to sign about this." The lawyer looked back and forth between the two. "Now, do you both then agree on the timeframe of one week—by next Wednesday—in which to find some sort of will?"

Both cousins murmured agreement.

"After which, if said timeframe has passed and nothing is found, then you both agree that one of you will buy out the other?"

Quinten gave a short, sharp nod and stood. He pushed aside growing panic. He wouldn't let himself think about the possibility of the company actually going bankrupt. If that happened, he couldn't afford to buy out Elliot's half. There had to be some sort of documentation in Grand-ma Viv's things. *Had* to be.

Elliot nodded too, but stayed seated. "There's no will to find. I own half the business now, anyway. So I'll just wait until Quinten comes up empty-handed. A week from now, the business will be completely mine."

NICKY TAPPED HER unpolished fingernails on her jeans-clad thigh and sighed.

She'd sat on the porch of the music shop for awhile after she'd found it empty but then realized she looked pretty conspicuous, so she headed back up the street to the Orient Hotel.

After she'd played a round of croquet on the back lawn with a couple of other guests and the wife of the owner, she'd headed to her room.

Which was why she was sitting here now staring at her laptop and a blank Word document.

She picked up her smartphone and logged on to her social media account.

Hmmm. Were there any more editors who had mentioned story pitches in their feeds? Nicky scrolled through. Sometimes she'd gotten work that way. Didn't look like it, nope. But Susan from the *Historical Woman* had begun to follow her. That was good news.

Well, she'd update her status anyway.

Working on a new story! she typed. *#amwriting.*

Nicky paused. Speaking of writing, had *Ivory* magazine deposited her money yet?

She tapped her banking app. Hmm. Nope, didn't look like it. She frowned and tried to nudge aside mounting worry mixed with annoyance. When was she going to get that money?

She frowned again as she glanced at her

savings account balance. After paying for this plane ticket, she had about one hundred fifty dollars left in it.

Frustration built inside her. That contract had stipulated, much like the one she'd just signed, that she would be paid forty-five days after article submission. And it was well after forty-five days now. She drummed her fingers on her thigh as the frustration grew. What was going on?

She went back to her social media account. This didn't make any sense. The frustration swept through her as she typed *#journalistsneedtogetpaid* and hit refresh. She sighed in satisfaction as her status updated again.

She'd emailed the magazine multiple times but had received no response. And the magazine's receptionist assured her someone would return her calls. No one had.

Maybe they'd respond to a social media post? Doubtful, but worth a try. She clicked onto their page. *#IvoryMagazine, I haven't received my payment from the story I wrote for you. When can I expect it, as it's now overdue. Thanks!*

Maybe she had some money from those photos? She opened Shutterstock. Looked like a few people liked those pictures she'd uploaded on Tuesday. Her royalties tab actually had a couple of dollars in it.

She put her phone down and wished she could set aside her concern as easily.

But she'd better get productive here. After all, there was nothing she could do about that late payment at the moment. She worried her bottom lip between her teeth.

She just had to keep going with the current piece. They'd pay her soon enough. Right? Probably just busy and running behind.

She turned back to the Word document.

What would be the best angle to approach this?

That first paragraph needed to hook her readers and really get them interested.

And it needed to be great. This was her chance to really make an impact, to make a difference. To write about something important. Someone important to history. A voice from the past that touched people's hearts in the present...

She needed to do Vivian justice. Needed to be able to paint a picture of her that would bring her to life, yet be true to her life.

She needed to understand where Vivian had been coming from.

Well, in order to do that, she needed to hear from Vivian herself. Or at least, the closest person to it. She got up and headed outside.

BACK IN VICTORIA, Quinten shut the driver's side door of his silver Acura and got out. He breathed a sigh of relief to find that the journalist—Nicky—wasn't waiting for him on his front porch. He rubbed a hand across his face. He didn't think he could handle anything like that now.

He headed across the porch, opened the screen door, and stepped inside.

Dappled sunlight filtered in through one of the west-facing windows and caught the varnish on the guitars and violins that were on display. A baby grand piano stood at the opposite end of the small space.

He didn't sell too many musical instruments; and those that he did have on hand were stringed ones. The bulk of his income came from piano repair and tuning.

At least, it had.

Maybe he should just focus on instrument sales? But he loved working with the vintage pianos. Bringing new life to old instruments. Bringing smiles to people's faces. Bringing people together around something besides a computer or a television. Uniting them in something that had meaning, importance, emotion, feeling, heart...

He rubbed a hand across his jaw and looked around the store. His grandmother had to have written down some mention of who would get the business. She'd been a tad disorganized but tended to write things down. Usually. That is, until dementia had taken over...

He flipped over the small wooden sign that hung from the screen door so that it read *closed*. He'd been in such a rush that he'd completely forgotten to close up properly earlier in the day.

He needed to start going through her paperwork. Through everything of hers, really. And the attic was probably the best place to start.

A FLUFFY GRAY long-haired cat snoozed on the cane-back rocker as Nicky walked up to the porch of Mabel Hendricks's house. She stroked the cat's head and then rang the doorbell.

It wasn't long before she heard the shuffle of feet. An old woman with perfectly permed, bright white hair answered the door.

"Hello there, dear. Who are you?"

"My name's Nicky Stendahl. I'm sorry to drop by unannounced..." She held up her pen and pad. "But a couple of people—Mrs. MacPhail and the lady down at the visitors' center—told me that you'd be the person to talk to about Vivian Robinson-Leard."

"My reputation precedes me, I can tell."

"I wanted to ask you when it would be convenient for you to talk with me about her?"

The old woman waved a hand. "I'm ninety-seven and a half years old. Got nothing but time these days. Never mind making an appointment. Come on in. I always like a good visit."

She opened the screen door wide and Nicky stepped into the house.

"Come on into the living room. That's where the most comfortable sofas are."

Nicky followed Mabel as she took a sharp left into the living room.

The old woman maneuvered easily

around several cat toys and a pile of newspapers beside a large cardboard box that had, from Nicky's quick glance inside, a jumble of odds and ends in it.

Must be donating some items? Or maybe she just needed them close by for who knows what.

Mabel took a seat on the couch. Nicky sat down on an armchair nearby and pulled out her pen and notebook. "I was just wanting to ask you some questions about her life."

"I'm the only one who remembers now. She wasn't well the last few years, you know." Mabel shook her head. "At the very last, poor Quinten had to take care of her all by himself. Only child, that one." She pursed her lips.

"He's a good man, Quinten. Always helping everyone he can around here. That's what makes this place more than just another small town. It's really one big family."

"I can imagine," Nicky murmured.

"Did you know he stayed up 'til 3:00 a.m. one time just to make sure that my neighbor here—" she pointed a thumb behind her "—got home safe from the pub? Another time, he waded out into the freezing cold water in the dead of January to help my other neighbor up the road find her car keys when she'd lost them. He's always doing stuff like that. A good man," Mabel repeated and looked at Nicky as if she would deny it.

Was it her imagination or was everyone she met here trying to set her up with Quinten?

She couldn't help but wonder what this place was like if you actually lived here. The corners of her lips tugged upward. That might be kind of fun to find out.

"So," Mabel continued, "I think Quinten would really be the best person to talk to. But I've rambled on enough. What do you want to know from me?"

"Well," Nicky said, and glanced through her list of questions, "I understand she worked in the signals department of the SOE during World War II and I—"

"Never heard tell of it." Mabel sat up straight. "Nope. She never mentioned anything like that to me at all."

Nicky's shoulders drooped. "She didn't?"

"Nope," Mabel said. "Never in all the fifty years I knew her."

"Well, what did she say about her time during the war?" Nicky persisted.

"Only that she spent time in London.

Mentioned something about being a file clerk."

Nicky bit her lip and tapped her pen on the blank page.

"We never really talked about the war. Our generation, you see," Mabel paused as if gathering her thoughts, "never felt it was right to talk about such things."

Nicky started to put away her note-book.

"Now, just a second. Right after Viv died, my daughter Anna helped Quinten clean out his basement—that house was where Viv and Wallace lived, you know— and Anna found a few things of Viv's she thought I might want, so he let Anna take them for me."

She waved her cane at the cardboard box that Nicky had noticed earlier. "Just there, in fact."

"Oh?"

"Take the whole box," Mabel said, "if it'll be of any use to you."

"Uh...if you're sure?"

"You, well, I think your heart's in the right place. So I don't mind, and I don't think Viv would've, either."

"Wow, thank you so much. I'll bring it all back once I'm done."

"I'm sorry I don't know what you need

answering. Quinten really would be the person to answer your questions about Vivian."

"Okay, I'll keep that in mind."

Mabel added, "There was a journal or a diary or something in that box there somewhere. I didn't read it, though. It was locked—all rusted shut—and I didn't have the key and it never seemed right to just pry it open."

She studied Nicky a moment. "I think you're trying to do good. So if you're doing a piece about her life, well, then you'd be the one to look at that little diary. Might need someone to help you open it up, though."

Nicky knelt down by the box. "I'll take a look through it right away." She started to pick up the box.

"If you're looking for a story..."

Nicky paused and looked at Mabel.

"The Nazis were here," the old woman murmured.

Nicky's eyes widened.

Mabel's eyes closed. "It was about 3:00 a.m. ..."

She continued, lost in memory, as if Nicky wasn't even there. "...I'd woken up but I couldn't get back to sleep. The moon was bright, bright and full that night; it shone on the water so that it reflected right into my bedroom window on the second floor. It was early May, I remember. I was lying awake in my bed when I heard rustling downstairs. It was just me and my younger sisters here in the house." She waved a hand to indicate the old Edwardian they were in.

"Being the oldest, I knew I had to see what was going on. So I got up and picked up my flashlight that I always had by my bed. I crept down the stairs, careful to avoid the three that creak. The rustling continued. From the kitchen.

"I pressed against the wall, the flashlight clutched in my hand like a baseball bat. I slowly tiptoed my way down the hall toward the kitchen door. The rustling stopped but the loud pounding of my heart hadn't, and I wondered if whoever it was could hear it.

"I'd gotten to the kitchen by then. Peered into the room. Saw that the pantry light was on. Knew I'd turned it off when I went to bed. The pantry door was open a crack, too.

"I held my breath the whole way across that black-and-white tiled floor. Afraid any second someone was going to jump out and, I don't know, shoot me. Ever so slowly, I nudged the pantry door open with my bare toe. The bulb's pull chain was still swinging back and forth. But no one was in there.

"Oh, I was so relieved. What could've I done with a flashlight?" She chuckled and shook her head.

"But then I saw that the ham we'd planned to have for Sunday dinner—gotten it in trade from a neighbor for some of our potatoes—was gone.

"I'd just reached up to turn off the light when I saw a glint of something silver on the floor."

Mabel opened her eyes suddenly and met Nicky's gaze. "That's why I know Hitler's treasure is here somewhere."

"What do you mean?" Goosebumps rose on Nicky's arms. "And what did you find on the floor?"

Mabel rapped her cane emphatically. "Sit back down, dear. It's time you heard the legend."

QUINTEN HEADED OUT back and grabbed the aluminum ladder down from the loft of the little shingle-sided blue barn painted with white trim around the windows and doors.

Though currently Quinten's storage shed, the small barn had originally been in a different spot in town and was sometimes used for spelling bees back in the twenties and thirties.

Now it sat in his back yard. He'd inherited the corner lot with its 1820s house from Grandpa Wallace.

He put the ladder over one shoulder and wove his way through the neat piles of various items that had collected over the years.

There was the group of four wooden school chalkboards, complete with roll-down maps, that Grandma Viv had gotten from the old schoolhouse up the road after it had been decommissioned.

There was the stack of his neighbor's paddle boats that were in the opposite corner of the shed, waiting for the perfect July day and the gaggle of tourists that would come to rent them.

There were the bags and boxes of his father's things that he'd somehow not had the heart to part with, even in the years since his dad's death.

He shook his head at himself. Sometime he really needed to go through all this. Figure out what he wanted to keep and what he didn't. Elliot was always hounding him to make way for the new, to get rid of the old.

But he couldn't, somehow, just throw it all out. It was his connection to those people, those places, that he wouldn't get back again...

BACK IN HER room at the Orient, Nicky put Mabel's box on the side table. The leather-bound diary was one of the only items in it. A battered shoe box was another.

Nicky lifted the lid on it and saw a jumble of papers. Receipts. Recipe cards. Utility bills. Hmmm. Wouldn't hurt to go through that later.

She picked up the diary and held it in her hand. The place to start would be here. She examined the book and felt a surge of curiosity mixed with a pang of guilt. Going through Viv's personal things...? But it was an opportunity to hear from the woman herself. Mabel had given her permission to take the box, after all. But shouldn't Quinten be the one to look at this? Then again, he'd given the box away to Mabel. The items in the box must not have meant that much to him...

She felt a nudge of regret. Quinten

hadn't even seemed interested in helping her out. Or in finding out about his own grandmother.

But maybe that wasn't a fair assessment? He'd seemed pretty stressed out. If what the woman in the visitors' center said was true, well, Nicky supposed she couldn't blame him for being a little...touchy.

She thought again of the way his eyes had caught the sunlight when he'd first looked up at her. That hint of vulnerability...the sense that he had deep roots and solid strength.

Something nudged at her heart but she turned her attention back to the small cream-colored book. She picked it up and tugged the zipper pull.

It slid easily open across the top of the book. But as Nicky pulled it around the corner, it stopped. She frowned. Looked like there was a piece of rust there.

She tugged harder. But now the zipper was stuck fast. She didn't dare pull any harder or the whole thing might fall apart in her hands.

Her brow furrowed more.

Even if she got the zipper all the way open, the diary was still locked. And she certainly didn't have the key.

She withheld a sigh. She had to be patient. This was important; and if she could just get at the information inside, then she'd be able to really do justice to this story, to this woman.

Quinten needed to at least know that. Even if he refused to help her, she at least had to try.

She picked up the small book and her keyring and headed out the door.

TODAY WAS THURSDAY, which meant Quinten needed to sort out the recycling. Usually it got picked up on a weekday. But with the storms they'd had not long ago, things had gotten behind. So pickup was scheduled for this Sunday instead.

With his free hand, he snagged a few clear blue plastic recycling bags from the box on the shelf near the shed door.

He headed outside and back over to the house. He set the ladder down by the porch, then went through the front entrance so he could put the recycle bags on the counter for easy accessibility.

After he started going through things this afternoon in the attic, then he could make some headway on organizing it for

the recycling and—

"Good, you're still here."

Quinten's eyes snapped to the front porch. The woman he'd shared a table with at Island Chocolates now stood on his doorstep.

He leaned against the counter in an attempt to feign nonchalance. But his heart thudded in his chest. Right. She was just like a customer. That's all. A customer.

"Sorry, we're closed," he said.

"But you're still here."

"Right. Because I'm the owner." Part owner, anyway...

He crossed his arms. "Can I help you?"

Nicky opened the screen door and stepped just inside the threshold. "Mabel sent me. She insisted that you would know the most about your grandmother."

Quinten felt a nudge of impatience, but hid it in his friendly tone.

"Well, Mabel's a good friend of the family," he admitted. Sometimes too good. "But she can get a little over-enthusiastic."

Nicky fiddled with the straps on her purse.

"Listen," Quinten said, "have you tried the visitors' center?" Maybe she'd read between the lines of the meaning of his suggestion and leave. He continued in case she hadn't. "They might be able to give you what you need. Or even the library in Charlottetown." Far away from here. He mentally crossed his fingers.

Nicky grinned. "Everyone in this town is so helpful. Friendly. It's so refreshing compared to New York." She put her hands on her hips. "The thing is, the lady at the visitors' center told me to come see you, too."

Quinten took a breath. He couldn't agree to this. She'd go poking around, asking questions, creating drama. He didn't have the time for it on top of going through all of Grandma Viv's paperwork... Even though he felt every nerve in him straining to say yes.

Just because that way he'd be liked. He'd be accepted. He'd be—"I'm sorry." He headed over to the screen door and held it open for her. "Nicky, was it? I'm on a tight deadline and have to go through a lot of paperwork." Better to avoid committing.

She stepped back over the threshold on the porch. He moved to latch the screen door shut and caught the flowery scent of her perfume.

He mentally shook his head. He shouldn't be noticing things like her perfume.

But he blinked and came up short when she held up something right in front of him.

"Maybe you'd be interested in this?"

Chapter Four

$\mathcal{S}$HE HELD A small cream-colored book with the words *Five-Year Diary* emblazoned across it in faded gold lettering.

A gold zipper around its edge looked like it'd seen better days and was fastened, Quinten saw, with an oval lock. Where on Earth had that come from? He'd never seen it before.

"Sorry," he repeated, "but I, uh, really have things to do." He turned to the ladder he'd set down by the porch railing.

"It was your grandmother's," she added as she followed him across the porch. He winced. He hoped not too many neighbors were watching this. Lace curtains twitched across the way. Too late.

Despite himself, a thread of curiosity wound through him. What was in his grandma's diary? It would just be a distraction, though. Like Nicky. He picked up the ladder. "I'm sorry to disappoint you, but I'm very busy at the moment with certain obligations and don't have the time to spend to talk about my grandmother."

He had to find the will. He wouldn't be able to focus if Nicky was around. He wouldn't be able to accomplish much if he was distracted by her. He'd be wondering how he came across, worrying about what to say to her...

Nicky bit her lip.

He took a breath. "I don't know that much anyway, okay? Besides, she wouldn't have liked a lot of fuss made about her, let alone some sort of article written up."

Nicky opened her mouth to say something but he continued. "All I can tell you is she was an excellent businesswoman—ahead of her time—"

"But—" Nicky started to say.

"Have you tried ancestry.com?" Quinten plowed on. "Maybe other, more distant relatives will be able to help you out. Now if you'll excuse me."

He picked up the ladder, opened the door and made sure to lock it behind him.

QUINTEN HEADED FARTHER inside, careful

to maneuver the ladder around the ornately carved newel post at the foot of the stairs.

He sighed. He didn't like to disappoint people. He recalled the way Nicky had bitten her lip. A sliver of guilt niggled at him. He should've said yes. Agreed to help her.

Maybe he'd been too hasty? After all, how long would it take, really, for her to ask him a few questions?

No. He shook his head. He was too busy. He had to find a will, or at least something that would clarify this mess.

He headed up the stairs, mindful the ladder didn't knock into the framed family photos along the stairway.

But those photos, like the piles of stuff in the shed, he couldn't seem to throw away.

He reached the landing on the second floor. After he set up the ladder, he climbed it and pushed open the small hatch to the attic.

He went through the hatch and sat down on the rafter stringers. A cloud of dust caught in a beam of sunlight made him sneeze.

He should probably find a better place to store Christmas and Thanksgiving decorations. Well, while he was up here, maybe he could start going through those things, too.

Grandma Viv had loved Christmas, and there were a lot of extra decorations he didn't need.

He set out the plastic bags he'd brought up with him, and got to work.

A few hours later, he was covered in dust. His stomach rumbled and he glanced at his watch. Getting close to five o'clock. Time flew when sorting junk.

But he'd made progress. One corner of the attic was now neatly organized and he had several bags full of recycling.

He sighed and raked a hand through his hair. But there was nothing about a will. And no paperwork to speak of.

He reached for the last box shoved into the north corner. It looked pretty old. He swiped at the thick layer of dust and coughed.

Hmm. This wasn't a cardboard box. It was a buff-colored suitcase.

A vintage suitcase, from the look of it.

He wiped off more dust and noticed that there was a lock on the case.

Odd. He'd never seen this suitcase up here before. Kind of like that diary...

Could Grandma Viv have been hiding

things from him? Or had she just forgotten, thanks to the dementia? His heart twisted.

Granted, this suitcase had been kind of hidden behind all these other cardboard boxes and piles of decorations...

He set it down so it lay flat, then flipped the latches and tugged on the lid.

Nothing.

He put a bit more muscle into it. With a screech of the hinges, the suitcase opened. Huh.

He rummaged through the contents. More Christmas decorations. Really *old* Christmas decorations. Along with Halloween pumpkins and a cardboard cut-out of a turkey colored in with crayon in the shape of a handprint that looked very familiar.

One corner of his mouth lifted as he rubbed a thumb across the faded image. That had been Grade 1 or 2, if he remembered right.

But how did it get in—

Quinten's eyes were drawn to a crumbling yellowed clipping from the Charlottetown newspaper that had somehow attached itself to the bottom of the turkey.

As he tried to carefully loosen and then examine it, the old paper started to crumble under his fingertips.

> —U-boat was sighted in Char-
> lottetown harbor early yesterday
> morning. Two destroyers were
> sent out to intercept but the
> sub slipped away before a firm
> lock could be gotten on it.
>
> This is the first sighting
> of U-boats this close to the
> capital city but not the first
> report of German activity in the
> Northumberland Strait or the
> Gulf of St. Lawrence.
>
> Authorities encourage lo-
> cals—

So Mabel had been right. He clenched his jaw. At least about the Germans. He had thought it was just conjecture and hearsay. Apparently not.

But as for his grandmother being in love with a Nazi, well, that couldn't be true. She'd loved his grandfather, Wallace.

He thumbed the edges of the page, which crumbled off and fell away. Patches of handwriting showed through. He felt his pulse quicken. There was more here?

He nudged aside the crumbling flakes. Yes. It looked like someone had pasted another page underneath...

The yellowed, dried glue simply let go under his touch to reveal a letter, obscured, in some places, by the article. In others, by time and deterioration.

Apri 5,   43

Dear t Viv,

*   even as my   mind grows grave,*
my love, fo   future of German   friend
Fritz talks   about Socialist Party but I
have an uneasy feeling i   That's why I
join   he cause   f things.
*   time I find myself longing*
fo   past. For what   ave been my con-
cert   areer.   Thou   have not put
m   s   e ivories of any piano in suc   le,
I   if I did, all of this unrest w   inter-
fere.
*   glad I can be certain of our*
love   I am sure you   the
extent   my feelings for you, and
I   confidently to our future to-
gether. I   hope Germany's
future   fare as well!
*   your other*
tion,   a Polish princess,
.   not   German queen.
*   You might be surprised to know that*
though I   German   t name, I am

indeed   nt, and can trace my lineage
back to that   line of
*   In fa   ss married the king of*
France but the mi   disappeared until my
great-gr
*   found   and now I*
have   locked away — as
suc   aluable object   be,
along   ith th   wry—on my family
estate.
*   B   was before the SS came knocking*
All my love
—A

Wait a minute. Quinten drew in a sharp breath. Could Mabel be right?

Part of him refused to believe it even though he held this very real piece of history in his hand.

He started to put the fragile page back into the suitcase but it crumbled into tiny pieces with the motion.

His eyes widened. This was more glimpses of a Vivian he never knew. Would this letter give him the answers he was looking for? He cocked his head. Give him a chance to be closer to his grandmother? To get to know the person she was before she'd come to P.E.I., before dementia had robbed her of her memories...

He took out his phone and snapped a few photos of the remains before he continued through the case's contents. He riffled through the long pouch on the underside of the lid and discovered a ream of Christmas music.

He flipped through it idly. He already had a big book of the classic carols sitting on the piano downstairs and didn't needed any more yellowed copies of that. Yep, all the Christmas favorites were here...

Huh. A few other pieces must have gotten mixed in. There was "The White Cliffs of Dover" and something called "Marsch Impromptu" by some German composer he'd never heard of.

Yep, these would be great to add to Sunday's recycling. He shoved the pages into the clear blue plastic bag as well as the crumbled bits of the newspaper article and letter.

His stomach rumbled again and he glanced around the attic. Shadows had lengthened across the floorboards and evening light filtered through the small window. He rubbed his neck. He'd been up here long enough for one day.

Well, he'd made enough progress for

the moment. He grabbed up the now-full, clear plastic bags and eased them all through the hatch.

He descended the ladder and put the recycling out in the foyer. Then he headed into the kitchen to make himself a late supper. His mind returned to his grandmother.

Hmmm.

What if the diary Nicky had found helped him find out more about Grandma Viv? Surely, she hadn't really fallen in love with a Nazi...

Perhaps it would also help him figure out the whereabouts of the will? Maybe, somewhere in it, would be a clue?

And what if the letter he'd found could help Nicky in some way? His heart pounded. Could he agree to work with her? But what if she rejected him? He shook his head. No. This wasn't personal. It was strictly business.

She was writing an article about his grandmother, that's all. Maybe she wasn't being a nosy journalist; maybe she was just doing her job well. She'd said she'd done research on the woman, so his grandmother's life would have to be her business. Parts of it, anyway.

He supposed he could talk to her.

Working with her wouldn't be a distraction, but a way to bring things into focus. Help him connect with his grandmother.

He straightened his shoulders. It was business. That, he could handle. He took a breath. He'd just be professional. Polite. She didn't need to know he felt a bit attracted to her. He could easily hide that.

He pulled out his phone again along with the now-crumpled business card Nicky had given him.

NICKY STARTED TO read through the Word document on her laptop. But her phone buzzed with an incoming text message before she could continue. From Quinten?

Why don't we meet at the music shop tomorrow morning? You're right, I'd like to look at her diary.

Without hesitating, she texted back.

Sounds great. See you then.

She put her phone down. Hmm. Battery was getting low again. Needed to charge it.

She turned her attention back to the story. She needed to look in the diary. What was inside? She felt a tingle of excitement go up her spine. And, well, she wanted to know...was Quinten *always* like that? Or was the lady at the visitors' center right?

She glanced back at the page. She'd made a little headway tonight on the story. Transcribed some of her notes on what Mabel had told her. That incident about the stolen ham would be a good one to layer in, somehow. Maybe as a sidebar?

She turned her attention back to the open document. She'd typed about a hundred words when her thoughts strayed again.

If she wasn't careful, she could think of several excuses to stay longer. The scent of the fresh sea breeze, the taste of salted caramel on her tongue... And Quinten Leard agreeing to help her?

No. As much as she needed the information and was grateful to Quinten, she knew she couldn't allow herself to be attracted to him. It would interfere with her carefully laid plans. She only had a few days here, after all.

She lifted her chin. She needed to stick to reading spy thrillers.

The romance genre was one best steered clear of. It wasn't realistic. It didn't do anyone any favors. Least of all for people like her who'd believed in romantic notions and then got them completely smashed when they discovered that real life, real love, wasn't the same as it was in a paperback.

She sighed. If only...

If only, nothing. She had a story to write, and a very good lead to follow now, what with Quinten's agreeing to help her. That was all.

QUINTEN GLANCED OUT the window Friday morning. Golden light spilled through the trees and cast dappled patterns on the pavement of Main Street.

Some tour buses were scheduled to come into the village later this morning, and he needed to be open for that. But he had a little time now.

He noticed Nicky as she walked toward his house. She said hello to a few people who headed up the street.

Sunlight caught the reddish highlights in her hair and burnished them a fiery copper.

Such a strong color. Kind of like her personality. His heart jumped. He wished he had strength like that. What was it like, to not hide? To say what he felt freely, without worrying what others thought?

He saw Nicky say something to one of the older ladies outside—was that Mabel? Looked like it. Acting like a local, practically.

Pretty soon she'd be buying a summer cottage here; a good chunk of the village was seasonal residents. Thank goodness none of the houses were for sale in the central core here. But the suburbs were another story.

He frowned. He didn't know Nicky well enough to make assumptions. He didn't know her at all. He winced. Strong personalities meant drama. And drama meant unnecessary attention called to himself. He needed to stay away from all of that.

"Hi Quinten," Nicky said as she walked up the steps of the porch.

"Thanks for coming."

"Thanks for finally deciding to help me." Nicky laughed and put a hand on her hip.

He shifted his weight.

"So." She met Quinten's gaze.

He could see the hints of green in her hazel eyes. He cleared his throat.

"Like I already said," she continued as she came closer to the screen door that divided them, "this is her diary. You want to know what's inside?" He saw a gleam of daring? challenge? in her gaze and couldn't help the half-smile that flitted across his lips. He kind of liked the fact that she took charge. That she knew what she wanted.

He opened the door.

She stepped inside.

The lace curtains across the street twitched.

Nicky now stood only a few feet away from him and for a second, they simply looked at each other.

Her hair was slightly windblown, and the turquoise blouse she wore looked vintage. It made her skin look—no. That was a detail he was going to pretend he hadn't noticed.

He swallowed and took a step back.

"The zipper's stuck. The lock doesn't have a key." Nicky bit her lip. "And I'm sorry to say I couldn't bring my tool box with me. Do you happen to have a pair of small pliers?"

"Uh..." Quinten blinked. "I think so. If you—" No. He didn't want to make her uncomfortable by asking her to come to the back room. He cleared his throat. "I have some in the workshop. Let me just check."

He exhaled softly as he walked into the back room. Breathe. Just breathe. She was just another person. She was just needing his help. He was just being a good neighbor.

But curiosity and heat nudged at him despite himself. She looked *really* good in that blouse.

He rummaged around in a drawer on his workbench. Here was a pair. He picked them up and headed back out to the store front.

"Found them," he said unnecessarily.

Her eyes lit up. "Great." She handed him the diary. "Here, maybe if you hold it, I can get a good angle."

"Okay. Uh, sure." He took the small book from her and studied its cover. Would there be anything in here that would clarify things? Or mention a will?

Why hadn't Grandma Viv ever wanted to talk about her life before she'd come to the island? Had she really been...hiding something? He felt a small stab of hurt in his heart.

"Hmm, I think it'd be better if you flipped it over," Nicky said as she reached for the book. She stood so close to him that he could see a small freckle on her collarbone. He moved his gaze to the diary instead.

She gripped the pliers in one hand and held onto the book with the other. Their fingers were nearly touching. He noticed the ring on the forefinger of her left hand.

He cocked his head. Another vintage piece. She appreciated things with history, he noted with approval.

That ring, though...it looked somewhat familiar. And in a flash, he remembered. That old black and white photograph of Vivian that she'd shown him when she was in the nursing home.

He caught his breath. She had been wearing that ring when the picture had been taken.

But how...?

He put the speculating out of his mind as he tightened his grip on the book and watched Nicky grasp the zipper pull with the pliers.

Gently, she tugged on the zipper. At first, nothing happened. But then, slowly, slowly, the zipper began to move.

He held his breath as the zipper inched its way down the long side of the book and then across the bottom.

"We did it!" Nicky grinned at him.

"Looks like it." He found himself grinning back. She didn't give up, did she? He could appreciate having someone like that to work with.

"Well," Nicky leaned in and he could feel her breath on his skin as she said, "we have to find out what's inside, don't we?"

"CAN I JUST..." Nicky indicated the diary with her free hand and Quinten startled. "Uh, sure."

He released the small book and Nicky opened it as far as it would go.

"But the lock's still there. See? It went underneath the flap that keeps the diary closed, and then the clasp locks over on top of that," Nicky said.

"Hmm." Quinten studied the small lock. "Well, I have a bunch of keys somewhere in a mayonnaise jar. Be back in a second."

He turned and headed up a stairway that Nicky hadn't noticed before, tucked as it was in a nook near the cash register.

Nicky heard floorboards creak overhead. A minute or so later, he came back down the stairs, mayonnaise jar with the label ripped off, in hand.

He placed the jar full of keys of all sizes on the counter where the cash register sat. Nicky saw a package of yellow jelly beans beside it. "Do you sell those too?"

"That's a good idea I hadn't thought of." He chuckled. "No. I actually bought those for my cousin's little girl. Her mom's birthday's next week and I wanted to give Rosie something to make sure she didn't feel left out."

Nicky's heart fluttered. That was sweet of him. "I've been a fan of jelly beans since my very first Easter."

"Me too. The chocolate shop here has a great selection. I've always bought mine there."

"I'll have to keep that in mind." She turned her attention back to the keys. "Let's see. Might be easier if we dumped it out."

Quinten glanced at her as a small smile formed on his lips. "I was just going to say that. Great minds think alike."

Nicky couldn't help but respond with a smile of her own at his compliment.

She picked up the jar and upended it. Long, thin, ornate skeleton keys were jumbled together with newer flat brass hotel room keys that looked like they'd been forgotten in purses and pockets. Some even had fobs imprinted with motel logos and room numbers.

"Quite the collection you have here,"

Nicky murmured.

"Grandma Viv was a bit of a pack rat," Quinten admitted. He began to sort them out by size. "Makes sense to look for the tiniest keys possible..." He trailed off as he concentrated on the jumbled pile.

Nicky came to stand beside him to help sort. "They all look pretty much bigger than what we need."

"Mmm." Quinten deftly kept sorting. "Sometimes you just have to be..."

He rummaged around between a pile of bolts that had somehow gotten mixed in, and a set of what looked like five or six motel room keys on a fob.

"...persistent." He grinned as he held up the tiniest key Nicky had ever seen.

The happy look on his face probably echoed her own, Nicky realized. Excitement filled her. It was fun to try and figure this out together. "Let's give it a try."

Nicky put the book on the counter and Quinten fit the key into the lock. But it was too small.

"Damn," Quinten muttered.

"Like you said, we just have to be persistent." Nicky scanned the pile of keys again. She reached out and picked up another small key. But that one didn't fit either.

For the next thirty minutes, they went through almost every key that could possibly work. Except none of them did.

Nicky shoved her hands into her pockets in frustration. "Now what?"

"Well," Quinten said, "we could just cut through the leather."

Nicky's eyes widened.

"Or not," Quinten hastily added. "That would sort of wreck the historical aspect of the book."

Hmmm. She appreciated his perceptiveness.

"Well," Nicky said in a joking tone as she pulled her hands out of her pockets and came up holding her keyring. "We could always try these." She laughed as she jangled them.

Quinten chuckled. "As long as we're trying far-fetched ideas, I might as well get out my own keys, too." They went through all of his keys, and most of hers.

"No luck." Nicky smoothed her bangs. "Not that I seriously expected anything to happen."

"What about that tiny little one on your keyring?"

"This one?" She shrugged. "Okay." She plucked up the tiny key and fit it into the lock.

Quinten leaned closer to watch. Nicky could feel the warmth of his nearness that carried a hint of his lemony cologne.

There was a snick as the key fit and a click as it turned.

Nicky gasped.

Quinten whistled. "There's no way—where did you *get* that key?"

"Inside a hidden inner pocket of a vintage jacket I bought on P.E.I. last summer. I just thought the key was cute, so I put it on my keyring as a knickknack."

"Oh?" Quinten raised his eyebrows.

"But now that I think about it, it makes total sense that this little key would fit Viv's diary."

"Why?"

"Because the jacket must've been Viv's, so..." Nicky said, almost to herself.

"The key obviously was too," Quinten said.

"She must've forgotten about it in the jacket pocket. Or purposely hid it there, since the pocket was concealed?" Nicky tapped a fingernail against her chin.

"Either way," Quinten said, "it worked to open the diary."

"Mmm. Come to think of it, that letter was in there too."

"Letter?"

"Written to your grandmother during the war."

Quinten glanced at her, a guarded look on his face as he said, "Was it signed with just the initial 'A'?"

"Yes. But how did you know that?" Nicky said.

"I saw a letter written to her too," Quinten said.

Nicky grinned. "We'll have to compare notes on the letters at some point." She turned her attention back to the diary. "But maybe for now we should see what's inside here?"

"Sure."

Nicky kept her eyes on the diary but couldn't ignore the slight buzz in the pit of her stomach from the brush of Quinten's breath against her cheek.

She gently opened the front cover and saw the faded words.

For Vivian

Love, Mother

Christmas, '38

Quinten traced a finger along the name and then flicked his eyes to hers. He moistened a fingertip and turned the page over in one fluid motion.

June 3, 1939

The heat has settled over London something fierce. Today was my first day in my new position at the Office. I suppose it won't hurt to say that I'm thrilled.

But more than thrilled, it's the feeling that we are achieving some purpose here. Me and the other girls. Though the room I'm in with them gets quite hot even with the fans blowing. And all the papers have to be weighed down or they would blow around and that would be a sorry muddle!

My skills are actually put to good use – maybe more so than they would've ever been had I taken a high school math position back in New York as Mother wanted – and hoped – I would. But war has a funny way of changing things, doesn't it?

So the fight must go on. We must win. And I intend to do my part, whatever the cost.

Quinten met Nicky's gaze and he wondered if her heart was racing too. He noticed her pulse beat at the base of her throat.

He forced his mind back to the journal. This proved that his grandmother had been involved in the war effort in England. Somehow.

"It's your grandmother," she said softly and handed the book to him.

Something about the look of compassion? empathy? in her eyes made him say, "You know, I never felt like I knew who she really was, exactly." He hesitated, then glanced her way and added, "She always seemed to have this part of her that somehow...eluded me."

"That must have been hard."

He felt a nudge to keep going, to say something more, to respond to her openness. But he couldn't. She'd judge him, tell him he was wrong to show emotion, to feel what he felt. Just like his father had judged him.

So he only nodded and thumbed the edges of the pages. Bits of ink showed themselves to him and he felt his pulse quicken. Wait a minute. Quinten drew in a sharp breath.

Nicky glanced at him.

There might be more about Grandma Viv in that letter Nicky had. She'd said they could compare notes on the letters, anyway. Hmmm. What if they went through all of his grandmother's things more thoroughly? Together? Maybe in there somewhere would be some sort of documentation that would help Nicky? And some papers his grandmother had written, indicating a successor?

It was worth a try.

"I'm sorry to stop here but I have to open up my shop in not too long. Tour buses coming in. I do have a day off tomorrow. Pretty much all my grandmother's stuff is packed away, but it might have more answers that would help us both. So why don't we meet at the chocolate shop in the morning, get some good coffee and then dive in to all those boxes together?"

YESTERDAY NICKY HAD left the diary with Quinten at his music shop. He said he'd be more comfortable with it there.

And she couldn't argue with that.

Nor could she argue with herself when she indulged in a memory of how his breath had brushed her cheek; the look of his solid chest as he'd stood so close; or the thrill up her spine when they'd unlocked the diary together and he'd met her gaze.

But more than that, she'd appreciated his persistence in their key hunt. Reminded her of herself when she chased down a piece of research. She also liked his perceptiveness... She toyed with a strand of hair. They'd worked well together yesterday.

She needed to concentrate. She'd gotten about fifteen hundred words down of a first draft. She checked her watch. Already Saturday. And nearly 9:00 a.m. She was making pretty good time.

Once she got to read through all the entries in the diary, she'd have a much better picture of Vivian.

After reading that first entry, it felt as if Vivian was talking right to her. In a way she was, Nicky mused.

And that was the type of story the magazine's readers loved. One that showed humanity, vulnerability... and, well, history. The *Historical Woman* believed that history was no different than the present, that people were people no matter the era.

And that was exactly what Vivian's diary would prove.

Nicky made a few last-minute notes to herself on the steno pad by her computer before she shut the lid.

She glanced out the window. Buttery yellow sunlight streamed through the gauzy white curtains; and the crystal clear blue sky seemed brighter than she'd ever seen it.

She changed out of her pajamas and pulled on a pale pink cashmere sweater.

She paired it with a pair of dark wash denim jeans—her favorite—that had a rip at the knee and were so soft and worn in that they felt nearly as good as cashmere.

Her phone bleeped and she glanced at the notifications. A text from her landlord. She bit her lip and opened it.

Nicky, don't forget the rent money by the 19th. That's in ten days.

She fought down a flutter of panic. She'd get the money. *Ivory* magazine had to come through. She chewed on a hangnail for a second. She'd tried again to get ahold of them but they *still* hadn't responded. They hadn't replied to that post she'd left on their social media platform, either...

She picked up her hairbrush and pushed down the nudge of worry. She couldn't do anything more about it, she told herself, as she ran the brush through her hair and fluffed her bangs.

What good would worrying do? Nothing. It would only make her nervous. She slicked on some lip balm and grabbed her purse with her notepad, keys, and her Nikon, then headed out the door and up the street to Island Chocolates.

QUINTEN WALKED UP the steps of Island Chocolates. Not too busy yet this morning. He opened the door.

The staff was working on a big batch of chocolates. He could see Gemma's brother Derek busily filling molds through the workroom window.

But Quinten wasn't the only one inside.

"...on my tab. Two espressos for now, please," Nicky said to Gemma.

"Quinten's usual, eh?" Gemma said with a grin.

He saw Nicky head to his favorite table by the window.

"Thanks. I could've bought them." He winced. That sounded far more accusatory than he'd meant. He followed her to the table.

Nicky shrugged. "I wanted to. Besides, I have to butter you up somehow as a thanks for helping me." She sat down. "And between you and me, I could use a cup of strong coffee at this point. I've been up for awhile. Got a start on a draft, anyway."

"Oh, good," Quinten said.

"You two want any cream?" Gemma came over with a small tray that had a tiny jug of cream and two spoons on it.

Both Quinten and Nicky nodded.

On impulse, Quinten found himself saying, "Gemma, can you bring us some chocolate waffles, please?"

"Two orders then?" She looked from Quinten to Nicky and back again.

"Yes, please," Quinten said.

"They're delicious," Gemma told Nicky as she put the tiny cream jug down on the table.

"Great," Nicky said. "I love breakfast. And I haven't had any this morning."

Gemma left them to their coffee and Quinten cleared his throat.

"So." He shifted slightly in his chair.

Nicky picked up her demitasse cup and wrapped her fingers around its steaming contents. The ring on her finger caught the light.

"That's a really intricate pattern of vines and leaves. It's pretty," he found himself saying.

"My ring? Thanks." A look of pleased surprise flicked across Nicky's face. "I love vintage jewelry."

"Where did you get it?"

Nicky glanced down at it and then extended her hand, fingers spread wide. "At a flea market in Nobo a couple summers ago. My friend, and former boss, Maggie—oh, hey, you might know her? She's from P.E.I. Kilhoughery's her last name."

"Mmm. Don't think I do."

Nicky shrugged. "Had to ask, 'cause you never know. So, yeah, she said it's pretty valuable. Apparently medieval Polish."

Quinten's brows shot up.

Nicky slipped off the ring and held it out to him.

He took it, the metal still warm from her skin. "Someone knew what they were doing when they made it, that's for sure," he commented.

"I know, right? That's what I love about vintage jewelry."

Quinten leaned toward her. "That's the thing with historical pieces. The crafts-manship's always excellent." He studied the ring. "That's partly why I got into the piano tuning business, actually. Because I love history. Being able to preserve that sense of heritage and pass it down to future generations. It's important."

"Right. To keep that connection to the past so that we know where we've come from."

"Exactly." He raised his eyes from the

ring to her face. "It's more than that, too. It's being able to share it. Share the stories embedded in the wood, in the strings, in the whole piece..." He tensed and busied himself stirring his coffee. Had he said too much? Exposed too much of himself?

He risked a glance at Nicky and saw a flare of excitement in her eyes as she said, "That's how I feel when I'm writing my articles. Sharing stories, the truth, with the world."

Quinten's shoulders relaxed as a few moments passed in silence. Maybe he was safe to open up a bit?

He cleared his throat. "There's a photo my grandmother showed me when she was in the nursing home. She's wearing this exact ring. Or, if not this exact one, then one that looks identical to it."

"Wow."

"I'd never seen her wear it but the photo looked as if it was taken in the 1940s. And on the back of the picture, all it said was 'Last day at the Office.'"

Nicky's brows furrowed.

But before she could comment, the waffles arrived.

"Yum. These look delicious," Nicky said.

"Told ya." Gemma grinned. "Need

anything else?"

Quinten shook his head. Nicky did too.

"Enjoy, guys."

Quinten spread honey butter over the waffles. Fresh whipped cream and a handful of island blueberries were scattered across the waffles. Rich, creamy, warm Nutella had been drizzled over the entire concoction.

Nicky took a bite. Then four more. "These are amazing," she said around a mouthful. "Especially the honey butter. I could eat all of this in one bite, practically."

He took a sip of coffee but his gaze lingered on her lips as she wiped off a trace of honey butter. He preferred to savor things...

He forced his eyes away, lest she catch him looking. "Eating them for the first time's almost as good as eating them every Sunday for brunch like I do. I always eat them by myself. But it's more fun to enjoy them with someone." He tensed as soon as the words left his mouth. What was he doing? Why had he just confessed that to her? But the admission had felt good.

To distract himself, he took another forkful of his waffle and the rich chocolate taste lingered on his tongue. But that didn't help.

"So what do you think it means, us having the same ring?" Nicky's words cut into his thoughts. She had finished her whole waffle and studied him over the rim of her coffee cup.

He tried to look busy as he finished the first half of his waffle. "What do I—oh, about the ring? I'm not sure. You know, I'd call it coincidence, but I don't believe in that sort of thing."

A speculative gleam came into Nicky's eyes. "Well, with what you said about the writing on the back of her photo, I'm thinking 'the Office' meant the Special Operations Executive headquarters at 64 Baker Street in London where she worked with a group of other cipher girls."

"Really?"

"Yep." Nicky grinned as she leaned forward and rested her forearms on the table. "The SOE actually recruited quite a few civilians for the codes department, which is something I hadn't realized until I looked at Viv's file."

"Mmm-hmm." Quinten rubbed a hand across his jaw to hide a smile. Her enthusiasm was cute. She loved history, didn't she?

"There's even a photo attached to her SOE file. But it's only a headshot, so I can't see if she's wearing any jewelry."

Quinten put down his fork. "But if she was wearing that ring in that other photo, maybe she got it from somewhere in London?"

"Or from someone in London?" Nicky grinned at him.

"True."

Nicky took a sip of coffee. "Then somewhere along the line she decided to get rid of the ring? Or maybe she had to sell it because she needed the money? Times were tough back then—the Depression was before the war. Or maybe she lost it somehow and it made its way to that flea market?"

Quinten picked up his coffee and said quietly, "She did, at one point, mail all her valuable jewelry to the Salvation Army." His fingers tightened on the cup's handle. "But like I said before, I..."

"It's okay." She hesitated a second, but then touched his hand.

He sucked in a soft breath as her fingers made contact with his skin. He opened his mouth, then closed it. What was he saying? He couldn't remember.

He met her gaze.

Her expression was one of empathy mixed with sadness. His heart softened and his throat tightened. Had she lost someone close to her, too? He swallowed. What would happen if he opened up more to her?

No. He couldn't risk that. He had to focus. With an effort, he managed, "Thank you."

"You're welcome."

He drained the last bit of his coffee and stood up. "Ready to go?"

He picked up both of their plates and carried them to the register, which was right by the doorway to the kitchen.

"Thanks, Quinten," Gemma called from around the corner of the door.

He pulled out his wallet. She waved a hand and then stuck her head around the doorframe. "No need to pay for the waffles. Already on your friend's tab."

A surge of pleased surprise coursed through Quinten.

Gemma added in a conspiratorial tone, "She told me to add on whatever else you might order before you came in."

He darted a glance at Nicky, who stood near the front door and examined what looked like a small piece of paper she'd pulled from her purse.

He grinned. "Oh, uh... Right." He put away his wallet.

"Have a good day, Quinten," Gemma said with a note of laughter in her voice.

"You too," he replied. He noticed that Nicky looked conflicted about something. But she put the scrap of paper back into her purse as he headed over to her.

"Shall we?"

Nicky, her expression now resolute, picked up her camera. "Let's."

THE STAIRS CREAKED as Nicky followed Quinten up the narrow steps. "I still have the ladder up here because I was going through Christmas decorations for the recycling. Which is due to be picked up tomorrow." Quinten glanced over his shoulder at her. He looked slightly sheepish and the tips of his ears turned red. "And now I'm rambling."

She couldn't help but notice he wore exactly the same expression as his photo on the stairwell beside her. What was he there in the picture? Twelve? Eleven? Something like that. Nicky hid a smile. His embarrassment was kind of cute. Some things don't change. "Hey, no worries. I do that a lot myself sometimes." They reached the landing and Quinten set up the ladder.

That cobalt blue shirt was such a great color for him.

What was she thinking? She had a story to write. Information to gather. That's all she was doing here.

She wasn't going to evaluate the merits of the way he filled out his button down. Even if it was very nicely, she admitted to herself, with another sidelong look. Or the way he seemed to appreciate her view on history. Something Ben hadn't appreciated in her at all.

A blush crept over her cheeks as he glanced at her. That cobalt color really brought out his eyes. "I'll just remove the trapdoor hatch here."

Nicky couldn't help but admire the play of his back muscles as he put action to words. He turned and offered her a hand up the ladder.

That was considerate of him. She took his hand and tried not to think about the implications. Was he interested in her? No. He just wanted to make sure she didn't fall and break a limb, that was all.

As she maneuvered through the opening, he said, "Watch yourself. It's a bit tricky to navigate if you're not used to stepping over roof rafters."

"Thanks." She paused. "It'd be great if

we could find something, wouldn't it?"

"Mmmm." Quinten raised and lowered his wide shoulders as he joined her.

Nicky felt a stab of annoyance. Was he always this noncommittal? But the man had to have emotions way down deep somewhere...didn't he?

She forced herself to focus on the task at hand. "So all these boxes were hers?"

"Most of them, yeah. I haven't gone through ninety-nine percent of them."

Nicky felt her stomach flutter. "So we have a lot of digging to do."

Quinten glanced at her. "We need to proceed with caution. Like I said, she didn't exactly talk about anything about her time during the war. She made a reference one time to almost having met Churchill. When I pressed her about it, she acted like she hadn't heard me. So I let it go." He paused. "Of course, that only made me more intrigued."

He picked up a box marked *Viv's Things.*

Nicky came to join him.

Quinten looked inside. "Not a whole lot in here. Just a bunch of photographs—you know, I think the one I mentioned should be here—and a few letters she wrote to her mother back in the States."

"Can I take a look?"

Quinten handed them to her.

Nicky leafed through them. "Just daily chatter."

Quinten poked around more in the box. "That's about it for this one...some gloves, stockings, and a hat or two."

Nicky put the letters back. "Can I look at the photos? I'm going to need some for my article and since she isn't here anymore, I can't take her picture. So if we could run the article with some of these, that'd be great."

"Sure." Quinten took out the photos and handed them to Nicky.

They were mostly candid shots, out of focus with parts of people instead of whole bodies. "She wasn't much of a photographer, was she?" Nicky mused.

Quinten shook his head. "She loved math. Puzzles. Crosswords. That sort of thing. She could do square roots and long division in her head. She had pretty much a photographic memory. I was always asking her how she did it and she would just shrug and say it came naturally. She went to school to be a math teacher but ended up with the music store business instead. That was something else she loved—music. Almost as much as math. But," he continued, "there's actually a lot of math in music if you think about it."

"Yep, that's true." Nicky jotted a few things down on a tiny notepad she'd pulled from her back pocket. She thumbed through the rest of the photos. "Here it is. You're right." She pulled out her Nikon and snapped some shots of the photo from close up and farther away. That way she wouldn't have to scan the image into the computer but they could still run it.

She held the photo closer. "That ring does look identical." She studied the ring on her own finger. "Huh."

She threw a sidelong glance at Quinten. "Did Hitler's gold and diamonds really end up on P.E.I.?"

"I can see Mabel's been talking to you. She's utterly convinced." He tugged at his earlobe. "That's what the rumors say."

"So you don't believe it."

"You sound disappointed."

"Just want to cover all the angles for my story."

Quinten crossed his arms. "That stuff about Hitler's treasure buried here is just an island legend. Being a journalist, you should know the difference between fact and fiction."

Now Nicky crossed her arms. "But

what if it's true?"

"And what if it isn't?"

"What if I have proof?" Nicky countered.

Quinten raised a brow.

Nicky held up a small silver coin. It glinted in the light.

Quinten's eyes widened. "That's a *Nazi* coin."

Chapter Five

QUINTEN LEANED FORWARD to examine the coin and Nicky caught the slight citrusy scent of his cologne. Something in the way he studied the coin, how he seemed to take in every detail like he wanted to really understand it, made longing swoop through Nicky. What would happen if she let him know her, understand her, like that? No. She was only here for the story.

A strand of his blond hair fell across his forehead as he looked down at the coin now resting on her palm.

As he reached out and picked up the coin with his thumb and forefinger, his fingertips brushed Nicky's palm. She couldn't ignore the fact that she liked the sensation.

"Where did you get this?"

"Mabel had it. She told me I could—"

"—use it to convince me to go treasure

hunting with you?"

"Something like that," Nicky smiled.

Quinten laughed and murmured, "She's always been a matchmaker. Half the island, I think, has benefitted from her convictions about true love."

Nicky shifted her weight and tucked a strand of hair behind her ear as she avoided Quinten's eyes. Mabel's matchmaking skills wouldn't be put to use here, that was sure. He was too stoic—which made him too much like Ben—for her liking. Wasn't he?

"So?" she said.

Quinten blinked.

"Hitler's gold," Nicky supplied.

"There's nothing to that. Even with this Nazi coin." Quinten handed it back. "It could've come from anywhere. There was a German POW camp up in New Brunswick, after all."

"But there were supposed to be U-boats in the waters around P.E.I." Nicky put her hands on her hips. "That's what the online database of archived Charlottetown newspaper articles told me."

"You've been doing your research, I see." Quinten gave her a sidelong glance.

"I *am* a journalist." Nicky tapped her finger on the notepad.

Quinten sighed. "You're not going to let this go, are you?"

Nicky's eyes gleamed. "Not if I can help it. It's the perfect add-on to the article about your grandmother."

"Why? She had nothing to do with Hitler's gold."

"I have a hunch there might be a connection. A good journalist examines all possible related angles. Besides, Mabel didn't say your grandmother was in love with a Nazi for nothing."

"So she told you that, did she?" Quinten's shoulders stiffened. "It's entirely untrue. The whole thing."

Nicky made an expansive gesture. "You don't know that for sure."

"Neither do you."

Nicky pursed her lips. "You just don't want to believe the evidence that's staring you in the face."

Quinten crossed his arms. "It's circumstantial."

Nicky lifted her chin. "There's only one way to find out for sure."

"What are you saying?"

"I'm saying we find the treasure."

Quinten laughed. "There's nothing to find."

"And you're not taking me seriously."

Quinten held up his hands. "It's not you I'm worried about. It's Mabel. It's this whole village. There's a propensity to believe what you hear, around here."

Nicky raised a brow. "So?"

"So," Quinten repeated, "there's nothing to it. There's no gold, there are no diamonds, and it certainly had nothing to do with my grandmother."

"BUT—" NICKY STARTED to say, but the sound of a chime from downstairs interrupted her.

Quinten glanced at his watch and swore. "That'll be the first busload of tourists. I need to go tend the shop."

Nicky tucked her notepad into her purse and hiked her camera bag over her shoulder. "Right. Of course."

They headed down to the kitchen on the first floor of the house.

"Here," Quinten said. He handed her the cream-colored book. "I thought we'd have time to go through this after we finished in the attic. But since we didn't get a chance to, why don't you take a look at it? If you find anything, let me know."

Nicky took the small book. "You're

sure you want to let this out of your sight?"

Quinten studied her for a second. "I'm willing to take a chance."

She blushed under his gaze. "Thank you. For the journal, for letting me take the pictures, and for your time."

"You're welcome. That's what I do around here—help people out."

She crossed into the showroom, Quinten behind her. "Once I finish a draft, I'll have a few more questions for you."

"Sure." Quinten held the screen door open for Nicky. As she left, the tourists came inside.

NICKY PICKED UP her laptop from her room. She headed across the back lawn of the Orient Hotel, careful to avoid the croquet wickets, and then down Nelson Street.

She could type up her notes on the boardwalk. There was a nice bench in the sun that she'd spotted yesterday. From what she recalled in one of the Victoria-by-the-Sea pamphlets, it was near the customs house.

She sank onto that bench a few minutes later and looked around. To her right, she noticed the customs house, its bright red siding faded and its windows boarded up. Wouldn't it be nice if someone restored it?

Her thoughts turned to Quinten. Her shoulders drooped a little as the sun warmed her. She'd hoped he would've at least considered the possibility of the treasure...

But it didn't really matter what he thought, now did it? This was her article. But it was his grandmother.

She chewed on a hangnail.

But what she'd told him back in the attic was right. This would provide a great twist to the story. Give it real depth if she delved into the supposed Nazi treasure aspect.

What if they found out the truth about all of it? Didn't Quinten deserve to know if his grandmother had been mixed up in it? Vivian deserved to have the truth known about her. And wasn't it up to Nicky to put that all out there for the world to decide?

Nicky watched the seagulls call and dive over the water. Yes, she realized, it was. And that was exactly what she was going to do.

She picked up the journal.

The second entry was dated two years after the first.

February 2, 1942

It's been so busy at the Office – it's hard to believe I've been here nearly two years now. Time has a strange way of contracting yet feeling unbearably long as well... But I know we are making a difference – I know we are.

Every little piece counts. Everyone here has a specific task, and I know mine. And though sometimes it feels like the war will never end, I need to have faith that it will – that we will come out victorious.

Because the alternative is not an option. And though the girls sometimes disagree about where to aim the fans – oh, how it gets hot in those vast rooms with so much paper and so many hushed conversations as we work to make heads and tails of everything – the overall sense amongst all of us is kinship. Women working toward a common goal, a common good – valued for our minds and our skills; at last.

Though some say it won't last – this newfound freedom we have gained – I prefer to think that perhaps, just perhaps, we could influence our daughters and our granddaughters – to usher in a bold new era.

But I go on too much now!

Nicky turned the page.

March 29, 1943

I have to share my news, if only with myself. I have been meeting him for nearly a year now. It feels treasonous to say so, but it's true.

I am in love with him. And he, with me.

And even though we were specifically told not to acquaint ourselves with those whose work we are entrusted with, it is what has happened.

I did not intend for it to happen. It simply did. I can close my eyes and picture him, standing there, in the hours before he left. In his moss-green jacket, the collar turned up against the London rain, his brown eyes full of warmth. Trust. Hope.

Hmmm. Vivian worked in the codes department, which handled agents' traffic. So it stood to reason that whoever this was couldn't be a Nazi. Why, then, had Mabel said Vivian had been in love with a Nazi?

Nicky rubbed her temples. She could wonder about that later. Right now, her primary focus needed to be getting clear on the truth about Vivian, not sidetracked by who she was in love with—as tantalizing as that was to speculate about. She read the rest of the entry.

I take some comfort in the fact that the politics within the Office here are such... that certain things have the outward appearance of rule-following when, indeed, they are not so. Things are done behind closed doors. People turn a blind eye; say one thing and do another. Such it is in a time of war. I blush at the recollection of what I myself saw one particular midnight!

Nicky looked at the next page. But the entry wasn't in English. She squinted at it. In fact, it wasn't any language she recognized...

She turned the little book this way and that. No. It wasn't in a language at all. It was some sort of cipher or code. She'd have to tell Quinten about this. Maybe he'd have an idea as to what it was. He had good suggestions. She liked that he seemed to be reliable like that.

Well, she'd start with these first two entries, anyway...

Several hours later, Nicky stretched and looked up. She rubbed the back of her neck. It had gotten a bit chilly out and the wind had picked up.

But she'd gotten a completed rough first draft. She grinned. Very rough. Lots of holes she'd have to go back and fill in with relevant quotes and more in-depth research.

At least now she had the shape of the story. Something she could look at, work with, mold until it was exactly right. Until it conveyed exactly what it needed to say. Until all the voices were heard.

Speaking of...

She uploaded and saved the photos she'd taken of Vivian's picture onto her laptop. She studied them a minute. No distortion or discoloration. They'd work just fine.

Job done, she got up and tucked the laptop under her arm. Her heart lifted as she watched the fishing boats bob in their moorings at the wharf. It was so charming here.

She glanced around. A line of tourists and locals snaked out the door of the Lobster Barn Pub & Eatery. Must be near dinnertime. She'd heard their lobster rolls were excellent. Her stomach rumbled as she headed over.

Nicky passed a tiny wharfinger's hut as she crossed the first few hundred feet of pavement toward the pub. She walked over yellow letters that read Fishers' Parking Only as she passed stone crab traps piled up along the edge of the wharf.

She reached the end of the line at the pub. Its shingle siding was a naturally weathered gray. But the bright turquoise trim set off the building's best features.

The chatter of tourists drifted to her along with the scent of fried clams and French fries.

Her mouth watered as the line inched forward. Nicky finally made it inside and told the girl at the bar she wanted a table for one.

"Usually it's a three-week waiting period for dinnertime in our busy season. But October's a good time to be here. A bit quieter. So more seating options."

She led Nicky to a table by the window that overlooked the water and a bluff that had a smattering of houses. The server noticed Nicky's glance.

"You can see Crescent Beach and our new subdivision from here."

"Nice." Nicky took the seat facing the window. "Think I'll enjoy the view."

The chatter of other diners and the clink of silverware washed over Nicky. The long, wooden table beside her held a group of laughing, loudly chatting people. She recognized a few by sight and waved. They waved back.

She turned back to her table and twisted the amber ring around her finger. Why had Vivian been wearing it? How had she gotten it? Maggie had said it was from medieval times... Nicky pulled up the search engine on her phone and typed in *medieval Polish amber rings*.

She scrolled through the results. Hmmm. Amber price and value information. How to assess vintage jewelry. Three ways to clean amber jewelry. Oh. *That* could be useful. She bookmarked the page and continued to scroll. Amber jewelry and souvenirs from Krakow, Poland.

Hmm. Nothing was really—

Wait. Her fingers hovered over a link that read Polish Art Center: The History of Amber Jewelry.

She tapped the link and scanned the headline. A history of the use of amber in jewelry in Poland. She skimmed the article and her eyes caught on the final subhead.

*The Stolen Riches of Princess
Magdalena Jola Piast*

It's been compared to the theft and disappearance of the Amber Room during the Second World War. But few have heard the story of Princess Magdalena Jola Piast's stolen riches.

In 1241, Princess Magdalena Jola Piast of Poland married Philippe Capet, a cousin of Louis IX of France. Her wedding dowry—diamonds, a beautiful jewelled mirror, and several pieces of amber jewelry, including a large, rare, green amber ring with matching ear-bobs, as well as an untold amount of gold—was commissioned and sent along with her to France.

Nicky leaned forward in her chair and kept reading.

Amid the back and forth of European royal intermarriages over the next several centuries, the dowry came back into Poland. It ended up with the prominent Gobell family, direct descendants of the princess's line.

Because the pieces originated in the Middle Ages, some started to believe a legend that said the jewelled mirror held the power to reveal the secrets of lasting love.

But after the fall of Poland in 1939

to Germany, the entire dowry went missing.

Some speculate it ended up as a private collection in North America after being smuggled onto a U-boat during the height of the war.

Other scholars believe the dowry was used as a bargaining chip by Hitler's personal secretary, Martin Bormann, to raise funds to support Hitler's secret plan to create a Fourth Reich.

Still others think the dowry remains in Germany, since its last known location was the Reichsbank in Berlin, Germany in 1943.

Whatever the case, the fact remains that the dowry, and all its valuable cultural and historical significance, has been lost.

Much like the Amber Room, after the war, the dowry simply vanished. No mention of it, nor its location, has ever been discovered.

Nicky scrolled a bit further down and saw a painting of a beautiful, black-haired woman wearing a gorgeous, burgundy silk gown.

The caption read *Princess Magdalena Jola Piast*.

Nicky noticed the small jewel-encrusted silver mirror the woman held in one hand. That same hand also sported a large green amber ring set in a sterling silver band with a pattern of vines and leaves.

Nicky's heart pounded. She glanced down at the stone set into the ring on her own finger. Her eyes widened. Every detail was exactly the same.

Nicky's lobster roll sat forgotten on her plate as her mind whirled.

She had to tell Quinten. He had to believe her now. But was her hunch right? Did Vivian *really* have something to do with all of this? Or had she simply seen the ring, thought it pretty, and bought it unawares?

Either way, Nicky was going to find out.

QUINTEN MADE ONE final adjustment and examined the piano. Pretty much it for this one.

He smiled in satisfaction but then his lips tightened as he fought a sinking feeling. He wasn't going to jump to negative assumptions.

The will had to be somewhere. Or at least, some sort of documentation. They just hadn't gone through all the things in the attic yet. Monday was a few days away yet. There were still more papers to look through...

The tourists milled around the small space. Quinten dusted some shelves behind the counter and rearranged a stack of sheet music.

With so few customers last month, he'd had lots of time to fine tune all the instruments in the shop. So if anyone bought them, they'd be in perfect playing order.

But for some reason, this month was quite profitable. Which was good. Because from his most recent conversation with his accountant, it looked like he'd need a fair amount to get the business back into the black—

"Excuse me? How much?" A man in a Panama hat pointed to a hand-carved miniature piano. Quinten checked the price and told the man.

"I'll take twenty. You have?"

"Sure. Let me get the rest of them from the back."

When he came back with the lot, the man pulled out his wallet. "You ship?"

"Yes." Quinten rang up the sale. This would certainly help things along, added to the increase in sales margins he'd seen over the last couple weeks.

A few more tourists bought some sheet music and then the cluster of people dispersed.

As Quinten started to close up the shop and quiet settled over the space, his mind wandered.

What was Elliot up to? Would he actually buy this place out from under him? He couldn't let that happen.

Quinten started to count the till.

There was always another option, another way. He drummed his fingers on the counter as he finished the till count.

Wait a second. He'd helped Mrs. Mac-Phail's husband Al upload that video for his crowdfunding campaign to rebuild his vintage Harley. Could Quinten do something like that for this business?

His heart beat a little faster as he

turned to his computer. It was worth a shot. He'd set up his own page right now. He could make it something about Victoria heritage. Make people aware they could help save a historic, family-owned business from going bankrupt.

The squeak of the screen door's hinges made Quinten look up from his computer. His heart jumped when Nicky rushed in with windblown hair and a gleam in her eyes.

Quinten straightened the hem of his shirt and brushed a hand over his hair. "What is it?"

She waved her phone in his face. "This thing goes even further than I imagined."

"Oh?" He came around the counter and took the phone she handed him. After he scanned the article, he glanced over at Nicky. For a moment, he said nothing. "How do you even know this is true?"

"How do you know it's not?" she countered, as she took a step closer to him. "It's the official website of the Polish Art Center."

He reread the article. "That ring certainly seems like it could have something to do with all of this."

Nicky nudged him. "Just seems like? You're not entirely convinced, are you?"

Quinten couldn't help but chuckle. "You got me there."

"Well." Nicky began to tick points off on her fingers. "First, we have the fact that my ring was Viv's ring."

"Mmm."

"Which, thanks to this portrait, we now know was originally Princess Magdalena's ring."

"Uh-huh."

"And then," Nicky said, "the ring went missing during the Second World War."

"So you think," Quinten said, as he raised his brows, "that because my grandmother had this ring originally owned by this princess, that means Hitler's treasure, which is rumored to contain this princess's dowry, is hidden somewhere on P.E.I.?"

"Exactly. Have you heard anything about this jewelled mirror?" Nicky's brows furrowed.

"The only thing I'd ever heard was about Hitler's gold and diamonds. As for my grandmother being involved in all of it, well..."

Nicky made an expansive gesture. "That's why it's time to go on a treasure hunt."

"Whoa, whoa. Treasure hunt? I admit, the evidence is compelling. But it's probably just circumstantial."

Nicky rolled her eyes. "That's why we need to prove it. Follow the facts and hunt down the truth. Think of it as a quest for truth, instead of a treasure hunt, if that makes you happier."

Quinten tugged at his earlobe. "Mmmm. That *is* a point." His heart jumped. What would happen if he spent more time with her on this?

He saw Nicky glance down at the article on her phone again, then pull up the photo of his grandmother and study it.

Vivian looked happy. Excited, even. What had she been up to? 'Last day at the Office.' Maybe she was deciphering messages. But maybe...

"She *must've* known something about the treasure." Nicky breathed.

Quinten's heart pounded. "What makes you so sure?"

"Well, I was going to show you at the chocolate shop earlier but thought you might change your mind about helping me, so..." Nicky said.

"What is it?"

"If you don't believe that legend about gold and diamonds, you're going to—" She interrupted herself and started to rummage through her purse. Her reddish-blonde hair fell in a smooth curtain that hid her face as she looked down. Ironic, really. Because she didn't hide at all. She wasn't afraid of her vulnerabilities. He respected that.

He thought back to her expression of enjoyment as she took her first bite of waffle. And the excitement on her face just now.

Every emotion was so clearly telegraphed. That took a certain kind of courage. Quinten rocked back on his heels. He had to admit he admired that simple, yet powerful ability in her.

He shoved his hands into his pockets. She had the kind of courage he wished he could express. Would he ever be able to?

He noticed the small frown between her eyebrows as she rooted around in her purse.

Could there actually be something to that legend? He hadn't heard too much about it growing up, really. Just that Mabel was sort of the village eccentric and was liable to say anything just for the stir it caused.

But then his mind flitted back to that old article he'd found about the U-boats. That was certainly fact. As was that crumbling letter to Viv...

He rubbed his jaw.

"Here it is," Nicky said. She held up a tiny scrap of paper. "I didn't really know what to make of it. But then that was before."

She pointed to a tiny black circle.

"That looks like a period at the end of a sentence."

"That's what they want you to think." A glint came into her eyes. "But it's called a microdot. They used them during the Second World War to pass information. Confidential information."

"You mean secret messages?"

"You said it, not me." She picked up her notepad and flicked through it. "Let's see. What did I... Here." She pointed to the page where she'd copied the lines. "I found these phrases on this microdot."

Quinten leaned forward and read Nicky's handwriting.

The secretary marches
To a tune unplayed
But the pianist's journey
Mirrors a plan well-laid.

He shook his head. "I still don't understand."

"The microdot was on the scrap of paper. That scrap of paper was concealed in this ring." Nicky held up her right hand. Then she tapped the photograph. "And this ring? Your grandmother had it."

"Oh," Quinten said. He raked a hand through his hair. "*Oh...*"

Some sort of trick? But Grandma Viv hadn't been a trickster. She'd always been a practical, plain-speaking, if somewhat romantic at times, person who believed in facts and figures, not rhymes and secrets.

But this...he darted a glance at the microdot again...was possible? His grandmother did love puzzles.

He shook his head and crossed his arms. That was a completely fanciful notion. Or was it?

"I mean," Nicky said, "you're right. It could just be circumstantial. It could even be that someone entirely different put that there and it had nothing to do with Vivian at all."

"That's exactly what I was going to say."

"I know. That's why I said it," Nicky replied.

Quinten rubbed the back of his neck.

But if this riddle was valid, and if there was some sort of connection to his grandmother, well, that meant he had to do something about it.

It would be like helping Grandma Viv. And maybe, just maybe, it would help him put to rest the regrets about her that haunted him.

He uncrossed his arms. "It sounds like some sort of rhyme or riddle or—"

"—code?" Nicky said.

NICKY SAW A flash of excitement in Quinten's blue-gray eyes as he studied the lines.

"Did you know that a coded message," Nicky said, "is what people usually mean when they say an enciphered message? But they're actually two very different things."

"Really?" He looked up, a gleam of interest in his eyes.

"Yep. A coded message means that there's significance in the words themselves—one word actually means something else. Like they did with the BBC broadcasts during the war. The SOE agents would tune in to the BBC's service station and listen for pre-arranged phrases from the broadcasters. Those would confirm arms, supplies drops—"

Nicky suddenly forgot the rest of her sentence. Her pulse fluttered as Quinten studied her, a look of admiration plain on his face as he said, "You know a lot about this stuff."

"Thank you." A swell of warmth filled her. "I'm doing a lot of reading. I love research. It really brings people from history to life. Especially if I find something like your grandmother's journal. That's what makes this whole thing so exciting to me."

He was a good listener. Didn't interrupt to interject his own viewpoint. Didn't try to get her to hurry up so he could go back to his sports show or science magazine. "I also believe in being informed," she said.

"Knowledge is power, and all that," Quinten murmured.

All Nicky could do was nod as her breath hitched. He could see more of her than she'd ever shown anyone before, couldn't he? It was like he wanted to know who she really was. Her heart hammered.

There was a beat of silence as they simply looked at each other. Heat rose to Nicky's cheeks. "But I'm getting side-tracked here. We're supposed to be solving this riddle."

Quinten cleared his throat as he turned his eyes back to the piece of paper. "We're pretty sure this is a code then?"

"Which probably has to do with the treasure? I think we can safely assume that, yep. Your grandmother's job description was deciphering messages. So her writing a coded message isn't that much of a stretch. And, like I said earlier, the ring was in her possession. Not only that, the dowry had disappeared. And German U-boats had been spotted around the island here, which is also where the treasure was supposed to be lost. Plus, in that love letter to Viv that I have, whoever A is makes reference to shared secrets, and something about having been trained to withstand the enemy."

"Right," Quinten said. "So do you think A was a Nazi?"

"Mabel seems to think so." Nicky paused. "But in your grandmother's diary, it implies she was in love with someone she worked with. And in that letter I have, it seems he got captured. So I think A is an SOE agent, not a Nazi."

"Mmmm."

"My theory at the moment is that maybe he was an agent using a code name for the letters. After all, your grandmother was assigned to several agents. One of them had the code name Ash."

"Oh."

"But to make it even more confusing, each agent was assigned not only a code name for their time in the field, but also one for reference when their traffic was being handled."

"Yeah, I can see how that'd be confusing." He rubbed his chin. "But I like your theory."

"Thanks." She blushed. She couldn't help but remember the look of admiration he'd given her a minute ago. No.

Everything was going better than planned. She couldn't afford to get distracted by Quinten. No matter how much she appreciated his listening skills. She'd be gone in a couple of days.

Nicky pushed those thoughts aside and turned her attention back to the riddle. She tapped a finger against her chin. "Let's see. It might be a good way to approach it if we work backwards line by line."

For several minutes they studied the lines in silence.

"*Mirrors a plan well-laid,*" Quinten murmured. "I think we know what plan."

"Yep, seems pretty clear," Nicky

agreed, "thanks to that Polish Art Center article."

"The plan to use Hitler's gold and diamonds to fund the Fourth Reich," Quinten said.

"Exactly."

"What about this?" Quinten tapped a finger on the word to underscore his point. "*Mirrors*. It's being used as a verb in this sentence, but what if it is really a noun?"

"A reference to the jewelled mirror."

"Right," Quinten said.

Nicky's pulse fluttered. She liked this. Playing detective with him. Working together to put the pieces into place. "The mirror was part of the dowry, after all," she added.

"Mmm-hmm." Quinten grinned.

"We work pretty well together." Nicky grinned back. His eyes were almost the color of a stormy day at sea, weren't they? Yet on him, there was a softness about the shade that—Focus.

She needed to focus on the work. On the words. She took a breath. "So the line above: *the pianist's journey*... Well, the slang term for a W/T operator was a pianist," Nicky said.

"W/T operator?"

"That's a radio operator. W/T stands

for wireless telegraphy."

"Hmm." Quinten rubbed his jaw. "That could fit but I—Oh."

"What is it?" Nicky touched his arm.

"Hang on just a sec." He pulled out his phone and started to scroll through his photos as he murmured, "No, no...Okay. This one." He showed a picture to Nicky. "You know how I said I had a letter from A to Viv?"

"Yeah."

"I found it in an old suitcase up in the attic in pretty bad shape. It basically fell apart after I read it. I did manage to snap a photo, though. Look at this line." He zoomed in on the bit of text and showed her.

Nicky leaned toward him. A thrill went up her spine at his nearness. "From what I can make out there, it seems like he's saying he was an actual pianist."

"Which means the pianist reference is probably talking about A," Quinten said.

"And so if the pianist went on a journey...this A was going somewhere," Nicky said.

"P.E.I."

"Bingo," Nicky said.

"Also, Viv would've known he was a concert pianist. And if we're assuming Viv wrote the riddle, which makes sense since it was secreted in her ring, then this line *has* to be referring to A."

"You know, music keeps getting mentioned all through this riddle. That must be significant."

"Viv loved music. That's why she and my grandfather started the piano tuning business." Quinten rubbed his jaw. "She was always playing music. I have reams and reams of sheet music that I've actually just put in the recycling because there's so much..."

"Really?"

"Yeah." He pointed to an upright in the corner. "Every day she'd sit at that piano."

She turned to the window and caught her breath. "That's some piano." Light gleamed off its polished wood surface.

"It's a Princess Royal. Supposedly modeled after one in Buckingham Palace. From what I've heard, they made the original for the princesses, Elizabeth and Margaret."

"Really? Wow. So do you think any of these musical references have something to do with that piano?" Nicky blurted out.

"Maybe," Quinten said. "But I've been over pretty much every inch of it... Found a crumpled scrap of paper with a few letters scribbled across it, but that wasn't anything musically related that I could tell." He shrugged.

"Hmm. Okay. Well, let's look at the first two lines."

"*The secretary marches/to a tune unplayed.*" Quinten mused.

"An unplayed tune..." Nicky said. "Since we figured out that the pianist is this A, then could an unplayed tune mean some sort of plan of his that went wrong?"

"Or maybe it's some sort of signal that means...something?" Quinten spread his hands, fingers wide.

Nicky cocked her head. "Maybe that part'll make more sense if we figure out the first line: *A secretary marches.*"

"If we're talking World War II, there were lots of secretaries doing lots of things."

"But not probably marching to a tune unplayed." Nicky made a wry face.

"No," Quinten agreed. "Probably not."

"But..." Nicky said. She picked up her phone again and opened the web browser. "Wait a minute. In the Polish Art Center article—didn't it say something about a secretary?"

As she scanned the piece, her eyes widened. She glanced at Quinten and then read aloud: "...*Some scholars believe it was used as a bargaining chip by Hitler's personal secretary, Martin Bormann, near the end of the war.*"

"So the secretary in the first line must mean Martin Bormann," Quinten said.

"It must. Now if I do a quick search for Martin Bormann..." She started to type, turned her phone horizontally, then back vertically. "Maybe that'll pull something up."

"Here." Quinten strode over to the door, flipped the open sign to closed, then walked over to the doorway to the workroom.

Nicky watched him disappear into the back. He reappeared a moment later with a silver MacBook Pro laptop in hand. "This is better than that tiny phone screen. Plus it'll be easier for both of us to see at the same time."

"Good idea. Thank you."

Her heart swooped at the warm way he said, "Happy to help." He opened the computer and made a few keystrokes before he hit the enter key.

Nicky was too busy watching the smooth play of muscles in his forearms to pay full attention to what he was saying.

"—we get."

"Huh?"

"I said, let's see what we get."

"Right. Sorry." She blushed. "There's a bunch of hits here." She leaned in to read over his shoulder. "Let's go with the top result." It read, *Nazi Loot for a Song?*

Quinten clicked on it and skimmed a finger down the screen. *"The Nazis started to get nervous and decided they needed to put aside funds—gold and diamonds."*

"In case the Third Reich fell—" Nicky murmured, as she resisted an urge to put her hand on his wide, strong shoulder, *"—the Nazis could reorganize in secret and come back to power by creating a Fourth Reich. They stashed the gold and diamonds in a location that was known only to Bormann."*

Quinten read the next paragraph. *"The only clues to the Nazi loot were on a piece of sheet music Bormann had. After Hitler committed suicide in the Fuhrerbunker, Bormann fled the bunker and tried to get out of Berlin."*

"But," Nicky finished the passage, *"he died before he could escape. The sheet music was lost but it supposedly points to the location of the gold, a collection of Hitler's personal diamonds, and the dowry of Princess Magdalena Jola Piast."*

Quinten ruffled his hair.

Nicky sat back.

There was a beat of silence.

After a second, she spoke again. "You know what this means, don't you?"

"What's that?"

"It means this is more evidence the treasure exists. That it includes the dowry, which Viv had a piece of. And," Nicky lifted her chin, "that she and this A were involved in it somehow."

"I can't argue with that. So, *The secretary marches/to a tune unplayed* has to be referring to that piece of sheet music Bormann owned."

"Exactly." Nicky caught her breath. "So this means—"

"—we need to find the sheet music," Quinten finished.

Chapter Six

$\mathcal{S}$HE AND QUINTEN spent the rest of the evening making speculations. Then she returned to the hotel.

A glow filled her. Quinten was good at figuring things out. He might not be overly talkative but he'd asked thoughtful questions. He'd taken the time to ask her what she'd thought, too. She appreciated that. His attention to detail. His attention to her opinions, her ideas.

But they'd been so busy doing research about Nazi loot that they'd gotten carried away and totally missed the obvious primary source. Viv's diary.

Nicky picked it up and sat cross-legged on her bed in the Orient. She'd changed into a pair of ultra-soft yellow cotton pajamas.

She traced a finger along the cover before she opened the diary again.

She flipped past the unusual encrypted

entry and read the next one, pencilled in neat, tidy handwriting.

May 31, 1943

My heart is breaking. But I must hold my head up and be strong. It does no good to wring my hands when I came to England to roll up my sleeves, against Mother's advice.

It's her homeland, after all. And I love it nearly as much as a native Englishwoman. Because of Papa, though, I am forever American. Thank goodness for the other girls at the Office.

I am grateful for my duties, for the distraction the numbers and letters bring.

Oh, it's so easy, though, to dwell on the love that we shared, and mourn what now shall never be. I am glad mathematics cannot break a girl's heart. I pray we not find ourselves in too deep over here. I must not think on it overmuch.

I am not sure I will find myself writing on these pages again. Too many memories.

Nicky turned the page.

Oct 7, 1945

The war has finally ended and I cannot help but feel a strange burst of sadness as to what my future holds.

I believe I will get a high school math teaching position after all, as we women are expected to resume our "regular lives." As if anyone could do that now, after all we have experienced. We have been sworn to secrecy so only I will remember what I have been involved in...

I have also decided I shall marry Wallace. He is a good man. A Canadian. From Prince Edward Island.

We met at the train station just after victory had been declared. Somehow our suitcases had gotten mixed up. He had mine and I had his. The way his blue-gray eyes sparkled with amusement when he'd realized what had happened made me think, wish, hope...

He proposed not long after.

I know I can make a good life for myself on the island. I do love him, and I believe I shall love it there. He has described the tiny village of Victoria to me and I am looking forward to seeing it ever so much.

Nicky turned the page but there was nothing there. At some point, it seemed, the glue had given way and the remaining pages had fallen out when someone had opened it.

Nicky turned to the very back of the diary.

A piece of lined spiral notebook paper, folded in thirds and then folded in half again, was wedged between the last page of the little book and its back cover.

It looked much newer than the journal. She saw, as she reached for it, that it was written in blue ballpoint pen.

She plucked it up with a pounding heart.

May 29, 2000

It must be something about this time of year that brings him to mind. The scent of the spring rains on the wind. Or the sound of early morning birdsong...

Whatever it is, always, this time of year, I remember.

I remember the night he told me. He'd just come back and then he'd had to leave again. We'd shared a Coca-Cola and a cigarette. I'd tried not to look at the gold signet ring on the pinky finger of his left hand. He only wore it when he was getting ready to leave. Because it contained his L-tablet.

I'd forced myself to smile when he'd turned to me with those brown eyes of his and took my hand. "Sweetheart," he'd said, "I don't want you to worry. That's why we need to arrange something between us because I'm taking a little trip."

"Oh?" I'd said, lifted an eyebrow: a fragile effort to make light of what surely was a dark situation.

He'd nodded. "Thirteen letters. That's what it'll be." He'd touched the gold signet ring and swallowed. Then he'd gently touched my face. "If I, well, am somehow...delayed. You get my meaning?"

"Yes." I'd whispered. He would use a key word of thirteen letters in length if he was taken by the Nazis, to signal to me that his cover had been blown and he was taken prisoner.

I'd understood his meaning perfectly that night.

And today, well, I can finally say it.

Nicky glanced at the date of the entry, 2000. By then, the official oath of secrecy had been lifted, so being able to tell about what she'd gone through must be what Viv was referring to in the last line of this entry.

She reread it.

L-tablet. That was shorthand for cyanide capsule. So this entry proved beyond any doubt that the man was an agent for the SOE.

In fact...this person had to be the A of the letter. Nicky put the diary in her lap, picked up her purse, and pulled out the letter. Yet if the A in the letter was also the agent whose code name was Ash, then why did Mabel talk about Vivian being in love with a Nazi? Perhaps she'd just made up the whole Nazi lover thing.

Nicky skimmed the entry's lines again. They must have run into each other when he'd been at SOE headquarters at some point.

Though according to her research, it was against the rules for girls in the codes department to know the real identity or any other information about the agents whose traffic they deciphered...

Obviously, someone had been ignoring the rules. When it came to love, you couldn't really confine it with rules. In fact, that was when it most easily died.

Nicky frowned. At least in her own experience. She sighed and put the page back where she'd found it.

What was she going to do now that the rest of the diary pages were missing?

Her brows furrowed. Maybe Quinten had some idea. She could show him the encrypted entry, too. But that would have to wait until tomorrow.

She put the diary on the nightstand beside her phone, which she'd just plugged in to charge.

She picked up and reread the letter to Viv. Finally, she put it down, leaned over to the nightstand and clicked off the lamp. Nicky closed her eyes and tried to calm her mind, but lines from the letter kept repeating in her head.

> *...the summer wind in our hair and shared secrets in our eyes...they cannot know what is in my heart...they cannot destroy my soul, though undoubtedly, they shall try...I have a cause to fight for...*

Nicky's eyes flew open. Why hadn't she seen that connection before? Viv hadn't just been in love with this agent—she'd handled a lot—probably *all*—of his traffic, too. Whoever he was.

In Viv's file, it listed the code names of agents whose traffic she'd deciphered. Oak. Ash. Maple.

She was pretty sure A stood for Ash. But... Nicky sat up. Her heart pounded. If she cross-referenced all three of those code names with more SOE agent files...she might be able to find out A's real identity.

Not only that, if Nicky could find his enciphered messages sent to Baker Street HQ, she'd know exactly what Viv and this agent knew.

Did the National Archives in England have copies of the SOE agents' traffic? She'd have to find out. Maybe that would explain what was really going on.

SUNDAY MORNING, NICKY took a sip of the thick rich hot chocolate she'd ordered.

She adjusted her seat at Island Chocolates so that she had a better view of the street and the leaves that had begun to fall in the light breeze that smelled of sea air and limitless potential.

She inhaled a big breath. She could get used to a place like this. Okay, who was she kidding? She could get used to *this*.

She loved it here. She loved the fact that everyone was so friendly. That when you walked down the street, people said hello to you—she was tired of the anonymity of New York City.

And more than that, she wanted to be seen, to be acknowledged, to be noticed for who and what she was. For what she offered others. And people really seemed to appreciate that here.

Especially with all the local shops and artisans and just the overall *feeling* of the place. People actually seemed to care here in Victoria.

She took another deep breath and looked around.

Sure, people here had their problems—just like people everywhere—but here, at least your neighbor would probably help you out with it rather than climbing over you to get to the next rung on the career ladder.

She winced. Okay, that was pretty cynical but—she shrugged a shoulder—that was how she felt right now.

She took another sip of hot chocolate as she riffled through her notes. From what she'd been compiling and gathering, and from her first draft, well, things were really shaping up into a second draft. Excitement zipped through her.

She'd threaded in what she'd discovered from the journal, as well as the love letter. Perhaps she could even feature as a secondary side bar a bit about the history of the SOE and the role that women played in the organization. Just some facts and figures to give the story some more depth and dimension.

She had enough research information here to write a book, practically. Her lips lifted. That was the mark of a good journalist. Gathering as much research and as many primary sources as possible so as to write the best article possible.

She pulled up the National Archives website and typed her message into their contact form.

Hello,

My name is Nicky Stendahl. I'm a journalist in the U.S. with the Historical Woman magazine. I'm looking for information regarding the messages that Vivian Robinson deciphered during her time with the SOE from 1940 until 1945. Specifically, I'd like to review the traffic related to the three agents she'd been assigned: Oak, Ash and Maple. I don't know their true names or any other information about them. Thank you!

Regards, Nicky

Looked like the response time was usually four business days. Well, with the time difference, it was practically Monday over in England now anyway.

She tapped her fingers on the tabletop. Hopefully, they'd get back to her within that timeframe because she only had about a week left 'til the deadline.

How should she work in the treasure angle? That wasn't the original gist of the story, exactly.

She would run it by her editor, but it would no doubt be fine. After all, the woman had said to get as much in-depth information as possible.

If she incorporated the parts about the treasure into the article about Viv, that actually made the story more important from a cultural and historical standpoint. Especially if Viv and this A were trying to recover it.

She pulled up her email and sent her editor an update.

A BLAST OF cool, fall air stirred Nicky's hair and she looked up. Quinten had walked in to the chocolate shop.

Her heart jumped as he saw her and nodded his acknowledgment. No. She couldn't get carried away. Being single was just fine.

He ordered something from the front and then approached her table.

"Is this chair taken?" There was a twinkle in his eye as he said it.

"Yep. By you."

He sat. "How's it going then?" He indicated the stacks of books and piles of papers that covered nearly the whole tiny table's surface.

"Really well. I've done a second draft of the article."

"That's great. So you're making progress then."

"Yep." Her heart warmed at his acknowledgment of her efforts. "I thought I'd look up this A that Viv had received that letter from."

"And?" Quinten leaned forward in his chair. A strand of hair fell across his forehead and she resisted the urge to reach across and brush it out of his eyes.

"Still waiting to hear back from the National Archives in England," she said instead. "Could take awhile."

"Well, while you're waiting...do you want to go to Charlottetown with me?"

Nicky sat up straighter. "Sure. But," she paused mid-sip and cocked her head, "what for?"

"Are you always this suspicious?"

She laughed. "Just being a journalist."

"The U-boats." Quinten glanced around and lowered his voice. "I was thinking about it in the context of Mabel's story.

That the Nazis were here on P.E.I. Well, if we want to find some sort of solid lead on that, and how it might connect to the sheet music and Viv, the library might be a place to start."

"Okay," Nicky said, and drained her mug. "Let's go."

Nearly an hour later, Quinten pulled into a parking spot along Queen Street in the downtown heart of Charlottetown.

Nicky got out and followed Quinten up to the library.

Bright yellows and oranges of marigolds swayed in the light breeze. The sun warmed Nicky's face and the chatter of outdoor diners drifted to her from nearby Victoria Row. And suddenly, she wanted to take Quinten's hand, wanted to hold onto this moment, this feeling, forever.

Quinten must have felt her looking at him because when he glanced over, she saw warmth in his eyes.

"Thank you," she said suddenly. "I appreciate your help."

"My pleasure."

He held the door open for her as they headed inside the library and up to the reference desk. An older man with wire-rimmed glasses and a slim build looked up from his computer.

"How can I help you?" His staff badge read 'Jerry.'

"Well," Nicky said, "I'm looking for some information about P.E.I. during World War II."

"Great! I'm a bit of a World War II buff, so you've come to the right person."

"Did you ever hear of Nazis on the island?" Nicky asked.

"Or anything about a piece of sheet music in relation to that?" Quinten added.

"Nothing about sheet music." Jerry paused for a second and his eyes narrowed. "As for Nazis on the island, you have to untangle the facts from the fiction with that tale."

Nicky and Quinten took seats on the chairs in front of his desk.

"The story about Hitler's gold and diamonds hidden somewhere on P.E.I. fits in with the local Nazi lore. The facts, though, go something like this:

"One specific German submarine, U-262, was on a mission to rescue German naval officer POWs from a prisoner of war camp in New Brunswick, near Fredericton, called Camp 70. Apparently, the sub planned to rendezvous with them in North Cape."

He glanced at Nicky. "That's at the

northern tip of P.E.I. Up west, as they say around here. I imagine the sub didn't meet the POWs in New Brunswick because the Germans didn't want to go any farther into enemy territory than they had to. Anyway, U-262 was actually the *second* sub they'd sent on this secret assignment. The first one, U-376, was reportedly sunk off the Bay of Biscay in France earlier in '43. April, I think it was."

"Okay," Nicky said.

Jerry continued. "So the second sub was tasked with the mission called Operation Elster. Means magpie in English."

He paused and took a breath. "Odd thing was, even though the second sub made the rendezvous point, the POWs didn't. A persistent piece of island folklore even says U-262 got caught in a pretty heated naval battle near the northwest tip of P.E.I. before it headed back to Germany. But *that's* the sub rumored to have been carrying Hitler's gold and diamonds."

Nicky's eyes widened.

"Now, whether that's actually true?" Jerry chuckled. "Well, that's part of the allure of the story." A gleam came into the librarian's eyes. "Personally, I like to believe that it's possible. Makes life interesting. What actually happened, though, no one knows for sure because no conclusive evidence has ever been found. Have you tried searching on the internet for that sort of thing?"

Nicky shifted in her seat. "No. I did see some archived articles but never came across anything like that specifically."

Quinten spoke up. "I found an original article about U-boats on P.E.I. from what I'm guessing is the early forties." He paused. "But it didn't mention anything about these two."

"An original, wow," Jerry said as he reached for a Post-It and a pen. "Here are the web addresses of a couple of online archives: the Robertson Library at UPEI and Charlottetown's paper—*The Guardian*." He handed the sticky note to Nicky, who tucked it into her purse.

"We also have a file down in the basement about the POW rescue attempt. I can go grab it for you." He straightened in his chair.

"Sure," Nicky said.

"That'd be great," Quinten echoed.

About ten minutes later, Jerry returned with a slim manila file in hand. "This is all that we have on record here. It goes into a bit more detail on what I just told you.

Some newspaper articles in there, too. You know what? I almost forgot. There's also a P.E.I. heritage database called Island Voices that has a lot of World War II stuff that's searchable." He jotted that web address down on another Post-It and gave it to Nicky. "So. If you check out all those digitized archives, you should at least have a good starting point. You can photocopy whatever you like out of there." He gestured to the manila file folder. "Just be sure to bring it back."

"Here," Quinten said, "I can go run a copy."

Nicky's heart melted a little. Mabel was right—he was a good guy. "That'd be great. Thank you, Quinten."

A few minutes later, Quinten returned. He handed the file back. "Thanks so much, Jerry."

"Yes. Really appreciate your help," Nicky added.

"You two come back any time if you have more questions. Or want to solve any more mysteries," Jerry said.

Nicky followed Quinten as they stepped out into the warm sunshine on Queen Street. "That Jerry guy really knows his stuff."

"Yeah, he's been the head reference

librarian there for a long time." Quinten stuffed his hands into his pockets. His habit of doing that was kind of cute, Nicky mused, as they headed over to his car.

She felt a thrill as she gazed at the red-brick buildings from the 1800s, the iron lamp posts, and smelled the scent of sea air. This island just kept getting better and better.

Especially in October.

Bright yellow oak, rich red maple, and russet-brown horse chestnut leaves scattered on the breeze and swirled around the car as they got in.

Quinten turned the key in the ignition and then turned his attention toward Nicky. "Listen, it's just about lunchtime." He adjusted the cuffs on his maroon button down. "Do you want to get a bite to eat somewhere and talk about what we've found so far?"

Nicky couldn't help the look of surprise that flitted across her face. "Umm," she said, "I mean, yes, that'd be great." A surge of excitement ran through her. "Where do you want to go?"

"Wherever you'd like to go is fine with me. I'm not picky," Quinten said.

"Well," Nicky laughed, "I have no idea what's good in this town, so it makes sense for you to choose."

"I hate making decisions, so I find it's easier if I let the other person decide." Quinten looked a little shocked at the words that had just come out of his mouth. "Did I just say that out loud? I didn't mean to do that but I... Okay, now I'm digging myself into a hole. I'm going to stop talking."

THEY GOT OUT of Quinten's car and headed down the sidewalk.

Quinten saw Nicky look around with interest and couldn't resist playing tour guide. "You know, downtown here didn't always look like this."

"Really? When I came up here for Maggie's wedding last summer, I just assumed it'd been this way forever. Charming, quaint and trendy."

"Nope. Twenty, twenty-five years ago, Charlottetown's core here was pretty run down. The city's done a great job, though, in changing all that and bringing in tourists every summer and fall. That's one of the things I really love about this city, about this island. Islanders don't give up. We just look for ways to revitalize." He paused and murmured, almost to himself, "Which is what I need to do in my own life. I'd always thought I'd get a chance to do a bit of traveling, have some adventures in my twenties..." He darted a glance at Nicky. Best not to share too much. Right? "...but with all my schooling and then running the shop, I never did." He shoved his hands in his pockets.

"I know what you mean," Nicky said, as she fiddled with a strand of her hair.

Quinten couldn't help but smile at that rather endearing trait.

"I couldn't wait to get out of the tiny Michigan town I grew up in. But living in New York isn't really doing anything for me anymore."

"No? I've always wanted to visit New York," he said. "There are a couple musicals I'd love to see live on Broadway."

"Certainly a great theatre scene there. Guess the grass is always greener, and all that."

"Guess so."

They walked farther down the street. The scent of fallen leaves mingled with the salt air and the chatter of passers-by.

"This time of year with the leaves changing, people come from all over," he said. "Sometimes people show up in

September thinking the leaves have already changed. But that actually doesn't happen until October. September is basically a bonus summer month, since June's usually pretty cool."

They passed red-brick façades with hand-lettered signs declaring clothing boutiques and a jewelry store.

"Autumn's my favorite time of year," Nicky said.

"Mine too."

"I love how the sky looks bluer, the air smells like fallen leaves, and the coffee shops have pumpkin pie lattes." She laughed and looked so happy that a sudden swell of longing to connect with her surged through him.

"When I was growing up, Grandma Viv, Grandpa Wallace, and I would always go apple picking this time of year. I loved it. Used to race back to the house and make caramel apples with the fresh ones we'd just picked. Something about the combination of salty and sweet..."

"P.E.I. seems like such a great place to grow up. That sounds like a great childhood memory."

"I was pretty lucky to have them for grandparents."

"I've actually never gone apple picking."

"No? There are some great orchards around here. You should go."

With me, Quinten almost blurted out.

But before he could, Nicky said, "The restaurant's nearby?"

"It's just around the corner here on Sydney Street."

They crossed to the other side of Sydney Street and passed Sim's Steakhouse on the corner. The building's third floor contained his attorney's office.

His shoulders tensed as he recalled Thursday's meeting and Elliot's words. Quinten shook his head. Elliot wasn't going to get the business. Not if he had anything to do with it. His crowdfunding page had even gotten a few hits. No donations. But still, hits were a start.

They continued a little farther before they came to a three-story red brick house with a sign on its lawn that read The Gahan House.

"They also brew their own craft beer down in the basement," Quinten said. "I'm not a beer drinker, but it's kind of neat to see the machinery."

Nicky grinned. "Don't worry, I'm not a beer drinker either."

"No? I wasn't sure what to make of you."

"Most guys don't."

He headed up the short flight of steps to the house, Nicky behind him.

"Two for lunch?" the maître d' asked.

Quinten nodded.

"Follow me." She led them past the wood-paneled bar with its flat-screen TVs and over to a round table with brown velvet wingback chairs nestled up against a bay window that overlooked the street.

Quinten pulled out the chair for Nicky.

She glanced at him and Quinten couldn't help but notice the way her lips formed a perfect O of surprise.

He simply smiled at her.

He sat down in the seat next to her and picked up his menu. The server came and took their drink orders.

Quinten always got the same thing every time he ate here. The blueberry mixed greens salad and the chicken and chorizo penne.

Nicky ordered the maple balsamic salmon.

She took a sip of her raspberry iced tea and Quinten couldn't help but notice the way her bottom lip pressed against the curve of the glass's rim.

His eyes lingered on her mouth and he tried to think of something else. Anything else. But he couldn't. How long had it been since he'd kissed anyone? She'd taste like raspberries...

He cleared his throat. Forced his mind back to reality. "So how's the story going?"

Nicky's eyes sparkled. Quinten felt a glow of satisfaction. He'd asked her the right question. A swell of courage filled him.

She leaned forward. He caught a hint of her vanilla perfume as he leaned forward too.

"Really well," she said. "I hope my editor likes it. This is one of the first longer pieces I've written and I want to make sure I'm doing it right, you know?"

She cocked her head as she regarded him. She wasn't afraid to speak her mind— that was one of the things he'd begun to really admire about her.

"I do, yes. Because when a customer asks me to fix a piano that's been in the family for, oh, I don't know, a hundred years, I know that if I mess it up, I'll feel like..." Quinten averted his eyes and traced the pattern of the table's wood grain with a fingertip, "...I've destroyed a part of their heritage, a piece of their own story, in a way." He slowly brought his eyes back up to Nicky's face. Expecting to see a frown, a smirk, some sort of doubt or disagreement on her face.

But warmth and relief filled him when he saw only understanding.

"I know exactly what you mean. Because there's nothing that's more important to me than honoring people's stories, telling their truths, sharing that with the world, and being able to have people know that, see that, acknowledge that. For their own sakes, and for the sakes of the people being written about."

She paused. "I think that your grandmother was an important person. She did a good thing, a strong thing, during the war, and I think that people should—no—deserve to know about it. So that it can perhaps help people now. So that it can inspire people to perhaps draw strength from a time of darkness and know that no matter what, things indeed do get better; that no matter what, there is a light in the darkness. To give them hope. To give them some sort of...comfort. To drive them to do better in their own lives."

Quinten's heart felt full as warmth wound its way through him at her words. He opened his mouth to respond, but suddenly Nicky's phone dinged.

"I GOT AN email from the National Archives," Nicky said.

"Wow. That was fast," Quinten said, before he took a few more bites of his penne.

"I know, right? Guess the time difference doesn't hurt. Listen to what it says."

Dear Ms. Stendahl,

Thank you for your query. Finding records of agents' traffic is tricky. It will take some time to search and retrieve all pertinent documents. There will also be a fee, but as soon as you have paid that, we can move ahead.

I've looked up the agents whose code names you mentioned. Unfortunately, both Ash's and Maple's files are sealed until next year.

As for Oak, most of his records are sealed for another two years. But part of his file has been officially opened this year. As such, that section is now available and digitized. The link below will direct you to that information.

However, I must warn you that it is incomplete, as at some point, files for X section had partially succumbed to fire.

Regards,
Greg Scott
Research Curator
The National Archives

Nicky scrolled down to the link and opened it. Pieces of type and text were blackened or missing, obscured by the fire damage.

R M C.R.1.

TE: 7.41   INTERVIEWED BY: C. GU

Surname (in block capitals): *GOBELL*

Christian names: *Andrzej Dawid*

Rank or ti

  orations:

1. ORMER NAMES(I

2. PERMANENT ADDR
    TE

3. IF SERVING (Regiment)

4. DATE & PLACE OF BIRTH *9 November, 1917, Gdansk, Pol*

5.   ATIONALITY At birth *Polish*
    At present *German/Polish*

6. EDUCATION
    (a) Schools atte
    (b) Universities *University of Bonn, Ger Oxford University, England*
        rees taken *classical music studies (Bonn)*
    linguists degree (Oxford)

7. MARRIED OR SINGLE? *single*

9. RELIGION *RC*

10. PEACE TIME OCCUPATION *translator, concert pianist*

            ION SINCE 3.9.39 *translator*
            NGUAGES
        at languages do you spe
        an w fluently? *German — fluent, Polish — fluent, English — fluent,*

    1 WHA   NTRIES HAVE YOU VISITED?
Austria, Switzerland, Czechoslov
    (other than in passage)

15. <u>ANY SERVICE EXPERIENCE</u>? *German naval ensign, left for personal reasons*

16. <u>POLITICAL VIEWS</u>

17. <u>HAVE YOU MADE A WILL?</u> *No.*

18.   RSON <u>TO BE INFORMED</u> if you
bec   a casualty
     <u>ARANCE</u>
) height *6'1"*
  (b) ght *191 lbs*
     hair *brown*
  (d) Colour of eyes *brown*
  (e) Complexion *medium*
  (f) Distinguishing Marks *none*
      former neighbours
    know your whereabouts? *No.*

20. DO YOU:-
  (a) Ride? *yes*
  (b) Sail a boat? *yes*
  (& member of Oxford crew)
  (c) Fly an aeroplane? *No*
  (d) Read & transmit Morse? *yes*
  (e) Drive a car/motor cycle? *car*
  (f) Run? *no*
  (g) Box? *yes*
  (h) Mountaineer? *no*

21. <u>HAVE YOU ANY EXPERIENCE OF
PHOTOGRAPHY OR CINEPHOTOGRAPHY?</u> *no*

22. <u>HAVE YOU ANY KNOWLEDGE OF MAP
READING, FIELD SKETCHING, ETC?</u> *map reading
& field sketching during time in German navy*

<u>OWLEDGE OF WIRELESS?</u> *yes*

<u>WITH WHAT DISTRICTS ARE YOU VERY
FAMILIAR?</u>
      at home? *Gdansk*
  (b) Abroad? *London*

25. <u>SPECIAL KNOWLEDGE.</u>
  (a) Propaganda *No*
  (b) Technical *translator abilities*

26. <u>ACCOUNT OF PAST HISTORY</u> *particulars as
discussed*

F O R M   X/89612

Field name: Matthias Grynberg

Code name: Oak

Cover occupation: Nazi in the
German navy; rank, ensign

Real occupation: agent for X
Section, SOE

Dates of employment: January 17,

1941—June 7, 1943

Nicky blinked and looked at Quinten. "I just realized something."

"Oh?"

"A didn't stand for Ash." She raised her eyes to the ceiling and shook her head. "It stood for Andrzej."

"The first name of this agent?"

"Not only that, but June 7, 1943...I think that's the same date that the letter had been written to Viv." She pulled the letter out of her purse. "Yes. Which means that was the date he was captured... So. This must be the right person."

She continued reading.

```
Mission Status: Seven missions
compl
 urrent mission: Op    Black
Forest
                ee Form 6. b)
```

Nicky frowned. This section had been badly burned. She scrolled farther and noticed that in several places, it looked like names had been cut out of the document.

Notes:

    disagreed with principles and

```
ideals set forth by Fascist
regime

        t, an Oxford school
friend in London; was approached
for interview by

Accepted into SOE and dispatched
back to Germany as agent.
```

Quinten finished his penne and wiped his mouth with his napkin. "What is it?"

Nicky handed her phone to him. "I hit pay dirt. So. His real name was Andrzej Dawid Gobell. But the SOE's file on him is partially burned. And censored."

A gleam came into Quinten's eyes.

"Better than a spy thriller, isn't it?" she asked.

"Definitely."

A surge of excitement ran through Nicky. She didn't know if it was from the warmth of Quinten's gaze in her direction or from the fact that they were getting closer to real answers about Viv, Andrzej, and this supposed Nazi treasure. Probably both.

Quinten looked thoughtful as he handed her phone back. "It says he was a concert pianist. So this confirms we were right."

Nicky's heart fluttered as Quinten held

her gaze. They *would* figure out this historical mystery together. It didn't matter, did it, that he didn't always say everything he felt or thought. He said what he felt he should. That's what counted, wasn't it?

"What if we use his real name to do a check online for anything else about him?"

"Good idea." Nicky reached for her phone. A second later she said, "Here's a Wikipedia entry."

Andrzej Dawid Gobell, born November 9, 1917, was a secret agent during World War II. He worked for Britain's Special Operations Executive, X Section (Germany).

Because of the dangerous nature of the work at the heart of the Nazi regime, the SOE ran very few operations in Germany. Gobell was one of only a handful of SOE operatives in that country. For most of the war, the SOE's X Section worked with the Political Warfare Executive's German sector and concentrated mainly on black propaganda and administrative sabotage.

Gobell used the code name Oak, and the field name Matthias Gryn-

berg, from 1941 until his death at Nazi headquarters in Berlin, Germany, in June of 1943.

Trained as a concert pianist in Germany, he also had a passion for the water, and he served with the German navy before obtaining his degree in linguistics at Oxford University, England.

Little is known about his early years, but he grew up in Gdansk, Poland. (During the war, Gdansk was considered to be in Germany and was called Danzig.) Though he was Polish born, he was both a Polish and a German citizen due to the German-Polish border shift in that region.

But as the Second World War approached, he became disillusioned with Germany's politics and returned to England to work as a translator shortly before the war broke out.

His time in the German navy as well as his dual citizenship served him in good stead, as the SOE recruited him and sent him back to Germany to work undercover as an ensign in the German navy.

In the hope it would defer suspicion, Gobell's cover professed he was *a Nazi supporter. Gobell was quiet and reserved, but when needed, became charming and assertive—the perfect combination for a secret agent during World War II.*

Nicky glanced through the Wikipedia entry again. "That's interesting. Andrzej's cover had him pretend to be a Nazi supporter."

"So I bet that's why Mabel said Vivian was in love with a Nazi," Quinten said slowly. "It was part of his cover story." He was silent a moment as he rubbed a hand across his stubble. "Speaking of, I wonder if looking up the U-boat crew manifest would yield any additional information?"

"That's a genius idea." She reached for her purse and pulled out the photocopied article. "Let's see. This lists the name of the U-boat as well as the commanding officer. So if we look that up, we could determine if Andrzej was part of that crew..."

"...and then we could hopefully figure out what he—and Grandma Viv—were up to." Quinten finished.

"Once we find that out, maybe we can find..." she glanced around and lowered her voice "...the sheet music."

"If it's even still around," Quinten amended.

Nicky threw him a look of exasperation.

"Hey," Quinten said as he spread his arms, "I'm just trying to be practical. I'm part Scottish, you know—"

QUINTEN'S PHONE RANG.

He ignored it. Usually people knew not to call him at lunch. It rang again. He glanced at the caller ID. His lawyer. He'd better take the call. "Sorry, I have to get this." He answered his phone, pushed his chair back and headed to the foyer.

"Pardon?" He pressed the phone to his ear over the noise of the other diners. "I can't hear you. I was just in the middle of something and..." He made his way over to a quieter corner.

"Quinten," his lawyer said in a louder voice. "I'm sorry to interrupt your day but I have some more bad news."

Quinten swallowed.

"Elliot's come into the office again."

Quinten nodded. Then remembered his lawyer couldn't see the motion. "Okay," he said slowly.

"He's told me to tell you that he wants to null your agreement from the other day and buy you out now instead. If you give him sole control of the business, he said he'll get you out of bankruptcy." He paused. "Have you found some documentation that proves ownership?"

Quinten's stomach knotted. How had Elliot even found out about the bankruptcy so fast? Then again, why was he wondering? Word traveled fast in a small place. Plus, his crowdfunding page... "I haven't. But I hope I don't need to make a decision right this moment?"

"No. But it needs to be soon. Listen, think about it—but not too long—and let me know."

"Okay." Quinten ended the call. He wasn't going to give in that easily, he knew that much.

He schooled his expression to polite friendliness as he came back to the table. "Sorry about that."

"No problem." She studied him. "Everything okay? I hope it wasn't bad news."

Quinten's shoulders tensed. Had he showed too much of his true feelings on his face just now? "A bit of business is all."

"About your family's shop?"

"Yeah." He caught Nicky's steady gaze. Something about the expression in her eyes made him realize, suddenly, that he wanted to tell her. Connect with her more deeply. Unburden himself. He took a breath and said, "I guess I'm just a bit...afraid that I'll lose it." He rearranged the silverware. "Grandma Viv loved it and put her heart and soul into it. That's the other part of why I started to work at the shop. Because I feel like the shop is somehow...a connection to her." He looked across at her, saw softness and compassion in her eyes. A warm glow filled him. She understood.

"I felt that way about my aunt when she passed away," she said softly. "She had a beautiful vintage pin she always wore and when I lost it after her funeral, I thought I'd lost her, too." She swallowed and fiddled with her purse straps.

"That's, I, uh, thank you for sharing that," he said softly.

"You're welcome," she whispered.

The server came back to fill their glasses and Quinten's mind drifted back to the conversation with his lawyer.

He had to think of something to say to Elliot. But he had to come up with just the right thing. Time was ticking.

Nothing like putting things off to the last minute. He grimaced. That was a habit he should really get around to breaking.

Maybe tomorrow.

"So." He leaned forward and rested his forearms on the table. "We have something much more historically important on our hands than we ever thought. You think?"

Nicky's lips curved up and she raised her eyebrows at him.

A tingle zipped up Quinten's spine as she leaned forward in her chair too. "What do *you* think?" Her cheeks flushed with excitement and her eyes sparkled.

Quinten felt heat creep up the back of his neck as she held his gaze. "I've already told you what I think." He opened his mouth. Closed it. "Uh, I mean, um..."

Confusion flitted across Nicky's face and she sat back, a small frown between her brows.

Damn it. This was what being direct and speaking the truth did. It made things awkward. It messed up dynamics. It hurt people, strained relationships to the breaking point. Like it had with him and his father.

The silence stretched. He cleared his throat.

He'd put his foot in his mouth again. Why was he always doing that?

He shot a sidelong glance at Nicky,

who now looked a little bewildered. Or was it bemused?

Either way, she seemed to accept him. His shoulders relaxed. Another thing that he appreciated in her—No. This line of thinking wasn't going to get him anywhere. It was unproductive.

She herself had mentioned she was only in Victoria for this story. So what was he doing? Going down this road wouldn't help him stay safely away from her.

Quinten felt a tug of disappointment as he turned his attention to the server who'd returned with the bill. "Here. You've been working hard these past few days. Lunch is on me."

THE SERVER CAME back with Quinten's Visa. That was kind of him to buy her lunch. Nicky's heart fluttered. Another thing she liked about him—his generosity.

The two of them headed out into the street and the bright sunlight once again.

She followed Quinten across the pavement and couldn't help but notice the long lines of his back underneath his neatly tucked in maroon button-down shirt.

That color looked really good on him

too. Jewel tones suited him, she decided.

Over these past few days, Quinten had been so helpful. Kind. Working with her on the riddle. Listening to her thoughts, opinions, views. Tracking down research. Holding open doors for her... Maybe, just maybe, she didn't have to hold her heart back, with him?

Gah. She bit her lip. No. She was better off single. His issues, whatever they were, would eventually come up; so would hers. So this spending time with him was just...for the story. She was almost done with it. Well, at least, the original assignment, anyway. Then she'd have to leave. Wouldn't she?

Of course she would.

She just needed to figure out how this whole treasure angle could be worked in without having to write an additional 3,000 words and go way over the length limit.

Maybe it was a follow-up piece she could pitch to Susan? That could work. And now that everything was shaping up so nicely, once it was published, the article could really begin to grow her name and reputation.

Chapter Seven

QUINTEN DROPPED NICKY off at the Orient Hotel and drove back to his own place.

He headed to the back door of his house and over to his workbench. It'd be a good time to tighten the strings on that guitar his friend and neighbor Tate had brought in.

But as he worked, his mind kept returning to Nazi submarines and that crumbling newspaper article he'd found.

If there was any concrete connection between the Nazi treasure, P.E.I., and the U-boats, then that website Jerry the librarian had mentioned would be the place to start. That'd be a big help to Nicky.

He put down the guitar and opened his laptop.

He clicked open his web browser. Now, what was the name—

Oh right. Island Voices. The website popped up and he scrolled through it.

Looked like you could search for whatever piece of island history you wanted. It was divided up by years, dates, and types of people, as well as subject matter.

Mabel's legend was one thing, the silver Nazi coin was another, but these first-person eyewitness accounts to history were something else entirely.

He typed in World War II, Nazis, and U-boats and hit enter. Hmmm. There were lots of P.E.I. regiments' accounts of fighting in the European theater...

He kept skimming.

...Canadian naval officers, shore leave, liberating France...

What was this? He scrolled down to the final hit. German submarine on P.E.I. He clicked on the listen icon.

"Well, it was back in the summer, no, the late spring of 1943. I remember it well because the spring lobster season was promising to be a good one. I'd been fishing the waters off the eastern side of North Cape for near-on twenty-five years at that point, ya see.

I'd heard the stories—well, everyone in these parts had—about the U-boats in the waters. Been rumors even of a sighting near Victoria. Can't say as I believed any of it, mind. But well, I had fish to catch and lobster to trap. What else was I to do but take a chance, every day, on my fishing trips? That year turned out to be one of the best lobster seasons I'd ever have.

But where was I? Oh, yah. Was near midnight, I think it was the 3rd or 4th of May.

Terrible rainy. But I figured it'd blow itself out. The RCMP had just the prior week come round and told us to keep a watch out for U-boats. They'd been working with the Coast Guard, ya see? We were told, "If ya see 'em, report 'em straight away."

Sure enough, bad weather did blow over. Moon was just beginning to come out from behind a cloud.

Out on deck I looked northwest and saw something breach. Far, far off in the distance.

At first. I thought it was a whale, so I grabbed my glass.

But then I looked through it. Made the hairs on the back of my neck stand up.

A swastika, plain as plain. I nearly fell overboard, a-tremblin' as I was.

Pretty much just me out there in that little fishing boat, ya see.

Near as I could tell, it was headed inland and I caught a few numbers on its side: 262.

I think that the U-boat captain or whoever he was musta cashed in on the thought that no one was around, seein' as how the bit of cloud cover that night'd been thick as gravy.

But that little puff 'o wind did it, 'cause that was when I saw a flash. Out of the corner of my eye.

I turned about real quick. And sure as the nose on my face but that flash was comin' from something on shore.

Musta been north of Seacow Pond, near as I could figure. Way up the beach. Like moonlight hitting metal. Bright metal. If I squinted through my glass, I could see it looked like a couple of men in uniform standin' on the sand. Busy doin' nothin' but standing there. Like they were waiting for orders or the like.

Headed as fast as I could for shore 'n got myself back home. Telephoned up the precinct right quick and told 'em exactly what I'd seen.

They thanked me, I hung up the phone, I had my supper 'n that was that. But then, well, when I heard about the sub's supposed connection to Hitler's gold, well, my convictions grew that there was summat goin' on. I could never be sure, but I always did wonder.

Never got the courage to go dig up the beach or anything to see if I couldn't find something."

The recording ended there and Quinten's heart pounded. More proof.

Maybe the German Navy had declassified military records from the war that he could look up to see the cargo manifest for U-262?

Some World War II military buff had a whole website dedicated to German U-boats in the North Atlantic that he'd linked to the archival records from the German Navy.

After thirty minutes of searching, Quinten found the right manifest. He started to scan it. Crew rations. Extra diesel. Tanks of oil. Gas masks. Shovels. Pick axes. And one crate which had neither a contents description nor dimensions listed.

Hmmm...

What had the sub's orders been?

Looked like the orders had been sealed, so none of the crew knew what the actual mission was.

He brought up the crew manifest. There was an M. Gryberg listed. Had that actually been Andrzej, aboard to carry out a secret Allied mission? The one that it referenced in his file? Looked like the dates matched.

The jangle of the bell at the door cut through his thoughts and he shut the laptop. Good. More customers. Or Nicky? He hoped it was Nicky.

He stepped into the shop, a grin on his face. But he ran right into Elliot.

Quinten took a step back.

Elliot crossed his arms. "You haven't given me or the lawyer any answer yet."

Quinten averted his eyes, grabbed a soft cloth from under the counter and began to polish an already-shiny oboe.

"Quinten." Elliot's voice held a note of exasperation. "You can't keep procrastinating. You need to give me an answer."

Quinten just kept polishing.

"Your avoidance of the situation isn't going to make it go away," he continued, as if Quinten had acknowledged him.

"And your pushing me into a corner about it isn't going to make me decide any faster," Quinten replied, making every effort to keep his voice calm. "It's only been a few hours since I learned about your offer."

"Look, you know how much this business means to me."

Quinten's head whipped up. His eyes narrowed. "No," he said through clenched teeth, "I don't know that. Because you were never around. You never even once paid attention to Grandma Viv or anything to do with this business," he spread his arms wide, "until now. When it suits you. When it fits in with your agenda and your—"

"Go on, say it. I want to hear it from you." Elliot tapped his foot. "I dare you."

Quinten's mouth snapped shut. He'd already revealed too much of himself, of his real thoughts and feelings. His hands clenched at his sides.

Sometimes he let his stubbornness get in the way of his ability to self-protect. He sighed. "Listen, I—the last thing I want to do is argue with family. We should all just get along."

"Why, when we fight so well?"

A chuckle escaped Quinten and he

rubbed a hand across his jaw but kept his gaze averted. "I just need...more time."

"Fine," Elliot said and turned to the door. "You have forty-eight hours. Or else the business is all mine."

NICKY SAT ON the deck of the Landmark Oyster House on Sunday afternoon. She picked up her last oyster and drowned it in sauce before she popped it into her mouth.

She wished Quinten was here right now. He'd probably have some great brainstorming suggestions about that piece of sheet music supposedly owned by Bormann.

Where could they look for it? Hmmm. If Bormann had something to do with it, then perhaps she should do a bit of research on the man. She ordered another iced tea and pulled up her web browser. Time to settle in for some research.

An hour and a half later, after reading through several articles and resources about Bormann, Nicky stretched and yawned. She'd found some good background stuff. Enough for now.

She bookmarked it all and looked up from her phone. Hmmm. Quinten had said

Viv had loved music. All kinds.

...Wait a minute. He'd also said Viv had a huge collection of sheet music. Some of which he'd saved.

If they started there, maybe that would spark some sort of inspiration?

She picked up her phone and dialed.

"QUINTEN? SORRY, HOPE I haven't interrupted you in the middle of something important."

"Just about to close up shop for the day. Had a chat with Elliot. He's gone now, though."

"I was thinking about the sheet music, that we could brainstorm some things together." She sounded a bit breathless and excited.

"Oh?" He felt a tingle go up his spine. Would she ever sound like that over...other things...if he suggested them?

He cleared his throat. Forced his mind back to the conversation.

"Yes," Nicky continued. "I was thinking that you said Viv had a pretty big collection of sheet music. What if we meet up in say, twenty minutes, if that works for you, and start going through it?"

"That would work," he replied, as warmth washed through him. She wanted to spend time with him. She wanted his help. She appreciated his actions toward her.

"Great! See you then," Nicky said and hung up.

He whistled a few notes to himself as he put his phone away. He had to take out the recycling. Today was Sunday. He checked his watch—the recycling truck was due in about an hour to come pick it up.

He headed to the foyer, picked up the three clear blue plastic bulging bags of recycling and put them out by the curb.

TWENTY MINUTES LATER, Nicky walked into the shop. As she closed the screen door, the chatter of tourists drifted in behind her.

Quinten was cutting a square of wrapping paper. Must be that gift for his cousin's daughter. He was so thoughtful.

Though she tried to avoid it, her gaze traveled over him as she walked toward him, a grin on her face.

Hmmm. That yellow T-shirt he wore

looked really good on him. Something about the pale shade brought out the highlights in his hair. And accented his chest.

He looked up from the bag of jelly beans he'd just finished wrapping, his expression happy. "Hi."

"Hey," she replied. Her heart pounded and she fluffed her bangs. She was leaving Tuesday—the day after tomorrow. She couldn't get carried away.

"The sheet music stockpile is in my living room. Over this way." He led the way to a door that was at the end of a short hallway near the entrance of the house.

The rumble of an occasional passing car sounded in the background.

He opened the door and Nicky felt his hand brush hers accidentally as he held the door open for her. She wished he'd keep his hand there.

Because she wanted to stand in the doorway with him all day. A longing filled her. She didn't want to leave. She wanted to stay. To spend more time with him. To get to know him better. To have him show his true self to her. And to share her true self fully with him.

But she walked through the doorway instead. She'd need to go; it was inevitable.

The story was getting closer and closer to being finished, after all.

"WHAT'S WRONG?" QUINTEN touched her shoulder.

"I..." Her eyes widened and for a second, he saw a look of...panic? on her face.

Quinten's heart stuttered as a surge of protectiveness swept through him. He wanted to help her, take care of whatever it was that was bothering her. Fix it for her. Make it better.

Her eyes darted to and then away from his before she spoke. "I really like this place and don't want to leave." She shifted her weight. "And, your noticing my sadness about that, well," she met his gaze, "I really appreciate it." She bit her lip. "Everyone else—and by that. I mean men I've been involved with—wouldn't have wanted to listen to how I felt. That would've meant they might've had to talk about how *they* felt too. They found it easier to avoid hard conversations and lie about what they thought."

She looked at him for a brief second from under her lashes as pink spread across her cheeks. She put a hand to her mouth.

He squeezed her shoulder. "It's okay," Quinten whispered. "People have said I'm easy to talk to. I think it's because I like to listen. Somehow, it's very easy to just listen. So I do." He ducked his head and chuckled. "Guess it comes naturally. Sort of always has."

What he didn't add was how his listening to others made it easier for him to not have to share his own thoughts and feelings and fears with anyone.

"What about you?" Nicky asked. "How's it going with the business?"

Quinten's eyes darted to and away from her face. He shrugged a shoulder. "A bit stressful."

"That good, huh?" Nicky nudged him. "I think I saw Elliot up the street as I headed over here."

Quinten rubbed the back of his neck. "Probably did."

"Well," Nicky said, "I'm not exactly a student of human nature, but I've lived a bit of life." She paused and studied him. "And I'd say..." She paused again, "maybe you're afraid," her voice softened, "that if you lose this business, you'll lose your grandmother, her memory, and all of the love and legacy that she gave, that she put into this business. But the truth is, Quinten," Nicky put a hand on his arm, "her love for you will still be in your heart, no matter what happens to the business. You're just hurting yourself if you think otherwise." She searched his gaze.

He tensed and felt his defenses slide into place. Why did she act like she wanted him to say something? Far better to keep his mouth shut and not share more details than other people absolutely needed to know.

Because otherwise, it just put you in danger. Of being analyzed. Of being criticized. Of being judged—and thus, declared not good enough.

"I know you can figure it out."

Quinten shifted his weight.

"You'll think of something."

He took a breath. She was trying to help him. Understand him. Be there for him. "Thank you," he managed at last.

He studied the floor. By not saying more than what others needed to know, he could stay safe. He could stay in control. Of how people saw him. Of how he saw himself. Of his vulnerabilities. Because if he didn't show any vulnerabilities to the world, to anyone else, then he wouldn't get hurt.

He looked up again. His heart jumped into his throat at the expression on Nicky's face. She looked so...sweet. With her face turned toward him like that. So willing to share, to be vulnerable.

He swallowed hard. He could *show* her what he felt. His gaze flicked to her mouth. Raspberries. If he leaned forward, he could finally taste her lips and—

"So where's that piano again?" Nicky backed up a step.

Quinten hadn't actually responded to her last statements, had he?

She tried to ignore the clench of anxiety in her chest. He'd only shrugged and nodded. Hadn't actually told her how he was feeling. She swallowed. Just like Ben.

A flutter of panic filled her as she glanced at Quinten. What was she doing? She couldn't let her guard down; she couldn't get involved.

"Oh, um," Quinten cleared his throat. "Just, uh, to the left, by the window."

She forced aside her tumbled emotions and turned to the window.

"Elliot's bought it and had me do a last tune-up. He's scheduled to have the piano movers come to take it to his place on Monday. It was Grandma Viv's. She always told me it was special."

Nicky's fingertips brushed the glossy wood as it shone in the afternoon sunlight. Would Quinten's skin feel as smooth?

She forced her mind back to reality. "You have a few pieces of sheet music here." She waved a hand at the books of sheet music that lined the music rest.

"Those are all mine. I've picked them over the years. My grandmother's collection is here." He crossed to a small shelf right next to the piano and pulled out a thick stack, blew off the dust and set it atop the piano. "I've done a fair bit of culling. She'd owned things that I already had copies of. I didn't feel the need to keep it all, so I've recycled all the duplicates."

Nicky scanned the titles. "Bach. Handel. Schubert. Looks like she liked her German composers."

"Always did," Quinten said thoughtfully. "Maybe now we know why?"

HE SHOOK HIS head. "But that's kind of terrible, since my grandfather was a wonderful man, and she loved him very

245

much. How could you have room in your heart to love more than one person at a time?"

Nicky rubbed at a nonexistent spot on the flawless surface of the wood and then took a seat at the piano bench. She ran her fingers across the keyboard, careful to avoid his eyes.

He shuffled through the papers and cleared his throat, "I guess we're looking for German composers then?"

"Yep. That makes the most sense, since that article we read earlier didn't mention what the piece of music was called."

"We have to remember, while it said Bormann had the piece of music, he didn't actually compose it."

"Okay," Nicky said.

The beep of a large vehicle backing up pierced the silence. Sounded like the recycling trucks were on his block.

"So what are we looking for?"

"Pretty much anything that looks kind of unusual."

"Wait," Nicky said. "I don't know why I didn't think of this before, but if I look up Bormann and coded sheet music, I bet I could find out what it's called."

"Good point," Quinten said, as Nicky pulled out her phone. "There must be a copy of that sheet music floating around on the internet."

After a minute, she said, "Okay, I think I have something here." She turned the phone toward him. "Looks like, no, Bormann didn't write the music himself. He just marked up a copy of it."

The beep of the recycling truck came closer. Quinten noticed its outline through the kitchen window.

Nicky angled the phone so he could see it better. A whiff of her vanilla perfume floated to him. "You're right. It looks like the composer was named Gottfried Federlein." He paused. "Appears he was a German-American. Interesting."

"And the piece that was used looks like it was the second movement in—"

"Marsch Impromptu," Quinten finished. His eyes widened and he jumped up. "I threw it out."

"What?" Nicky's head shot up.

"I threw it out." Quinten crossed the kitchen at a jog. He saw the recycling truck pulling up to the curb outside his house. "It's gone. Unless we act now."

QUINTEN RACED TO the screen door at the

front of the shop, Nicky right behind him.

The recycling truck parked. Its side door was wide open. One of the workers got out.

Quinten shoved through the screen door. "Hey!"

The worker walked toward the bags of recycling.

Quinten pounded down the steps, Nicky close behind. The screen door shut with a bang.

"Wait!" Quinten shouted.

The worker glanced Quinten's way as he leaned down to pick up the first bag of recycling.

Quinten jogged over to the man. "Don't touch that one."

The man stopped and his head jerked up. "What's the matter? Got a load of gold in here you changed your mind about?"

"No, more valuable," Nicky called out as she darted past Quinten and snatched up the first blue bag.

"Okay, okay." The man held up his hands. "Don't get yourselves in a twist."

Nicky's heart pounded as she clutched the bag to her chest and looked over at Quinten. His hair was disheveled and he was slightly out of breath.

So was she. She watched him rake a

hand through his hair, which caused his bicep to flex. Her pulse sped up as she watched the motion.

His blue-gray eyes blazed as he slid his gaze to hers. For a second, she couldn't remember to breathe, couldn't remember anything except the way his eyes held hers. A shiver went up her spine.

"Got anything else?"

"What?" Quinten tore his gaze away from Nicky. "Oh." He rubbed the back of his neck. "Uh...no. Just, um, these two bags, thanks."

"Right." The worker shook his head, threw the two bags in the truck, and got back inside. With a lurch, the truck pulled from the curb and lumbered on to the next house.

Quinten closed the space between them with a couple of strides. "That was close," he said. He still sounded a little breathless. "But we did it."

Nicky's pulse jumped and she just nodded, unable to trust herself to say anything. She caught a whiff of the clean laundry scent that clung to his soft cotton T-shirt.

She held out the bag to him.

"No," he said, his voice gentle, "you take it." Something in his stance and the tone of his voice suddenly reminded Nicky of that moment when they'd first met. How he'd radiated that quiet strength. That solidness. Her heart hitched.

"We can sort through it in the house," he continued. "Don't want anything to blow away in this wind."

Nicky nodded again and they headed back inside.

A few minutes later, a rather crumpled piece of sheet music lay between them on the kitchen table.

"Wow," Nicky laughed. "Your grand-mother was pretty clever."

"How's that?"

"I just realized. That very first line of the riddle is *The secretary marches.* "Marsch Impromptu." The piece of sheet music is literally a march."

"You're right."

"The more I find out about her, the more I realize just how, well, vivacious she must've been."

Quinten's gaze softened. "She was, that. I remember how she'd insist on swimming at the wharf on the very first day of summer. No matter if the water was freezing."

Nicky grinned. "Wow. That takes guts."

"Good for the soul, she always said, with that little gleam in her eyes."

"I did something like that one time."

"Really?" Quinten leaned forward.

"Yep." Nicky laughed. "I'm from Michigan originally, and I jumped in a lake in December on a dare in high school."

"In high school I was pretty awkward. Never did any dares."

"No? They bring something out in you... At least they did for me."

"Sounds like you two would've gotten along great," Quinten replied, a light in his eyes.

"Thanks. I think maybe we would have..." A warmth curled through Nicky's chest.

"She was always doing things like that. Until she got dementia." His face fell.

"I'm sorry," Nicky said. She placed a hand on his arm.

Quinten looked from her hand on his arm to her face. "Thanks." He paused, then said softly, "It was really hard. I never expected to be in that position this early in my life."

"What do you mean?" Nicky saw a flash of vulnerability in his eyes as he looked at her and then away.

He took a breath. "My mom left when I was a toddler. And my dad died when I was in my mid-twenties. So I spent a lot of time caring for my grandmother by myself." He cleared his throat and glanced at her. "Anyway."

Nicky saw the guardedness come back into his expression. She took her hand from his arm and turned her attention back to the sheet music. "It looks pretty normal to me."

"That's the point," Quinten said. "To someone with no musical training, it would look normal."

Nicky's eyes widened. "So the idea is..."

"That this piece of sheet music is hiding something."

"The question is, what?" Nicky tapped a finger against her chin and studied the page. "Well, where should we look first?"

Quinten studied the piece of sheet music.

She couldn't help but notice the way that the sun caught the streaks of gold in his sandy hair. It looked soft. Touchable. What would it feel like to run her fingers through it and—

"Maybe the best place to start is here. Look at this." Quinten pointed to words on the page.

"What is it? Those are just the lyrics to the song."

"No," Quinten said. "Look again."

```
Edelweiss grows at the Black Forest
Where Matthias plays the chords
Northwest of the crown.
```

"It's another code," Nicky murmured.

"Exactly." A gleam came into Quinten's eyes and Nicky's pulse jumped in her throat.

"Just like the microdot riddle," she whispered.

"It must be."

"So who's the writer?" Nicky asked.

"Well, Bormann. Question is, how do we figure out what it really means?"

"Let's work backwards," Nicky suggested. "The last line, *northwest of the crown*. Northwest is a direction."

"Well," Quinten mused. "That fisherman did say U-262 was headed northwest."

"Fisherman?"

"I found a sound byte on the Island Voices database," Quinten said. "He recounted a story about seeing that U-boat in the waters near North Cape and some Germans on the beach there in May of '43."

"Okay. As for crown," Nicky said, "could that mean royalty?"

"I think you're right. In fact, princes wear crowns."

"And this is Prince Edward Island, after all." Nicky grinned.

"That fits perfectly."

"Plus," Nicky said, "if Andrzej was on U-262, which we know from the crew manifest you told me you found, then it's more than likely the treasure was on that sub."

"Right," Quinten said.

"So then the second line, what do you think about that?"

"Not sure."

"Matthias..." Nicky murmured. "Why does that name seem kind of familiar?"

Quinten's brow furrowed and for a second neither of them said anything. "Oh!" He looked at her. "Remember?"

"What?"

"His file. Andrzej's. Can you pull it up?"

Nicky did.

Quinten pointed to the lines. "See? Alias: Matthias Grynberg."

Nicky gasped. "And Matthias is the name used in the second line here, so that fits. But what does it mean, when it says *plays the chords*?"

Quinten shook his head. "No idea."

Just then, Nicky's phone beeped. She glanced at the notification. "Another email from the National Archives."

"Open it," Quinten said. "It might help us out here."

Nicky tapped the screen.

Dear Ms. Stendahl,

Thank you for your further inquiry into the traffic from Agent Andrzej Gobell. The fee has been received. The pertaining document has been obtained. The bulk of Gobell's traffic that Vivian Robinson deciphered was in 1943. The first part has been digitized.

However, we are still working to scan and upload the second and third parts for that timeframe.

As the volume is quite substantial, this may take some time. You will be notified when the second and third parts are completed. But I do hope that this first portion meets your needs.

Regards,
Greg Scott
Research Curator
National Archives

Nicky opened the attachment, turned the phone to Quinten, and they read together.

F O R M 6. B)

C.C. AGENT TRAFFIC
AGENT: OAK
COUNTRY SECTION: X
DECIPHERED BY: ROBINSON, V.F.
(File #5234)

INITIAL DROP SUCCESSFUL LOCATION
AT SAFE HOUSE ESTABLISHED ASH
AND MAPLE HAVE MADE CONTACT MORE
ARMS ARE NEEDED WILL WAIT FOR
NEXT MOON PERIOD TO SEND NEW
DROP LOCATION WILL BEGIN INQUIRY
INTO OPERATION ELSTER

OPERATION ELSTER AS COVER FOR
OPERATION EDELWEISS CONFIRMED.
USE OF STOLEN FUNDS TO CREATE 4R
CONFIRMED. PLAN FOR TRANSPORT
AND DEPOSIT OF CACHE OF STOLEN
GOLD AND DIAMONDS CONFIRMED G &
D USED AS FUNDING FOR CREATION
OF FOURTH REICH CONFIRMED CACHE
LOCATION UNCONFIRMED PLAN AND
FUNDING INITIATED BY BORMANN

PREPARING TO ABORT OPERATION
EDELWEISS AS ORDERED AND RE-
TRIEVE STOLEN FUNDS CACHE BEFORE
TRANSPORT ACROSS NORTH ATLANTIC
ACCESS TO U-BOAT GAINED ASH AND
MAPLE TO ACCOMPANY

```
UNABLE TO RETRIEVE CACHE AND
DISMANTLE STOLEN FUNDING SOURCE
ASH AND MAPLE TAKEN WILL FOLLOW
SECOND ATTEMPT AS ORDERED
ONBOARD U262 DEPART FIRST MOON
PERIOD IN MAY

AFTER U-BOAT MISSION WILL PRO-
CEED WITH ORDERS TO SABOTAGE
REMAINING ELEMENTS OF FOURTH
REICH CREATION BY BORMANN UPON
ARRIVAL BACK IN BERLIN BORMANN
DRAFTED CODED MESSAGE INTO
MARSCH IMPROMPTU TO SECURE LOCA-
TION OF GOLD AND DIAMONDS HAVE
BEEN PLACED IN CHARGE OF U262
CARGO
```

Nicky looked up from the screen and over at Quinten.

"Wow," Quinten whispered. "I feel like I'm there."

"I have goosebumps," Nicky whispered back.

There was a moment of silence.

"This is how you feel, isn't it, when you're writing." A mixture of awe and seriousness came onto Quinten's face as he looked at her. In that second, Nicky realized, he got it. He understood exactly what she meant. He understood *her.*

Emotion swelled in her chest.

"So, what do you think these transmissions mean in relation to the second line of the riddle?" Quinten asked.

Nicky tapped a fingernail against her chin. "Well, we know that Matthias was Andrzej's alias."

"And Bormann was the one who wrote these lines..." Quinten's brow furrowed. "Plays the chords." He looked up suddenly and snapped his fingers. "It's like, pulling strings. I bet it means Andrzej was in charge."

"That makes sense. Bormann must have trusted Andrzej to carry out his orders. And since this is a piece of sheet music, Bormann decided to cloak it in a musical reference."

"Exactly. Because see?" Quinten pointed to the phrase. "Andrzej says here he's been placed in charge of the cargo."

"Which contained the treasure," Nicky said. "So then what about the very first line? *Edelweiss grows at the Black Forest.*" She frowned.

"Black forest seems very specific," Quinten mused. "Do you think that it's supposed to represent an actual place or—"

"A meeting point." Nicky scrambled for her purse.

"What?"

Nicky dug out her phone. "I got curious and did a bit of research on Bormann earlier." She scrolled through her bookmarks. "It's here somewhere..."

Quinten leaned closer and Nicky could smell the citrusy scent of his cologne.

"Here it is." She skimmed it. "See? It says here that he headed some sort of secret Nazi meeting in the Black Forest in early 1943."

He studied the screen. "You're right. And according to these transmissions, Andrzej said Edelweiss is the name of Bormann's operation."

"So this line is Bormann's way of signing his name to this project, and this treasure, too. He's essentially saying that he created Operation Edelweiss at this Black Forest meeting."

"That makes total sense," Quinten said.

Her heart beat a little faster at Quinten's nearness and she couldn't help the heat that crept onto her cheeks. She liked this, she realized.

Being with Quinten, helping him to work out these riddles, it made her feel...alive in a way she'd never experienced before.

But it wouldn't last. It couldn't last. Because she was only here for the story.

With an effort, she turned her attention back to the riddle.

"So," Quinten said, as he got up to pace, "it seems like Andrzej was ordered to stop Edelweiss from going forward."

"And prevent the creation of the Fourth Reich," Nicky said. "Since the sub with the treasure was headed to P.E.I."

"And he went undercover as a crewman on the U-boat to try to prevent the treasure from being moved," Quinten said.

"And Viv knew all about it."

"So why," Quinten rubbed a hand across his chin and Nicky could see the flecks of gold in his stubble, "did she end up with this piece of sheet music that Bormann encoded?"

NICKY'S EYES WIDENED. "Because she was the one reading Andrzej's traffic."

"Andrzej probably knew that. Maybe he gave it to her?"

"And she knew that it was encoded," Nicky said.

"So then she wrote the first riddle," Quinten said.

"Because she knew what was going on and wanted to help," Nicky finished.

Quinten suddenly stopped pacing. "You still have the riddle from the microdot?"

Nicky pulled out the scrap of paper.

He examined it. "So she wrote this." His eyes raced over the lines. "But what if it has multiple meanings?"

Nicky frowned. "What're you saying?"

Quinten shook his head. "Not multiple meanings. I meant... Okay." He slowly exhaled. "Look at the third line: *the pianist's journey*. We know Andrzej was an actual pianist."

"Yep."

"But," Quinten held up a finger, "what if it meant another type of journey, too?"

"To P.E.I.?"

"No."

Nicky gasped. "He was a pianist, so you're saying we should take a musical journey. Play the song."

"Exactly."

"You have plenty of pianos." Nicky got up and headed to the door that led to the showroom. "Let's pick one."

"Well, that Yamaha has a nice tone." Quinten crossed over to it. "I have an antique Steinway in the back I'm refitting." He looked around the showroom. "But Grandma Viv loved to play on her Princess

Royal—Oh."

"What?"

"Princess Royal..." Quinten said slowly. "I think maybe there was more than one reason Viv loved that piano."

Nicky raised her eyebrows.

"The dowry was from a Polish princess," Quinten said.

"So you think the name of the piano is significant?"

"It's not a coincidence that the dowry's from royalty—a princess, in fact—and that the name of Viv's piano is Princess Royal."

"So you're saying...?"

"We need to play the song on *her* piano."

"Then let's—"

Just then there was a knock at the door. Quinten glanced at Nicky and made a wry face. "'Scuse me just a sec."

"Sure," Nicky said. She couldn't help admiring his retreating form as he walked toward the door. She caught sight of a gaggle of tourists farther down the street.

Two big burly men stood on the porch. Quinten stepped outside to join them. Snatches of conversation drifted to Nicky.

"...take it Monday."

"A bit of...mixed-up schedule."

"...over this way." Quinten opened the

screen door, followed by the two men with *MacBeth Bros. Moving* written across their navy blue polo shirts.

"Hi, how are yah?" one of the men said to Nicky.

"'Lo," the other one said.

"Hi there," she replied but hid a smile at their Maritime accents. She couldn't help but feel a bit of a thrill. This place was so much better than the city.

"So here it is, boys. But can you give us just a second? We were going to play one last song."

"Sorry, Quinten. We'll be loading it right away. On a bit of a tight schedule. You said it goes to Elliot's, yeah?"

Quinten nodded.

Nicky's stomach dipped and she started to open her mouth. Wasn't he going to put up more of a fight? Argue with them that it would only take a second? But she bit the inside of her cheek. It wasn't her place to say anything.

Quinten's gaze slid to hers as the movers started to load up the instrument.

Just then, the gaggle of tourists walked up onto the porch. One of them asked Quinten a question.

There wasn't anything she could do about the movers taking the piano and she didn't want to get in their way.

"Quinten," she said in an undertone as she approached him during a lull in the conversation. "I'm gonna head back to my hotel room to finish up my story."

"Okay." Was that a flicker of disappointment on his face? Or just the light shifting in the shade from the apple tree outside the window?

She clenched her jaw. Of course, she couldn't tell what he was actually feeling. He was too stoic for that. And that was why she had to protect her heart and stay away from him.

Well, she'd just go write up what she'd seen here and add it in to the final draft of her story.

She took a breath. It was better this way. She needed to concentrate, to get away from being distracted by Quinten's presence...

She picked up her purse. "But we can wrap things up here first thing tomorrow?"

"Sure."

EARLY MONDAY MORNING, Nicky hit save for the final time on her Word document.

Satisfaction curled her lips upward.

Done with the story. But a slice of disappointment edged its way into her mind. She'd had to modify it a bit. She'd had to take out the treasure angle, now that they'd hit a dead end.

She sighed. That would've been such a great secondary thread. But maybe she could file that away for a future issue? Maybe even a book? She had enough information about it, that was for sure.

But all in all, she'd done what her editor had asked. She'd completed the story about Viv. Almost a week ahead of deadline. She grinned. She'd send it off here in a second.

Then she'd need to stop by Quinten's to...say goodbye. A knot formed in her stomach.

A beep from her phone interrupted her thoughts. She pulled it out.

Some sort of email from Susan. Probably wanting to know the status of the story.

Well, she'd have good news for her. Though Nicky had sent her an update a couple of days ago. What if the word count had changed?

Or maybe she wanted to run the piece in a different issue?

Nicky opened the message.

From: susanolmsted@historicalwoman.com
To: nicky.stendahl@gmail.com
Sent: Mon Oct 11, 8:12 a.m.

Dear Nicky,

Nicky frowned. Susan never started her emails like this.

I know you're busy with the assignment, so I'm sorry to interrupt you with a message. But unfortunately, as the Historical Woman magazine is owned by Umbrella Group—

That was the same company that owned *Ivory* magazine, who *still* hadn't paid her. She turned her eyes back toward the email and kept reading.

—you will find attached to this message an official affidavit for a libel suit against you.

Nicky's hand started to tremble.

Your social media post to Ivory Magazine on Thursday, October 7, indicates to our lawyers your unhappiness and dissatisfaction with our payment methods. Furthermore, your implication that said publication, which also takes into account Umbrella Group, does not treat its writers with timely and professional financial dealings, is hereby considered libelous and further action will be taken.

As per the work-for-hire contract you have signed, though you no longer own the rights to your work, you are liable for all attorney fees and potential court costs incurred by said situation.

Additionally, as per your contract, your current story will not be run and you will not be paid.

I await your response.

Susan Olmsted
Editor-in-Chief
The Historical Woman Magazine

Nicky wiped her sweaty palms on her ripped jeans and reread the email. Once. Twice. And a third time, as anxiety and panic clawed up her throat.

THE SCREEN DOOR opened and Quinten grinned. "Nicky. You're right on time. Come on in. I know that the piano's not here now. But we'll think of some way to…"

He saw sadness flicker across her gaze but she gave him a smile anyway. "What's wrong?" Quinten touched her arm as he stepped out to join her on the porch.

"There isn't really anything else to think of." Nicky rolled a strand of hair between her fingers. "We couldn't play the song. And I have…" she bit her lip, "some bad news."

Chapter Eight

NICKY TOOK A jagged breath. "I'm being sued for libel."

Quinten's brows shot up.

Nicky shoved her hands in her hair. Wasn't he going to say anything to that?

She suppressed a tremble in her tone when she added, "I'm actually pretty freaked out about this whole thing." Relief filled her at being able to share her anxiety. "Has anything this unnerving happened to you?"

"Not exactly, no..." He trailed off and averted his eyes.

Worry nudged at her. Wasn't he going to say more? But she forced down the thought. He probably had his reasons. Right?

"What happened?" he asked.

She rubbed her forehead and said, "I made a mistake on social media. I was doing a bit of, uh, venting. It got out of hand."

"Okay."

"A periodical I wrote for awhile back, *Ivory* magazine, was behind on their payment to me. Beyond the contracted pay period." She began to pace. "So I posted a query, naming that magazine specifically, about how I wondered about my payment being late. They took it, apparently, as libelous. Decided to sue me for it."

"Mmmm," Quinten said.

"The thing is—" Nicky bit a hangnail "—that magazine and the *Historical Woman* are owned by the same parent company. Because of all that, my story on Viv has been axed."

Quinten's jaw tightened, but still he said nothing.

A flutter of panic raced through her. He wasn't responding to her.

"Since I don't have liability insurance," Nicky shifted her weight from one foot to the other, "I have to figure out a way to fork over money for lawyer fees and court costs related to that." She glanced at Quinten and twirled a strand of hair around her finger. "For something I don't even own anymore."

Quinten pressed his lips together and remained quiet.

The gnawing worry mixed with disappointment only grew inside her. Why wasn't he saying anything? "So I'll need to go back to New York and deal with this."

"Right now?" Quinten asked. He shifted his weight. It seemed like he wanted to say something else. And yet...

"I changed my flight to today, yes." Nicky glanced at him. She took a breath around the band of anxiety that had begun to tighten in her chest.

He shoved his hands in his pockets.

"It's just that, well..." Nicky fiddled with a strand of hair again, then tucked it behind her ear. She glanced at him and then glanced away. Cleared her throat. "It seems like I've been disappointed," she whispered, "so many times. After I moved to New York, I was so hopeful. Got that job with Maggie at her jewelry company. But that went up in flames. Then I drifted around pretty aimlessly for awhile. But when I got my journalism certificate, I was so excited. I'd finally found something that I love to do, something that I'm good at. And things were going so well, too. I'd begun to see my writing dreams come to life. But now?" She bit her lip. "I could lose that. All because of some tiny little thing I did that I thought had no importance. I feel like I messed everything up. I feel like if I had only done things a tiny bit differently, then I wouldn't be—"

Nicky's eyelids trembled as she closed her eyes. She took a breath and opened them again. "What I'm trying to say is this story is really special to me. Your grandmother is special to me. She had perseverance, persistence. She wasn't afraid to go out there and do what had to be done at such a dark time; she kept going despite fear, despite disappointment." Nicky took a shaky breath. "No one had any idea when or how the war would end. But to keep going in the face of all that? That takes a kind of strength, a kind of courage, that I'm not sure that I really have. That's why I admire your grandmother, that's why this story is so important to me. That's why I feel so drawn to her. Inspired by her."

Nicky stopped talking and shoved her hands in her pockets. She tucked her chin to her chest and studied the floorboards of the old porch. Paint had peeled off in some places, which exposed the bare, naked wood beneath. The only sound was the tinkle of wind chimes from a house up the street, and the rustle of leaves in the wind.

She'd done it again. She'd just made herself vulnerable, put herself and her emotions on the line...

Quinten swallowed.

...And he still wasn't saying anything in response. He wasn't going to, was he? The band of anxiety squeezed her chest tighter as it mixed with slivers of hurt and disappointment.

Who was she kidding? She'd been stupid to allow herself to start to feel anything for him.

Because if he didn't tell her how he was feeling or what he was thinking now, if they ever got involved, he wouldn't tell her how he felt or what he thought later, with really important situations and decisions that could impact herself and her own life. Just like Ben.

She tried to take a calming breath. Maybe Quinten just wasn't responding to her for his own reasons? Oh no. Full-blown panic hit. No. She *did* know the reasons. Very clearly. He was withholding from her. On purpose. He didn't have the capacity to be vulnerable. When it counted.

When she'd shown so much of her own vulnerabilities to him, the least he could do was reciprocate. Yes. He was purposely withholding what he really felt. What he really thought. Just like Ben had. And withholding was basically a lie of omission.

And then one lie would lead to another and another... Until she wouldn't ever be able to trust Quinten to tell her what was going on inside his head.

Her heart pounded. Because if Quinten had his guard up now, he obviously didn't trust her. And that was no foundation to build anything on.

The silence stretched on.

Nicky's lips quivered despite her best efforts. She tugged on the ends of her hair in frustration. If only he'd say something to her. If only he'd actually voice his opinion.

What would happen if they ever started a relationship? Not that they had. And now they probably never would. The hurt settled deeper. A relationship should be a two-way street—both people had to be willing to share equally.

"Why aren't you *saying* anything?" The question burst from her.

Quinten's head snapped up and his eyes widened.

"Like right now. About your grandmother. About what I just shared."

QUINTEN PRESSED HIS lips together. She

wanted an answer. Deserved one. But somehow, watching her be that vulnerable with him just stirred up all his own pain.

He crossed his arms.

He didn't deserve to have the story pulled out of him like this. All the ways he'd thought, wished, hoped that if only he'd taken better care of Grandma Viv then things...would somehow have been different between him and his father.

Because then he wouldn't be afraid to say how he really felt. Wouldn't be afraid to speak his truth. Wouldn't be afraid of being judged or criticized or told he wasn't good enough.

He shouldn't have to tell her that like this. Not when they were basically just friends. She hardly knew anything about him. And whose fault was that? His. He didn't have her courage. He didn't have her strength.

He tightened his jaw. He should be able to tell her when—*if*—they ever became closer. He had hoped they might've... Pain pinched in his chest. But now that she was leaving, that had no chance of happening.

He shouldn't have to tell someone he knew so little about the pain that he guarded so closely in his heart. He hated that. He hated being pried open like a nut or prodded like a turtle who had pulled its head into its shell.

It was none of her damn business. It was none of anyone's business what he'd gone through.

He felt the old pain bubble up into his throat, almost close off his airway, as he tried to speak.

Because that's what love did; it caused pain.

He swallowed hard. So he couldn't let Nicky get to him like this. He couldn't let anyone affect him like this. It was too risky, too dangerous, too vulnerable for people to know his secrets, to know his pain. He had to keep people away. He had to push them out to a safe, comfortable distance. He had to shut them all out.

Because if he let them in, he'd drown. He'd suffocate. He wouldn't be able to function because he wouldn't be able to know what was real, what was true, how to trust or who to trust...

Because his father—he pushed the thought away but still it intruded—hadn't loved him. He'd never said "I love you" to Quinten, so Quinten must not be very lovable. Had never praised him, so he must've never done much right.

His dad took out his own pain, his own

hurt, his own suffering about his wife leaving them, on Quinten. He'd been too trapped in his own personal hell, too stuck in his own unhappiness, to show his own son any real affection.

Quinten dragged his thoughts away from that, forced himself to focus on the present. Forced his mouth to move.

"She had dementia, all right? She didn't know who anyone was. Least of all me. I'd come in and she wouldn't recognize me. Wouldn't—" He broke off and blinked rapidly. "It was hard. Really hard."

He crossed his arms over his chest and the flash of hurt in his blue-gray eyes as he turned his head away from her brought to mind a little boy whose parents had gone missing.

She reached out to place a hand on his arm. "I'm sorry. I didn't—"

He flinched away from her. "Never mind," he said far too quickly.

She pulled her hand back as if burned. Her gaze darkened.

He had too many fears and too many demons in his own heart and his own mind for her to waste any more time trying to understand him, trying to reassure him, trying to help him.

He was too damn stoic for that. She held back angry tears. He wouldn't let her in. He wouldn't let her help him. He just had too many walls up to allow her to be close to him. He was too damn afraid to do that. Too much like Ben.

She wasn't going to do this to herself any longer. She was going to free herself from this whole ridiculous, sorry situation.

She was going to leave.

She glanced at him. His face was averted from hers and he was typing something into his phone.

Sparks of indignation lit her blood. He was exactly like Ben. She'd been stupid to think anything else.

She snatched up her purse. Fine, then. She would stay as cool and stoic as he was.

She slung her purse over her shoulder. "Thank you for your help." She forced the words out in a falsely bright tone. "I appreciate your time. And if there's any chance the story will actually be published, I'll do my journalistic best to attribute the letters and such to you and your family."

A shadow crossed Quinten's face but it passed so quickly Nicky knew it must be a trick of the light.

When he met her gaze, his expression was simply polite, his tone neutral. "Thank you."

She turned and walked down the porch steps.

QUINTEN SWORE UNDER his breath and dropped the curtain as he watched Nicky's rental car turn left and head out of the village.

He hadn't said anything. Again. He bit his lip.

And now she'd taken his heart.

He swore once more. This situation was entirely his fault. His fault. He couldn't fix his relationship with his grandmother. He couldn't fix his relationship with his father. And he couldn't fix this.

He'd tried. He'd thought, back in the restaurant, that maybe he did have the courage, the ability, after all. But no. He couldn't express himself. He couldn't explain how he really felt.

It was like there was some sort of vise around his throat, preventing the words, emotions and feelings from coming out.

He'd just let a woman who'd become pretty damn special to him, walk away—

well, drive away—from his life. And he'd
stood by and done nothing.

He slammed a fist onto the table.

He'd done *nothing*. Just like all those
other times before. When he'd listened to
his father's criticisms, or stood by his
grandmother's bed in the care home,
feeling helpless to do or say anything that
would make the situation better.

He took a breath. He needed to calm
down. He couldn't go back and undo the
past. He needed to move forward.

Well, there was one thing that was still
in his control, at least. Finding the will. Or
sorting through the rest of those things in
the attic anyway. He headed upstairs.

As he worked, he tried to fight off his
gloomy thoughts, but failed.

He'd lost Nicky. And he was about to
lose his business. He chewed on a hangnail
and surveyed the mess.

He'd go through everything else up in
the attic here. It was the best distraction he
could find that wouldn't remind him of
Nicky.

Except everything reminded him of
her.

He forced that thought away. There
had to be a ray of hope somewhere...

His phone beeped. He glanced at the

notifications. There'd been a donation to his crowdfunding page.

See? Things weren't as bad as he'd thought. He checked the app.

Twenty-five dollars. Well, it was better than zero dollars. He shoved his phone in his pocket and set to work.

NICKY BLINKED BACK tears as she walked out of JFK airport early Monday afternoon. The smell of rain on blacktop only made the scent of ocean air seem that much farther away.

She sighed. How had things ended up this way? No. She wasn't going to give in to self-pity.

It wasn't all bad. After all, she could sell the article to some other publication.

The story. That's what she needed to concentrate on now. Not on Quinten.

She forced an image of him out of her mind. He surely wasn't sparing any last thoughts for her, so why should she bother with thinking about him at all?

She clenched her jaw as she headed to the city bus that would take her back to her apartment.

What if it wasn't even hers anymore?

She still didn't have the rent money. Her throat constricted. She only had a week left. And now with this lawsuit hanging over her head...

She winced. It wasn't like she could ask her parents for money. They didn't have much.

She hated to bother her friends. And the bank wouldn't give her a loan because she didn't have regular, stable income.

She swore under her breath and rubbed her temples. It didn't do much to ease the headache forming there.

She blinked back tears as she stepped out of the bus and headed up to her apartment.

She sighed in relief as the key turned in the lock.

But as she started to unpack her carry-on, reality settled in. She'd kept her phone off for the return trip but now she powered it back up.

She also turned on her computer. Time to try to do something about this. There must be some lawyer in this town who did pro bono work? A tiny flicker of hope built in her chest. It was worth a shot.

THREE HOURS LATER, Quinten headed downstairs from the attic for a late lunch.

He paused mid-step. Maybe the reason he hadn't raised any money was because no one had known about the fundraiser.

He headed into the kitchen. Some homemade soup would be good. He reached for the tattered and stained cookbook wedged between a diet tome on one side and his grandmother's recipe box on the other.

Yes... Why hadn't he thought of this before? What if he posted it all over his social media accounts? Put up posters around Victoria—Charlottetown, too—as a way to build awareness of the crowdfunding for his "Save-a-Heritage-Business" campaign?

He pulled out the yellow-and-blue recipe book and flipped to the soup section.

That could work. If he told all his friends here in the village—Brian, Anna, Tate, Gemma, Mabel, Derek, Mrs. MacPhail—they'd pass along the word to their extended circle of friends.

That was something Islanders were excellent at—banding together in a time of crisis to help each other out. And certainly this village knew how to do that.

He now had less than forty-eight hours. He'd better get started on those posters.

He turned his attention back to food. Hmmm. He had chicken broth. He checked the fridge and walked back to the cookbook. So maybe cream of chicken soup...

He looked in the table of contents, then turned to the recipe page.

What on Earth? This looked like the same type of paper from...Grandma Viv's journal? Still held together along their back edge with ancient glue, from the look of it.

He felt a pang. She'd done that, near the beginning. When the dementia had started to close in on her. Car keys in the freezer. Cereal in the linen closet.

He picked up the bunch of blank pages and riffled through them. But they weren't all blank. There was writing here.

January 20, 1947

If I close my eyes, I can still see him in the hours before he left, that final time...

He stood there in the glow of the streetlight; the whoosh of traffic suddenly seemed very far away. His fingers, gentle on my face; his kiss, tender; his smile, sweet. He pulled a box from his pocket and opened it. "This is the last remaining link I have to my family's heritage, to my history."

As he slid the ring on my finger, he whispered, "Keep it safe for me, so that when I come back, we can make our own history—together. I love you."

There will always be a place in my heart for Andrzej, one that no other man could ever fill. But he is dead. I still have the amber ring he gave me on that night; oh, it seems so long ago—almost in another lifetime...

But I shall wear it. I do not have to say from where I obtained it, now do I?

Maybe some day I will find out what happened to the treasure. But I know I must put that part of my life aside, as I need to focus on my life here on the island and on my newborn son.

Quinten swallowed a lump in his throat and turned the page.

July 25, 1948

Oh, how my heart pounded as I saw the postmark. Berlin. June 7, 1943. No return address—of course.

I knew at once who it must have been from.

Five years is a long time for a piece of mail to sit. Though I simply cannot fathom how, he must have smuggled the letter out by courier. Had the courier addressed it afterwards?

I can only think that in all the turmoil since

the war's end, it must have been misplaced and finally found its way here. After Wallace and I were married, I did leave this as my forwarding address from New York.

It contained only three things, but I know which one is most precious—his final letter to me.

I will put them all aside for safekeeping; though I know in my heart that I cannot pursue this, as my son and my wonderful piano tuning and restoration business now take up my time and my heart. Perhaps one day I will pass the ring and its secrets along...

Quinten looked up from the words. Three things... The first must be, as Viv said, Andrzej's final letter.

But the second? Oh. Andrzej must've enclosed "Marsch Impromptu" with his letter, which was how she'd ended up with the piece of sheet music.

But what was the third thing? He had no idea. For a second, he wished Nicky were here. His gaze flicked to his phone. What would she think of these entries?

What if he called her? Told her about it and—No. That wouldn't do any good.

He sighed and leafed through the rest of the pages. What was this? He pulled out a brittle yellowed sheet folded in quarters.

The edges crumbled as he unfolded it to reveal an enciphered message.

NICKY STARED OUT the window at the darkening New York cityscape after she hung up with the lawyer's office Maggie had put her in touch with.

Their pro bono caseload had been a mile long. But they'd told her they'd put her on their waiting list.

At least it was a step in the right direction. Something she could respond to that email with.

She should have felt happier. She sighed.

All she could think about, though, was a particular shade of blue-gray. One that didn't match the gray tones of the busy city...

The gray sidewalks, the black wrought iron on some of the buildings, the rush and flurry of people, so many people. Too many people.

She sighed. New York. She was tired of it. Tired of its hurry. Of its buzz of activity. Tired of its anonymity. Tired of blending in, of not being seen, of just being another face in the crowd.

Her mind drifted back to Island Chocolates. That very first day, when Mrs. MacPhail had said, *"We're not above sharing tables with strangers here. That's how people make new friends."*

The sound of laughter and the crack of mallets hitting croquet balls on the emerald-green back lawn of the Orient Hotel. The way that strangers had treated her like a friend from the very beginning. The taste of salted caramel chocolates on her tongue...

And Quinten.

His eyes warm, his smile soft. How he looked at her as if he truly appreciated her, as if he really wanted to listen to her, to know her and who she was, what she was... That connection that they'd shared.

She clutched her mug tighter to stop her fingers from trembling. What had she done?

Why was it that she didn't miss things 'til they were gone, until they were too far away to ever be retrieved? She pressed her palm against the window as raindrops slid down the pane.

She wiped a few drops from her cheeks. She was being ridicu—

A sob broke through her resolve and before she knew it, tears streamed down her face. How could she just have walked away like that?

How could she have let her own issues, her own fears, build up to a point that *that* was all she'd seen; *that* was all she'd allowed herself to see, when in reality...?

In reality, she didn't know because she wasn't a mind reader.

In reality, she realized, as a hard knot formed in her throat and was difficult to swallow, she'd never asked him.

Her gaze strayed again to the window, to the walkers, to the raindrops, to the seemingly endless sea of black umbrellas.

She wished it was a different sea—the coast of P.E.I.—that she was looking at.

But she couldn't go back there. Not now. Not when she'd screwed everything up between them. She couldn't go back, either, because she'd made it clear she had nothing more to say to him, and he had nothing more to say to her.

And that was that. What else was there, when there was nothing to do but remember all the mistakes, all the missed opportunities, all the pain—

She exhaled sharply. She was giving in to misery. She needed to think about something else.

So she picked up her Nikon and started

going through the images. She paused on the black and white photograph of Viv. But she couldn't concentrate. She kept seeing the wharf in Victoria, the way the leaves had rustled on the trees, that particular quality of October light that was golden, that was beautiful, that was, at its heart, the essence of Prince Edward Island.

She put down her camera and picked up Viv's journal. She'd remembered to return Mabel's box. So why hadn't she remembered to give this little book back to Quinten? She sighed. She'd have to mail it back.

She opened the book and paged through it. There was that enciphered entry.

She traced a finger along the lines. She'd meant to mention the entry to Quinten. Or at least, try to figure it out herself. But with everything else that had ended up going on, it'd gotten a bit lost in the shuffle. But now...?

She looked again at the arrangement of letters on the page. Had Viv used one of the ciphers she had been trained to decipher, to write this? It was possible.

In fact, now that she thought about it, hadn't Leo Marks mentioned in his book that agents used the Playfair cipher sometimes? Yes.

She turned to the Internet for the decryption process and then pulled out a notebook and pen and set to work.

At last, she was able to read the clear text writing.

May 1, 1943

We are not supposed to speak of this but I simply must have someone to tell it to, even if it is only to this page. I have taken great care to encipher these paragraphs and hide this journal.

As I deciphered his incoming message, I felt my heart plunge, because the mirror, the gold, the diamonds, have been taken by the Nazis. Worse, there have been sightings of U-boats along the North Atlantic coast and perhaps he is even on one of them, as he spoke to me about joining the German Navy as part of his cover. (Yet another thing that is 'forbidden.')

The Nazis think they can simply take what they want—ruin lives, ruin whole histories, without the littlest regard for anything beyond their own interests. They have stolen his heritage, his culture, his family legacy. Just because of his lineage. In fact, he is proud of his closest guarded secret. Which he entrusted to me to keep. Which I shall.

That is why I promised him before he left last

week–his eighth time–that I would do what was in my power to help him. Even if he does not return.

Nicky looked up from the small book. His closest, most-guarded secret... Not that he was Polish. No.

Viv had meant—Nicky's eyes widened and she picked up her phone and scrolled to that Polish Art Center article she'd bookmarked—he was the descendant of Princess Magdalena Jola Piast.

Yes. The article even said the dowry ended up with the prominent Gobell family, direct descendants of the princess's line. Viv said *his family legacy* in this entry, too, which meant he must have inherited the jewelled mirror and—

The ding of a new email notification popped up on her laptop. Nicky's mouth went dry as she saw who it was from.

From: jwhite@umbrellagroup.com
To: nicky.stendahl@gmail.com
Sent: Mon Oct 11, 8:15 p.m.

We have not heard from you in re-sponse to our earlier message.

In the interim, we have spoken with our lawyers.

We have decided we do not wish

to tie up company time in legal bat-
tles. After consultation with our
lawyers, we would like to propose the
following:

1) That the lawsuit may be considered
   withdrawn if:

   a) you agree to never again write for
      Ivory magazine, the Historical
      Woman, or any of the
      publications the Umbrella Group
      produces

   b) you agree that your article with
      the Historical Woman magazine
      will not run and that you will not
      receive compensation for any part
      of it

   c) you agree not to run the already-
      agreed-upon article content with
      anyone else, as the work-for-hire
      contract for that material had
      been signed and agreed upon
      previously.

   Your decision must be made within 48 hours. Otherwise, we will press
charges.

Jonah White
Executive Assistant to
George J. Starr, CEO
Umbrella Group

Nicky chewed a cuticle. Of course. She'd forgotten that she'd already signed the contract. She sighed. There went her idea to sell the article elsewhere.

She stared at the screen. But what about all the work she'd put into the story? And all her extra research...

How could she just give up all of that?

Nicky pulled out the delicate air mail envelope and stared at Andrzej's final letter to Viv. She traced the neat handwriting with a fingertip.

She couldn't just give up on Viv's story, give up on Viv's life. It was important. Something that had to be said—and shared.

But in exchange for not having to go to court? She swallowed hard. That would be a lifesaver.

She hit reply.

QUINTEN STEPPED AWAY from the telephone pole and grinned as he surveyed his work.

The last poster was up. He'd plastered them everywhere between here and Charlottetown, it seemed like. Told all his friends. Posted like crazy on social media.

Now he'd just have to wait.

He shoved the sleeves of his teal blue shirt farther up his forearms.

He wished Nicky could be here to see the progress he'd made on this. She'd appreciate his work. She'd probably even post something about it on her own social media platform that she loved so much.

A sad smile flitted across his face as he remembered the way her eyes had sparkled as she'd sat across from him at Gahan House. The protectiveness he'd felt as she'd stood so close there in the doorway. The way she'd put her hand on her hip, so sure of herself and what she wanted, when she'd come into his shop with the diary.

She wasn't afraid to speak her mind. That was one of the things he admired most about her.

Quinten rubbed a hand across his stubble as he walked back to the music shop and went in the back door.

That was the trouble. His own fears and insecurities had such an iron grip on him. That was part of why he couldn't say what he truly longed to say to Nicky. Truly yearned to say to her.

Damn it. She didn't realize just how powerful of a connection he felt to her.

Somehow, his lips were sealed, his

throat wouldn't work. It went beyond an unwillingness to say anything. It was a visceral, almost primal need to *not* say how he felt. Not to risk being seen and thus, be rejected.

He shook his head. Probably related to his father and all those years Quinten felt that he wasn't important. All those years that his father had criticized him. Told him that he wasn't good enough. Told him that he'd never measure up.

His fists tightened at his sides.

That was ridiculous. But that was how it was.

He blinked rapidly. Nicky had been willing to be there for him. Willing to see him. But now she'd gone, he could never tell her.

He *wanted* Nicky to see him, wanted her to know him for who he truly was. He'd been wrong, back on the porch, when he'd been so sure they were just friends; when he'd been so sure he wouldn't—couldn't—open up to her.

He brushed the back of his hand across his face. He wanted...to let Nicky in.

But he didn't know how.

Chapter Nine

LATE MONDAY NIGHT, as Nicky lay awake in bed, she tried to ignore the nagging feeling in the pit of her stomach. No lawsuit. But at what cost?

She rolled onto her side and shoved the pillow over her head. But it didn't drown out the vibrating buzz that erupted on her nightstand.

She grabbed her phone, half-hoping it was Quinten.

It wasn't.

Dear Ms. Stendahl,

I have some unfortunate news. The files request you have made regarding Agent Andrzej Gobell's traffic has run into some difficulties.

The second and third portions, when they were retrieved from deep storage, have succumbed to mildew and water damage.

We have done our best and were able to digitize one piece of traffic. His final transmission. It is enclosed. Thank you, and best of luck with your research.

Regards,
Greg Scott
Research Curator
The National Archives

Nicky jumped out of bed and went over to her desk. She'd be able to see it better on her laptop. Besides, her phone battery was almost dead. Again. She really needed to replace it.

She pulled up the file.

```
SUSPECT COVER COMPROMISED
COULDNT ALERT OSS TO CACHE LOCA-
TION HAVE TAKEN PRECAUTIONS WITH
CACHE REMEMBER AMBER IMPRISONED
ON CROSSING BACK HAVE ESCAPED IN
BERLIN SAFE HOUSE BEING WATCHED
HAVE SENT SHEET MUSI
```

The message ended mid-sentence. Nicky's chest tightened.

If Andrzej had suspected his cover had been blown and the safe house was watched, then...the moment the message was being sent was the very same moment they'd been discovered.

The W/T operator must have been shot partway through the transmission. And Andrzej? Captured and tortured and then killed by the Nazis.

She stared at the last four letters. Goosebumps broke out on her arms. She rubbed them. Someone had died. More than one person, actually.

She couldn't just sit here and not do this whole saga justice. The public had to know. She needed to keep looking for the treasure. Because it had to be returned.

What about Quinten? Oh God.

She pressed her fingers against her lips and refused to let the tears fall. Quinten wasn't going to see her cry. Not even in her own mind.

She clenched her hands so tightly that the knuckles turned white. Damn him and damn her issues. She'd completely screwed it all up with him because of her stupidity and her fear.

She'd been too busy worrying about how he never seemed to open up to her to realize she'd been dangerously close to falling in love with him, anyway.

And now? It was too late. Too late to turn back. Too late to start again.

She couldn't go, she couldn't...

Go?

She narrowed her eyes. That's exactly what she *had* to do. Go back to P.E.I.

She lifted her chin and suddenly she could very clearly see everything about the island, everything about Quinten, and everything about herself that she hadn't seen before.

She'd let her perceptions overrule the truth. She hadn't let him show his true self to her when he'd been trying to, she realized now with a little gasp.

She'd been too busy labeling him, judging him, thinking she was so sure about him when all it would've taken was a little compassion, a little empathy, and—her heart skipped a beat—a little *love* in order to see him for who he truly was.

Yes.

She squared her shoulders. She had to talk to Quinten. And she had to follow through on the story. It didn't matter if no one published the article. What mattered was doing the right thing.

Who knew? Maybe she could rewrite it and put it up on a blog of her own? Maybe she could use all the extra research to write her own book about all of it?

Because she had to do this. For herself.

For Quinten and his heritage. And for Viv and Andrzej.

TUESDAY MORNING, QUINTEN picked up his phone. His forty-eight hours were almost up. All that work. The crowdfunding. The social media posts. It had helped. Unfortunately, not enough.

He'd have to call his lawyer.

He didn't want to sell to Elliot. But it looked like he didn't have any other choice.

Quinten's grip tightened on the phone as he dialed his lawyer.

"Is there anything you can do? I mean, I know I'm grasping at straws here but I have to ask."

The other man sighed. "There's nothing I can do. Legally, Elliot can buy out your half, seeing as how you haven't yet found any solid inheritance documentation."

"What about this bankruptcy solution Elliot's imposed?"

"I'll have to do some checking; and I'll get back to you by the end of the day today. Technically, your forty-eight hours don't end until midnight tonight. Remember that."

"Okay, I'll wait to hear from you." Quinten put down the phone and took a deep, yet shaky, breath. There was hope after all.

He rubbed a hand across his face. At least there was some hope. For his business anyway. But what about his love life?

"Nicky," he whispered to the empty room. "I'm sorry."

He had thought that by holding back, by not telling her what he now knew she most wanted to hear, that he was helping her, helping himself.

Doing them both a favor by taking out the messy emotions and the drama and protecting himself.

He sighed. Protecting himself. That's exactly what he had been doing by playing the tortoise and pulling his head inside his shell.

But that wasn't going to get him what he really wanted, now, was it?

He shook his head.

It was only going to get him more of the same. More pain. More silence. More lonely nights and long days filled with work but not much else. There was an emptiness in his heart that longed to be filled.

And the only person who could fill it was himself. There was no one else who got that job. He shouldn't—couldn't—ask that of anyone else.

He had to do that for himself. He had to create his own happiness. Nicky wasn't going to give that to him, nor was anyone else.

He picked up his phone again.

He had to tell her that. Somehow. He had to make himself do it. He'd been wrong. He'd put her through too much pain to hope that she'd forgive him, but at least he had to try.

He dialed.

NICKY PICKED UP her to-go hot chocolate off the counter at Island Chocolates late Tuesday morning and turned toward the door.

She pulled out her phone to check her messages but then realized the battery was dead. Again. This was the third time in a day. She'd have to buy a new battery for it—

"Nicky!"

"Mrs. MacPhail." She tossed her dead phone back in her purse.

"Sorry to startle you, dear." She patted Nicky's shoulder. "But I'm so glad I ran into you. You know, I haven't seen you around lately."

"I, uh," she cleared her throat, "was away for a bit." She took a sip of coffee. "But now I'm back." She glanced at the door.

"I've been trying to find Quinten today but you'll do just as well. I'm sure you'll see him so if you could give him this..." She started to dig around in her purse as she kept talking. "It's just that, you know, Quinten's crowdfunding campaign got me to reminiscing. His grandma and I used to write letters to each other, back when I was overseas teaching in Ethiopia."

"Uh-huh."

Mrs. MacPhail continued, "Well, I threw most of them out. Al didn't like all that junk, as he called it, just sitting around." She flapped a hand. "So what did I do but listen to him? Anyways, that was awhile ago." She paused. "But then just yesterday, I was cleaning out my kitchen. You know how you always have a drawer that sticks? Well, that one's in my kitchen. It was driving Al batty—frankly, me, too— so I decided to fix it."

Nicky hid her smile around another sip of coffee.

"Ah-ha. Here it is." Mrs. MacPhail pulled something out of her purse and held it up. "I found it stuck in a drawer. The darn thing wouldn't shut and when I pulled out this crumpled piece of paper, that's what it turned out to be. So here you go, dear." She passed the mangled page to Nicky and straightened up.

"Thanks, Mrs. MacPhail." Nicky tucked the paper into her own purse. "Nice to chat and, uh, hope to see you around later."

"I won't keep you now. But I just wanted to say that everyone in the village here, well, we're so happy that you decided to write about Viv. You know, if you're ever looking for something else to write, my mother was in the Women's Royal Canadian Naval Services during the war. Went over to New Brunswick, near Moncton, to a place called Coverdale. All very top secret, of course, at the time. But it was actually an outstation for Bletchley Park back in England. The women who worked there, including Mom, intercepted and transcribed German messages from the U-boats running around the North Atlantic, then sent 'em over to Bletchley to break."

"Wow," Nicky said. "I'll keep it in mind. I really should run now..."

"Alrighty. One other thing, dear. We're preparing for the annual Victoria Village Christmas Stroll. Happens near the end of this month." She patted Nicky's shoulder. "Maybe you'll be around for it?"

"I hope so," Nicky called over her shoulder as she hurried out of the chocolate shop.

QUINTEN CHECKED HIS crowdfunding app. His eyebrows shot up. People had actually donated more? He gave a shaky laugh. Things were looking up.

He would need to organize the prizes and get that together, but it should be easy enough to do. Maybe he didn't have to wait to hear back from his lawyer after all?

He glanced at his phone and tried to ignore the fact that Nicky had not replied to any of his texts. Or the call he'd made.

He had to harden his heart, snuff out that hope. At least things with his business were looking up—he should just focus on that and—

He jerked his head up as the floorboards creaked.

NICKY STOOD ON the porch of Quinten's music shop. She put her trembling hands in the pockets of her denim capris and shook back her hair in an effort to feel nonchalant.

It didn't work.

She took a breath, pushed open the screen door and stepped inside. Quinten met her gaze from across the counter.

Sunlight shone through the window and highlighted the gold in his hair. She wanted to reach out, touch it, smooth it under her fingertips and then lean forward and kiss him; tell him how she felt; tell him her deeper feelings and deepest desires.

She shook her head. Bit her lip. Those gestures wouldn't be enough. She had to show him.

So that he would truly know and understand, so that the embers in his heart would catch fire again and they could both be bathed in the warm glow.

She let out a shaky breath and twisted a strand of hair around her fingers. She began to speak very quickly. Maybe if she talked fast enough, he wouldn't kick her out before she'd said what she had to say.

"Listen, while I was back in the city, I had a lot of time to think. In between worrying about paying my debts." She gave a quick laugh. "I started to wonder why the song would have to be played on that specific piano. And since we're thinking it did have to be played on that specific instrument, well, that could mean there's something more to the song than notes. What if there was some sort of connection between the melody you were going to play and something unusual about the piano itself?"

Quinten opened his mouth to say something but Nicky hurried on.

"Because you'd said yourself that your grandmother loved puzzles, so maybe she engineered something about the piano to hide a clue? Or maybe she just used what was already there and connected the melody somehow with—"

"Whoa, whoa." Quinten crossed the room in a few strides and put his hands on Nicky's shoulders. "Slow down. We'll figure this out together."

Nicky blinked. "You're not...mad at me?"

"You sound disappointed."

Nicky made a strangled noise.

"Did you not get my text messages or

308

my voicemail?"

"My phone died and it doesn't hold a charge and I didn't have time to replace the battery or anything so I've just been using my laptop to check emails and such."

"Well, that explains that."

"Listen, I'm sorry, Quinten. I...I acted like an idiot and I need to fix this." She looked at him with a hitch in her chest.

His face was unreadable. For a moment Nicky felt the old anger, the old fear, return.

He blinked rapidly, averted his gaze, and shoved his hands in his pockets.

But then she realized, there in that second, that she'd read him all wrong. The lack of expression on his face, the stoicism, wasn't that he didn't care...

It was that he was working twice as hard to hide the fact that he *did* care.

"Oh..." she whispered.

QUINTEN JERKED HIS head back in her direction. Saw the look in her eyes.

She'd come back because she actually might care about him? Care about him so much that she'd been willing to be vulnerable with him, set aside her own fears, her own hang-ups, for the sake of reaching out to him.

That was real love. That was true love, he thought, as a bitter taste filled his mouth.

And he'd gone and stomped all over her sweet, good, kind intention, back when he hadn't opened up, been vulnerable, or reached out there on the porch. He'd shattered her heart, and his own in the process.

But he couldn't just apologize to her for that. No apology was going to change that, was it? Words weren't enough; action, hopefully, would fix things. Right? There was only one way to find out.

QUINTEN SQUARED HIS shoulders and cleared his throat. "You're right. There's something about that piano. We'll need to go see it at Elliot's."

"Um." Nicky shifted her weight. "We'll have to figure out how to...arrange...that." She tucked a strand of hair behind her ear.

"Looks like we're going to have to do a little—"

"—breaking and entering?" Nicky's pulse raced. She'd never done anything illegal before and it seemed a bit extreme.

He chuckled as he picked up a wrapped package Nicky recognized as the yellow jelly beans. "I was going to say pay a house call to drop this off." He hefted the package. "And check the piano now that it's been moved. Because, you know," he paused and lifted his eyebrows, "it could be out of tune."

Quinten grabbed his car keys out of the basket by the back door and "Marsch Impromptu" off the counter. "Let's go play a song, shall we?"

FIVE MINUTES LATER they came to a stop in front of a large old Victorian two-story house with a box-bay window and a wraparound porch.

Quinten got out of the car. "They moved this house to Dunrovin Estates here from my other grandparents' farm," Quinten said to Nicky.

"Wow. So picturesque." The yellow house stood on the edge of a small bluff that overlooked the Northumberland Strait.

Nicky followed Quinten as he walked up to the front door and knocked.

Elliot opened the door. "Did you come by to say you've decided sell to me?"

Quinten swallowed and took a breath. "Um, no." He glanced at his watch. "Technically, I still have until midnight tonight."

Elliot crossed his arms.

Quinten forced himself to sound casual. "I, uh, wanted to check that the piano made it through the move okay."

Elliot didn't say anything.

Quinten added, "I won't charge you."

A silent few seconds passed. Elliot tilted his chin in Nicky's direction. "Who's your girlfriend?"

Heat crept up the back of Quinten's neck. He thrust the wrapped package at Elliot. "I, um, also brought these for today. They're for Rose."

Elliot took the package and said a terse, "Thanks."

"Honey, who's at the door?"

Elliot turned at the sound of his wife's voice from the back of the house. "It's Quinten," he called back.

"Good, he can tune the piano for my birthday party. Come help me move the table before the guests start arriving, please."

"Sure, sweetie!" Elliot yelled in reply.

To Quinten, he said, "Fine. Come in then. I'll just be in the kitchen. Piano's in the living room." He opened the door wider to let them in. "You have ten minutes," he added in an undertone before he left.

QUINTEN PICKED UP the rather brittle and somewhat crumpled sheet of music and placed it on the piano's music holder.

Nicky couldn't help but admire his long, strong fingers.

He bowed his head a moment before he placed his fingers on the ivories. He glanced at her for a second and Nicky caught a wistful expression that lingered even as he turned his attention back to the piece of music.

He began to play.

Nicky watched as his eyes closed and he lost himself in the piece. Her throat tightened as she saw his concentration deepen, his focus narrow, his body sway ever so slightly in time with the melody. Her heart squeezed as she was again reminded of one of the trees along the street here. Solid, strong. Deep-rooted.

She closed her eyes too and listened as if the music notes themselves would tell her something, would reveal some hidden, deeper meaning...

But all she heard was beautiful music. What was Viv trying to say? What was Andrzej trying to convey?

The pianist's journey, she mused, *mirrors a plan well-laid...* What if there was no plan at all?

Was there even a treasure? Or was this some sort of elaborate diversion designed to distract the Allies from whatever the Germans were planning in relation to D-Day?

Nicky's stomach dipped.

Quinten played the final notes. They echoed in Nicky's heart as they faded into silence—

Her eyes snapped open. What was that? She held her breath. Had that noise been from the clock on the mantel? Or the piano? She listened again.

Now nothing. Just the chirp of birds and the rustle of the leaves on the maple tree outside the window.

She met Quinten's gaze. "You play very well."

"Thank you."

For a moment, neither of them spoke as the silence filled in the words between them.

Her heart pounded. Was he thinking the same thing she was?

As he looked at her, a softness filled his expression and she swallowed. Was she thinking the same thing he was?

But he was the first to avert his gaze.

"DID YOU HEAR that?" Nicky whispered and glanced toward the kitchen. The sound of Rose's laughter, the clink of dishes, and the murmur of Elliot and his wife's conversation drifted into the room.

"Hear what?" Quinten said in a low voice.

Nicky sat down beside him on the piano bench, so close her hair brushed his upper arm. "A noise at the very end of the song. Like, a click?"

She turned her head toward him. Quinten's heart jumped into his throat at the excited expression on Nicky's face.

He swallowed hard. She was so close. His gaze flicked to her lips. But so far away...

His mouth went dry and he swallowed. If he leaned forward an inch—

"I bet it's some sort of secret compartment your grandma rigged up," she whispered, her lips close to his ear. "And the compartment was somehow triggered when the last few notes were played." Her eyes lit up.

He shifted on the bench. It creaked under him as Nicky jumped up then crouched down to examine the piano legs. "I'm trying to remember exactly where I heard it." She frowned. "I think it was somewhere around here."

Quinten joined her. "Let's look for anything that's sticking out or seems oddly fitted," he murmured under his breath.

Nicky ran her hands over the glossy surface. "I don't see anything yet..."

A few seconds ticked by in silence.

"The piano's fairly free of ornamentation. There isn't much of a place to hide anything," Quinten whispered.

Nicky tapped the legs of the piano but shook her head. "Doesn't sound like they're hollow."

Quinten continued with his inspection of the piano. "I've tuned this piano so many times. I can't believe there's something that I've missed."

"Wait a minute," Nicky said, her voice tense and low. "Look at this."

She pointed to the front right piano leg's scalloped edge. "That wasn't facing in that direction before." She touched it, then motioned to Quinten. "I think..." He came nearer. "Playing those notes somehow made the leg rotate a few degrees. What do you think?"

Quinten ran his fingers along the piano's leg to the place that she'd indicated. Smooth. Satiny. Like her own legs...

No. He couldn't think about that now. He forced his mind back to the piano. "You're right. This leg's turned counterclockwise ever so slightly. I think we need to move it just a bit more... There's some sort of—" Gently and carefully, he swivelled the wooden piece just a hair. "—secret compartment."

Quinten met Nicky's gaze as he slipped his fingers into the darkness. Her eyes widened and he heard the catch in her breath.

Floorboards creaked and they both froze as footsteps sounded in the hallway.

Quinten plucked up what felt like two small scraps of paper from the cavity with his first two fingers.

He did a sweep around the remainder of the small space. No, nothing else.

There was a quiet snick as he rotated the piano leg back into place. Quinten gave a quick nod to Nicky and they both stood up. He tucked the papers into his pocket, then glanced over his shoulder.

Elliot's wife leaned around the door-frame. "How's it sound to you?"

"Great." Quinten dusted off his hands. "You're all set." He walked to the door, Nicky behind him.

"Wonderful," she said. "Thanks so much."

"You're welcome. And happy birth-day." Quinten waved as the door banged shut behind him and Nicky.

NICKY SANK ONTO one of the oak captain's chairs at Quinten's kitchen table.

"So. What did we find?" Her voice came out a whisper but her heart raced.

She held her breath as Quinten sat down beside her and pulled something out of his pocket. "It's two pieces of paper."

The scent of his cologne drifted to her as the breeze from an open window brushed her cheek.

"Oh." Nicky struggled to keep the dis-appointment out of her voice.

"You were hoping for some gold coins?" Quinten's eyes sparkled.

"Never hurts to hope." She wound a

strand of hair around her finger and avoided his gaze. "So." She cleared her throat. "What's on it?"

He unfolded the first brittle, yellowed paper.

Nicky peered over his shoulder and frowned. "What on Earth...?"

"It looks like some sort of diagram." Quinten squinted as he turned the paper this way and that. "I think it's from some sort of machine?"

"Two concentric circles. Maybe we can logic it out," Nicky said. "We know it's probably vintage World War II, whatever it is."

"And it's round."

"So it could be from a gun barrel?"

"These look like dimensions." Quinten tapped the page. "See the numbers?"

"I do. It almost looks like crosshairs or something..."

"Mmm." He studied the page. "I think it's bigger than a handgun."

"A tank?" Nicky guessed.

"I don't think..." Quinten picked up his phone and began typing. After a second, he showed the phone to her. "See? Looks like it's from a submarine."

Nicky sucked in a breath. "A German U-boat."

Quinten put his phone back in his pocket. "I think this is a diagram for the forward and aft torpedo tubes."

"But why stick it in there with..."

Quinten carefully opened the second piece of paper. "A piece of poetry? That's a very good question."

```
The moonlight shone
Down on your face
My heart leapt up
To take its place.

Watch, my love,
For my return.
Though tears fill your eyes,
Though your heart shall yearn.
```

Quinten frowned. "Why go to all that trouble for a poem?"

"Unless," Nicky grinned, "it's not a poem."

Quinten raised a brow.

"Well, it *is*. But it's more than that. Of course." She smacked her forehead. "Why didn't I think of that right away? Andrzej was an agent. He worked for the SOE. The SOE used poem codes to pass messages from enemy territory back to London. It was a system that unfortunately wasn't very secure even though it used double-transposition and key words..." She bit her bottom lip.

"Key words?"

"Five words, chosen at random from the poem, that the agent would use to carry the message. They'd put those five words through a double-transposition system. They'd number each letter of each of the five words and then transpose the resulting numbers into a grid... The SOE asked the agents to memorize their poems. They thought that would make the poems secure."

"But it didn't?"

"No. Leo Marks, head of SOE's codes division, eventually devised a more secure system agents carried with them on silk handkerchiefs that they would then cut away and burn. But they also continued to use poem codes as well."

"Mmm. That makes sense. Old habits die hard, and all that."

"Yep. And there was a lot of internal politics involved, too, apparently."

"But why weren't the poem codes secure?"

"Because the Germans tended to figure out the key words. Either through torture of a captured agent or through a lot of searching through books by trial and error on the part of the German cryptographers. And once they figured that out, well, they could figure out the resulting indicator groups and transposition keys and crack the messages."

"Okay."

"Plus," Nicky continued, "a lot of times the agents were given common poems, for ease of memorization, that everyone, including the Germans, already knew."

"Really?"

"Like Poe or Shakespeare. Once Marks joined the team, though, he got SOE agents to start making up their own ditties, as he called them. He wrote a lot of them himself, actually. Which made it slightly more secure."

"How do you *know* all this?" Quinten watched her.

Nicky felt warmth surge through her at the admiration in his tone. She fiddled with a strand of hair. "Research. And, I read a book called *Between Silk and Cyanide*. It's Leo Marks's memoir."

"So you think someone at the SOE wrote this?"

"It's possible Viv wrote it. Or Andrzej. Or neither of them... But whoever received it would've had, or known, the indicator group. That would've told them what the five key words were that were then used to transpose the message." Nicky glanced at the poem.

"Hmm." Quinten rubbed his jaw and Nicky watched the motion. A blush swept her cheeks. No. There wasn't time for thinking about that now. "Any guesses on what the five words could be?"

"Unfortunately, no." She tapped her fingers on the table. "Crap!"

"What?"

"This isn't going to do us any good even if we *did* have an indicator group. Because we need to have the enciphered message. Otherwise...there's nothing to decipher. We can't just make the message of out thin air."

"Damn. That's right." Quinten frowned. "Because the poem is what would give us the way to crack the enciphered message... But without the enciphered message, there isn't anything to solve."

"Exactly." Nicky sighed and put her chin in her hands. "We need to have the secret message." She bit a hangnail. "*And* the indicator group."

Chapter Ten

QUINTEN LOOKED AT the poem. "You said an indicator group..." He trailed off. "What does that look like?"

"Well," Nicky said, "the thing is, no one really knows exactly what type of indicator groups the SOE used. The best guesstimation is that they must have labeled the five key words using either letters or numbers. So the short answer is, it has to have either five letters or five numbers."

Quinten frowned and stared at the poem. "Five letters or numbers." Then his eyes widened. "Wait a minute. When I was tuning the piano before I gave it to Elliot, I found the oddest thing under the lid." He jumped up from the table. "It didn't make any sense to me, but I thought I'd try to figure it out later so I put it over here."

He strode over to the door where a low marble-topped cabinet sat. He rummaged around in a shallow wicker basket filled with house keys, sticks of gum and loose change. "Okay, here we go." He plucked out a small square of old yellowed paper and came back over to Nicky.

She extended her hand and couldn't suppress a shiver as his fingertips brushed her palm. She unfolded the paper.

BIOPW

"Huh." A slow grin spread across her face. "Exactly what we need." She met Quinten's gaze.

"It's my grandmother's handwriting," he said.

"Wow." Nicky traced a finger over the letters. "So Viv must've known what indicator group Andrzej would've used."

"You know, I bet there's an app for this," Quinten mused. He pulled out his phone.

"Even if there is, I want to do it the old-fashioned way."

Quinten put away his phone. "Okay."

"It's how they would've done it," she said softly. "I mean, can you imagine all that the agents and the wireless operators went through to get the messages back to London?"

Quinten traced a finger along the faded

letters as Nicky continued to talk.

"You had to somehow get your message to the wireless transmitter operator. When the Germans stopped people on the street for random searches..."

"Uh-huh."

"...and if you had anything on you that was suspicious, even just one tiny thing out of place, you were questioned."

"Whew."

"And then the W/T operators...doing the enciphering with just a stub of pencil...maybe in near-darkness in some cramped, airless space...heart racing, one ear listening for the Gestapo pounding down the door?"

Quinten shook his head.

"All the while trying to transpose the letters into numbers correctly when you hadn't slept in three days but you knew you had to concentrate, had to get that critical arms drop location back to London? But one tiny mistake could mess up the whole message."

"It wasn't easy for the W/T operators to transmit the enciphered messages by Morse, either," Nicky said, as she picked up the yellowed scrap of paper. "They had the most dangerous job. The units were usually big and heavy. The only way they could typically hide them were in suitcases. Pretty conspicuous. But they had to send the messages. They had to communicate with the free world."

"Yes."

"The agents and W/T operators didn't let anything stop them—the fear of discovery, the sleepless nights, the constant threat of imprisonment or worse. It's like, when I do this by hand, somehow, I'm part of history, I'm helping history..." Nicky touched a fingertip to the yellowed bit of paper. A few flakes crumbled away from the edge.

"History," Quinten echoed. "You know what...I think I just might have the enciphered message."

"What do you mean?"

He went and grabbed his grandmother's cookbook off the shelf. "Here."

Nicky's eyes welled.

Quinten gently put a hand on her arm. "So now what?" he asked.

Nicky gave a shaky laugh. "This means Andrzej must've sent Viv the secret message along with the final letter he wrote to her."

"Must have," Quinten agreed.

"But she didn't decipher it?"

"Mmm." Quinten shook his head. "I

don't think she did. Because in a diary entry of hers that I found in this old cookbook, she says something about not knowing what happened to the treasure."

"That makes sense." Nicky took a breath. "Okay. So in order to figure out the secret message..." She bit her bottom lip but couldn't suppress the happy thrill that ran through her, "...we need three things." She ticked them off on her fingers. "One: the poem."

"Check," Quinten said.

"Two: the indicator group."

"Check."

"Three: the enciphered message."

"And check." Quinten held it up. "So how do we solve it?"

"Well, that's why the indicator group is so important. We use that to figure out the five key words that the message is enciphered with." She took out a pencil and her small notepad from her purse. "So, first thing, you have to label the poem." She picked up her pencil. "You assign a letter to each of the words in the poem, starting with A. So the first word in the poem is 'the.' You write the letter 'a' above that."

"So we'd label the next word, which is 'moonlight' with the letter 'b' because it's the second letter." Nicky continued, "Then we do that for the whole alphabet." Nicky put words to action until the whole poem was labeled.

Quinten glanced from her notepad to the poem and back again.

B = moonlight
I = heart
O = place
P = watch
W = tears

Quinten rubbed his jaw. "Okay, so that tells us the five key words. I also noticed something... Each of the 'words' in the enciphered message is five letters long. Is that random or is there a reason?"

Nicky grinned. "It's to help out the W/T operator."

Quinten cocked his head.

"The enciphered messages were transmitted by Morse code. To make it easier for the wireless operator to send the coded messages back to London, the enciphered message was sent in 'words' that were five letters long."

"Ah," Quinten said. "Now what?"

Nicky tapped her pencil on the page in

her notebook. "Now we write these five words out all strung together. Like this."

| M | O | O | N | L | I | G | H | T | H | E | A | R | T | P | L | A | C | E | W | A | T | C | H | T | E | A | R | S |

"Then we label each of the letters with a number. We label each letter that's shown, in chronological order. So the first A—it's there in the word heart—we label that with the number 1. The second A, in the word place, would be number 2. There aren't any words with B, so we move on to C until we go through the entire phrase. That creates the transposition key." She started to write. After a few minutes she put down her pencil.

| M | O | O | N | L | I | G | H | T | H | E | A | R | T | P | L | A | C | E | W | A | T | C | H | T | E | A | R | S |
| 17 | 19 | 20 | 18 | 15 | 14 | 10 | 11 | 25 | 12 | 7 | 1 | 22 | 26 | 21 | 16 | 2 | 5 | 8 | 29 | 3 | 27 | 6 | 13 | 28 | 9 | 4 | 23 | 24 |

"So these numbers we've just generated underneath the letters," she tapped the eraser end of the pencil on the notebook page, "are what we're going to use to decipher the message. This is exactly what your grandmother would've done."

"Wow. I never knew." Quinten shook his head and cleared his throat. "You said it's double transposition. Which would mean we need to use this numbered grid twice?"

"Right," Nicky said. "Which also means we need some squared paper." She ripped out a clean lined page from her notebook and used a spare pencil she'd grabbed from her purse to draw vertical lines down the page so that the page was filled now with small squares. "To keep everything lined up," she explained.

"Okay."

"Now that we have our chart, we look back at the enciphered message. See the first five letters?"

Quinten looked at the page. "I T E I A."

"Right. We take each five-letter group in the enciphered message and put it in the chart. We write it vertically under the corresponding number's column."

"Okay."

"So, since the first five letters in the enciphered message are I T E I A, we put I T E I A under the column with number 1. That corresponds to the A in the word 'heart.' Like this."

M	O	O	N	L	I	G	H	T	H	E	A	R	T	P	L	A	C	E	W	A	T	C	H	T	E	A	R	S
17	19	20	18	15	14	10	11	25	12	7	1	22	26	21	16	2	5	8	29	3	27	6	13	28	9	4	23	24
											I																	
											T																	
											E																	
											I																	
											A																	

"Then you just repeat that process, putting each five-letter group from the secret message vertically under the correct numbered column, until the whole enciphered message is placed beneath the transposition key?" Quinten asked.

"Exactly." Nicky set to work. It wasn't too long before her pencil stopped moving. "So now we have the whole chart filled in. But that's just the first part of it."

"Right. Because you said it uses double transposition."

"Yep. In order to figure out the clear text message, we need to decipher the second part of it. The message, in essence, was scrambled twice. We've gotten the first unscramble. Now we need to do the second unscramble. Which, by the way, is actually the reverse of what the agent did to encode it. So, if I don't make any mistakes, this will give us the actual plaintext message."

She picked up her pencil again. "We take what we've gotten from the first transposition, and read those letters horizontally left to right, starting at the top left. See?"

M	O	O	N	L	I	G	H
17	19	20	18	15	14	10	11	
D	N	U	H	D	G	H	

Quinten nodded.

"We put those letters, which now appear horizontally in the first table, into the second blank table vertically in order to spell out the actual clear text message." She started to fill in the blank squares.

M	O	O	N	L	I	G	H	T
17	19	20	18	15	14	10	11	25
D	A	R	L	I	N	G		
N	I	A	M	G	O	N		
U	A	N	D	T	H	A		
H	E	M	I	R	R	O		
D	I	A	M	O	N	D		
G	U	A	R	D	T	H		
H	E	R	I	N				

Nicky's pencil stopped moving a little while later.

"So now," Quinten said, "it looks like we have to read the resulting letters here horizontally left to right...?"

"Right," Nicky laughed. "Right."

```
DARLING IF YOU ARE READING THIS
THEN I AM GONE PLEASE KNOW THAT
I LOVE YOU AND THAT I HAVE TRIED
TO RETRIEVE THE MIRROR THE DOWRY
AND THE GOLD AND DIAMONDS I HAVE
TAKEN STEPS TO SAFEGUARD THE
HIDING SPOT DONT FORGET THE RING
```

Nicky exhaled a shaky breath and turned to Quinten. "This confirms what we've been theorizing all along."

"You're right." Quinten looked thoughtful for a moment. His eyes widened and he sat up straighter. "So *that's* the third thing that Viv got..."

"Third thing?"

"In that diary entry I found in the cookbook, she said Andrzej gave her three things." Quinten tugged his earlobe. "Andrzej sent her that final letter, which she mentioned in the entry. He also gave her the sheet music. He must've also given her—"

"The poem code and the schematic," Nicky exclaimed.

"Right. So this means the treasure is definitely real." Quinten grinned.

"Question is," Nicky said, as she tucked a strand of hair behind her ears, "is it still there?"

"I know how we can find out." Quinten dangled the car keys from thumb and forefinger.

Nicky jumped up. "Let's go."

Quinten stood too. "Where?"

"That's easy." Nicky laughed.

"North Cape." Quinten chuckled to himself. "Because that's where everyone's been saying it's been for the last seventy-five years."

"And because that's the POW rendez-vous spot referred to in that *Guardian* article," Nicky added.

Quinten grinned. "Looks like we're headed up west."

"I'll drive," she said.

"Do you know where you're going?" A note of amusement crept into Quinten's voice as he glanced at Nicky in his driver's seat while he tossed a couple of shovels in the trunk.

She shot him a look with brows raised as he got into the passenger seat and stowed a pair of flashlights in the back seat. "I figure with your fancy Apple watch, you can navigate."

"True," he said. "But I'll probably use my phone. It has a bigger screen."

"Speaking of phones, can I charge mine up?"

"Here, I can do it for you." He took her phone and plugged it into the car charger.

"Thanks." She threw a grin at Quinten, put the car into reverse, and backed out of his driveway.

"Let's swing by my friend Tate's place. He has a metal detector he's let me borrow a couple of times. Might need one now."

After they picked up the device, they turned back onto the TransCanada before they changed to Highway 12 West.

"I haven't been up west in awhile," Quinten said, as the rolling hills covered in pine trees flashed by the passenger window in the early evening light.

"No?" Nicky said. "Looks like it's a pretty beautiful part of the island."

"It is. During the war, there was a station up in Tignish. You know, there was some wartime song... Let's see, how did it go?"

He hummed a few bars.

A companionable silence descended between them. He could get used to this, he realized with a jolt. Her. Him. The road stretching out in front of them. Savoring the journey together. He glanced at Nicky.

But did she want that too? His gut tightened.

"We still headed in the right direction?" Nicky asked after a while.

He certainly hoped so. In more ways than one. "Almost there, actually. Just pull into the parking lot here. This is where the lighthouse, restaurant and gift shop are.

Closed for the day now, though."

Nicky got out and stretched. "Pretty long drive."

"Yeah. About an hour and a half from Victoria." Quinten rolled his shoulders.

"So what's next?"

"Now?" Quinten pulled out a shovel from the trunk. "We see what we can find."

"But," Nicky said as she turned on the metal detector, "we have no idea where to look. The message just indicated North Cape, which is a pretty big search radius, from what I can tell." She glanced around. "And we're starting to lose daylight."

"No worries. That's what these are for." Quinten handed her a flashlight and pocketed the other. He put one of the shovels over his shoulder and headed toward the beach, Nicky beside him.

"From what that fisherman said on Island Voices, we know that the U-boat didn't come ashore. But part of the crew got the crate to shore somehow and..."

"Buried it. That's what Andrzej said, after all, in the message we deciphered."

"Only question is, where?"

"Right." Nicky came to stand beside him on the wide expanse of beach. Her vanilla perfume filled his senses. "I mean, it seems pretty random as to why a torpedo schematic would be included with the poem code. Unless it has something to do with it?"

Quinten pulled out the yellowed page. "But what?"

NICKY STUDIED THE schematic of the torpedo tubes but found herself distracted by Quinten's nearness.

If she shifted even a millimeter, she'd be pressed up against his solid chest, could wind her arms around his neck—

"Well," Quinten said, "does anything look different or unusual on this page?"

Nicky forced her attention back to the paper. "Not really."

"Hmm." Quinten studied the drawing again. "What do those numbers mean?"

"Those are just the dimensions of the fore and aft torpedo tubes. It's not—"

She looked up. Their gazes locked.

"I don't think those are dimensions," he whispered. "See? Along here?"

He pointed to the vertical and horizontal lines along the edge of each circle.

"I bet that's latitude and longitude." Nicky pulled out her phone and started tapping. "Yes." She pointed at the screen. "See? When I enter those numbers, it comes up with..."

"Nothing," Quinten finished, as he peered at her phone over her shoulder.

"That's weird." Nicky frowned. "Maybe I entered it wrong?" She tried again. "Still nothing."

"Here, let me try." But Quinten came up with the same result. He rubbed a hand across his jaw.

"But these have to be latitude and longitude." Nicky bit her lip.

"Unless they aren't."

Nicky made a wry face as she gently folded the yellowed sheet back in quarters, as it had been originally. "It's a wonder the paper hasn't completely disintegrated."

But Quinten didn't reply. He was staring at the page in her hands. "Hold it up again," he said, his voice tense.

Nicky cocked her head but did as he asked.

"Whoa."

"What?"

"It makes a compass."

Nicky blinked.

"See?" Quinten pointed at the middle of the drawing. "When it's folded up like that the lines intersect. That would create a heading..."

"You're right," Nicky breathed.

Quinten pulled up the compass app on his watch. "Let me just confirm it." He glanced up at the horizon. "Yes." He looked back down at his watch. "Right...over..." He consulted the antique paper and then his compass app again. "...there." He pointed to a piece of beach with a pile of red sandstone rocks that jutted out into the surf. "Come on."

Nicky followed Quinten as her heart pounded in her chest. This was really happening?

The scent of the salt air and the whoosh of the surf told her it certainly was real. Her heart skipped a beat as she glanced at Quinten and then back out at the horizon. The full moon had begun to rise.

A swell of happiness filled her and she realized, in that moment, that she belonged here. On this island. With this man. Her heart filled with happiness and joy as she looked over at Quinten. She bit her lip. But did he feel the same way?

"It's over here." Quinten pointed to a spot in the sand, glanced at his Apple watch and compared it to the paper one last time.

"Okay," Nicky said. She swept the metal detector over the area. It began to beep.

They started to dig.

The only sound was the whisper of the breeze, the call of the gulls, and the sound of the shovel turning over sand. And more sand.

"There's nothing but sand here," Nicky said, as she fought to keep the disappointment out of her voice. "I think we've dug down about three feet. We need to—"

His shovel hit something wooden.

"—dig this up," Quinten finished as he grinned at Nicky and knelt in the sand.

She sank to her knees beside him. They began to carefully push away the sand.

The exposed wood was rotten in places. Nicky switched on her flashlight and frowned. "It almost looks like a case."

"For?"

"I have no idea. Let's open it and see."

Together they pried the partially rotted lid open on its rusted hinges.

"A typewriter?" Quinten said and sat back on his heels, his flashlight in hand.

Nicky dusted off her hands. "Wow. Has glass keys and everything."

"What are these things for?" Quinten pointed to multiple thin black wires that were attached to the front.

"I'm not so sure it *is* a typewriter."

Quinten frowned. "But what else could it be?"

Nicky shook her head.

"And what about this? Above the keyboard? Looks like rotors or something," Quinten mused.

Nicky gasped. "It's an Enigma machine." She glanced at Quinten's raised brows. "I've watched a lot of World War II movies and TV shows," she murmured with a guilty shrug.

"Come on," Quinten said, "let's move it and see whatever, if anything, is underneath it."

"I don't think this is going to be light," Nicky said with a laugh.

Together, they cleared the sand away from all four sides of the wooden box that housed the Enigma machine and reached under it. Slowly, it began to shift as they lifted upward.

"Oof," Nicky muttered. "My grip is—"

"Oops, careful there," Quinten said, as the machine tilted sideways. He gritted his teeth to keep hold of his side. The motion jostled the wires.

"Sorry, I just—there, I think I've got it now—"

"Let's just—be careful and—ooh—this

is hard to—"

But Nicky's fingers slipped again, which caused one of the wires to jerk loose. "I think I have the wrong angle now—just don't—"

Quinten swore under his breath.

"What?" Nicky's cheeks flushed.

"Look down there."

"Oh God. Where?" Nicky's eyes darted around.

Through clenched teeth, Quinten jerked his chin at the hole.

Underneath the Enigma machine was a stack of TNT on top of a wooden crate. Wires attached the TNT to the Enigma machine.

Nicky's face drained of color and she almost dropped her end of the machine.

"I've read somewhere that the stuff gets more volatile the older it is." Quinten's jaw set as he grappled for a firmer grip on the heavy device. "And after seventy-plus years, I'm sure it's none too stable—"

Another wire popped loose.

A loud ticking noise started.

"What is that?" Nicky's eyes widened and her muscles strained as she held the machine.

Quinten swore again. "With those two

wires that just came loose, I think we've just—"

"—triggered a bomb." Nicky swallowed.

NICKY WILLED THE pounding of her heart to slow but it didn't work. "What are we supposed to do now? I don't think I can hold onto this much longer. My arms are getting really tired."

"Mine too," Quinten said. "We need to put it down as gently as possible. Don't want to risk jostling anything else loose."

Nicky nodded.

"On the count of three," Quinten said. "One, two..."

"—three," they said in unison.

They put the still-ticking Enigma machine back down.

"W-what are we going to do?" Nicky tried to force her voice to stay level but it wavered anyway. She jumped up.

"Don't panic." Quinten jammed a hand in his hair. "That's the first rule of survival. Don't panic." He swallowed.

"I don't suppose you know any bomb squad people?" Nicky said with a shaky laugh.

Quinten shook his head.

"Well," Nicky smoothed a shaky hand over her hair, "neither do I."

He swallowed again and looked down at the rotors. "We don't have much time, either. Hear how fast the ticking is?"

"That's not exactly helping my train of thought, you know."

"Sorry," Quinten said. He jumped up too and pulled out his phone. "We need to call someone—911. The police. An—"

"We need to solve it," Nicky said.

"Huh?"

"The Enigma machine encoded words five letters long using these rotors and pins. We need the right five-letter word that would break the code. We do that, the bomb doesn't explode, we don't die, and we can see whatever's in the crate underneath it."

Quinten rubbed a hand across his face. "Got any favorite colors that are five letters?"

"Not helping." Nicky bit a hangnail.

"Sorry. Just trying to lighten the tension." Quinten tugged his earlobe. "The right five letter word... Well, maybe it has something to do with Andrzej or Viv?"

"There are fifteen billion-billion possible combinations. But we only have one try."

"Don't remind me," Quinten said, as his eyes fixed on the rotors.

"WE NEED TO think." Nicky pulled at the ends of her hair in frustration.

Quinten began to pace on the sandy shoreline. "Andrzej and Viv. What did they have in common?"

"They both knew the treasure was here."

"Andrzej must have rigged this up. In that last transmission, he said he'd 'taken precautions.' This must have been what he meant. To prevent it from falling into the wrong hands...which doesn't really help us now. What else?"

"They loved each other?" Nicky said.

"Love is only a four-letter word."

"Damn it," Nicky said. "What about a name?" She looked up at Quinten.

Quinten kept pacing. "Some sort of name that they both would've known... Andrzej thought that Viv would come find the treasure because after he got caught by the Nazis, he knew that he wasn't going to make it."

"But what name?"

Quinten frowned and stared down at the ground. "Well, Andrzej is seven letters, Viv is three and—Oh!"

"What is it?"

Quinten's gaze locked on Nicky. "The secret message we deciphered said, 'Don't forget the ring.' At first, I thought it was something just sentimental, but I think the ring must have something to do with all this."

"Okay," Nicky said slowly.

Quinten gasped. "The last time I saw my grandmother alive, she looked into my eyes and said with the strongest conviction, 'Remember amber.' I just dismissed it at that point because I thought she was talking about a person. But," he shook his head "she wasn't."

Nicky's eyes widened and her voice lowered to a whisper. "The ring...is *made* of amber."

Quinten sank to his knees in the sand. "And amber? Well, it has five letters."

"I really hope you're right," Nicky said. With shaking hands, she keyed in the five letters.

As she hit the last key, she held her breath.

Quinten tensed.

The ticking stopped.

Nicky closed her eyes and let out a slow breath.

For a second, they both sat there in silence, the moonlight shining down, the only sound the rush of the surf.

Quinten met her gaze and opened his mouth but then closed it. He cleared his throat and said, "Should we find out what's underneath?"

Nicky nodded.

They carefully cleared the sand off of the small wooden crate. A swastika was stamped on the lid.

"It's nailed shut," Quinten said. "But I have a car kit that might have something in it. Be right back."

He returned a minute later with a hammer and put it under the lip of the crate's lid. Pieces of rotten wood flaked away. The rusty nails squealed in protest but finally came loose.

Together, Quinten and Nicky lifted the lid and peered inside.

Several piles of cotton bags leaned against one side, stamped with the symbol of the Third Reich. The bags were streaked with dirt and grime and smelled of seawater and stale dust.

Nicky reached down and pulled one out. She started to untie it but the rotten cloth fell away in her hands.

The shine of gold winked in the light from the rising moon. "Coins." She examined one. "Definitely Hitler's gold. The swastika is unmistakable."

"He must have melted down the Polish princess's gold and re-minted it. Looks like some of the other bags have silver coins. And these," Quinten lifted out a smaller silk pouch in the opposite corner, "must be the diamonds." He undid the drawstring. "Yep." He tilted it so Nicky could see inside.

"Look. There's something else," she murmured. A small wooden box, with intricate marquetry work on the lid and sides, and small, delicate gold-ball feet, was in the center of the small crate.

Quinten reached a hand out to help her carefully open the lid.

Nestled inside on a bed of plush deep blue velvet were a hand mirror, a pair of amber ear bobs set in silver with tiny diamonds, an amber necklace encrusted with diamonds, and an empty sterling silver ring box.

"The rest of the princess's dowry. We found it," Quinten murmured.

"And the jewelled mirror," Nicky whispered as she picked it up. Its silvery back, carved with a delicate pattern of flowers and leaves, inset with sapphires and pink diamonds, winked in the pale moonlight.

Quinten peered over her shoulder as Nicky turned it over. She could see both their reflections in the antique surface.

She met his gaze in the mirror. And in that second, she knew the secret of lasting love in her heart that she'd been withholding from herself.

Internal confidence, not external confirmation. She could be confident to let love in again, could allow herself to be known fully. She didn't need to have someone tell her everything on their mind; she could simply have confidence within herself that they cared. Quinten had inadvertently given her that gift, in all of this. She felt a glow, a stirring in her heart.

AS QUINTEN LOOKED into Nicky's eyes in the mirror while the moonlight bathed their shared reflection, he felt a deep knowingness rise up within him.

He didn't need to believe his fears anymore. That was just the fear trying to control what he did and didn't do, what he did and didn't say. Which just crowded out his own happiness.

He was done with all this hiding. He was ready to step out into the light of his true feelings, his heart's voice, his own pure, real emotions...

He could be vulnerable. He could speak his truth. That was the secret of lasting love. His fingers curled and uncurled. He swallowed.

He should've known—should've acted on that long ago, with Nicky, when it wasn't too late. But maybe it wasn't?

The soft whoosh of waves and the whisper of the breeze were the only other sounds besides their breathing.

Suddenly, Quinten's phone blared. He startled and fumbled with it as he pulled it out.

His lawyer? He took a breath, cleared his throat, and answered the call.

"So Quinten," his lawyer said, "you filed the initial bankruptcy motion with me."

"...Yes."

"Now, I've been familiarizing myself with what Elliot's demanding. And I've done some checking. It looks as if there might be a way to rectify things...if you act fast."

Quinten's heartbeat sped up.

"Now, since your grandmother's health was in decline and that had negatively impacted the business, along with the bookkeeping associated with the business, which was also affected by her poor health, there may be an opportunity to look at filing the necessary paperwork with the courts for something called a hardship discharge."

"Okay," Quinten said. "What does that mean?"

"Basically, if granted by the court, it can allow you to have the bankruptcy terms reduced or relieved entirely."

"Wow, that's great. What do I have to do?"

"Well, that's the more complicated part. It would help if you had found the will."

Quinten winced. His lawyer went on.

"Since Elliot's offering to take over the business, thus showing your debtors that they would get their debts repaid, it might be a bit more challenging. But, you still have a chance. You need to show the court official working on your case that you can't pay the debts. But it needs to be due to something outside your control, like job loss. In your case specifically, that situation would be the ongoing medical bills from your grandmother's illness and her time in the specialized care home that provincial health didn't cover."

Quinten exhaled a shaky breath.

"I hope you've kept good documentation about that," his lawyer added. "Because you'll need the medical bills and profit and loss statements to support this filing."

"I've kept everything."

"Good. I'll be in touch with Elliot and then go ahead and start on the paperwork. You'll need to come down to the office to meet with me."

"Okay. Thank you so much."

"You're welcome."

Quinten ended the call and Nicky threw him a sidelong glance. "Good news?"

He exhaled. "My lawyer's figuring out how I might not have to sell to Elliot. And how I might not have to file for bankruptcy."

"That's great." Nicky put a hand on his arm. His heart flipped.

"What about your situation with the article?" Quinten asked.

"Well," Nicky said, "I can't publish it anywhere. But that's actually a good thing because I really want to tell your grandmother's story in depth. And to do that, I realized, it needs to be longer than just some article—"

Her phone buzzed. She jumped. The notification said she'd gotten a message from Shutterstock. She pulled up the message and as she read it, she laughed. "Wow."

"What is it?"

"I uploaded some photos last Tuesday onto Shutterstock. They've gotten enough combined royalties now to cover this month's rent."

"What a relief, eh?" Quinten said.

"Definitely." She fiddled with a strand of her hair and met Quinten's gaze. "I've gotten so much good background information while I've been here on the island..." She paused, "...that I've decided to stay here for awhile and write a book about Viv and her life and Andrzej and the treasure." She grinned at Quinten.

"That's great." Quinten's heart jumped. She was staying. He put his hand over hers and squeezed. "I'm sure your book will be filled with some amazing history."

"Thanks!" Nicky laughed and Quinten's heart leapt again at the sound. He leaned closer to her. "Nicky, I—"

"Speaking of history...I almost forgot."

She pulled a mangled piece of paper out of her purse. "I meant to give you this earlier but in all the excitement I, uh, forgot about it."

"What's this?" He looked her with raised brows.

She pointed to the page.

Quinten unfolded it.

Most of the writing had faded away, and the ink had blurred. But the last few paragraphs of the letter were still legible.

I know you're not supposed to have favorites. But Quinten is my favorite grandson. I'm so proud of him. And so proud of having a hand in raising Quinten to be the fine young man he's become. That's why I know that when I pass on, there's no one else but Quinten who I want the business to go to.

Love,

Viv

Quinten wiped at the corner of his eyes with his thumb. "Thank you, Nicky."

Nicky placed a hand on his arm. "You're welcome. Mrs. MacPhail cornered me in the chocolate shop and wanted me to give it to you because she couldn't find you."

Quinten chuckled and shook his head. "Oh, P.E.I."

But his expression turned serious as he looked at the treasure. "We'll have to contact the appropriate organizations so we can make sure the dowry, the gold, and the diamonds are given back to the correct people in retribution for the war crimes of Hitler and the Nazi regime."

"It wasn't Hitler's gold or diamonds in the first place," Nicky murmured. "That was all part of the dowry, originally. And the ring. It's time for it to be returned to Poland. Viv and Andrzej went through so much."

"They knew it was worth it, though. They had to. Why else would he take on such a dangerous task unless he had a personal reason?"

"You're right." Nicky caught her breath. "Viv even said in one of the entries, *I will do what is in my power to help him.* After Andrzej died, Viv must have decided to write that riddle with the hope that someday, somehow, the treasure had the chance of being found and returned to its rightful owners."

"And now it will be." Quinten said softly. "She must've decided not to look for it herself, because in that diary entry I found in the cookbook, she said she had chosen to put that part of her life aside to raise her son."

Nicky slid the ring off her finger and placed it in the sterling silver ring box. "I think that's everything in here, then," she said, as she looked again at the crate.

"Nope, nothing else—wait. What's this?" Quinten leaned forward to examine the spot where the bags had sat for three-quarters of a century.

He pulled out a brittle, yellowed piece of tissue-thin airmail paper that had been wedged between two slats and carefully opened it.

August 29, 1942

Dearest Viv,

You know Fritz? Remember, you said, when I told you that story about him and the champagne cask, that his sense of humor was 'wild!' if I quote you correctly.

He had joined the Nazi Party early and attended their rallies often. He was an old friend of the family, so he knew about the mirror. But I'm afraid it's gone missing.

Our house had been broken into at the beginning of all of this—apparently Fritz let slip about my Polish ancestry, so the higher-

ups in the Nazi Party thought it best to liberate objects d'art and make several, shall we say, inquires. Starting with my family home.

I tried to get back there—I'm fearful for my family—what their fate may be, as well as that of the mirror. I have not heard from anyone in months and we're forbidden from trying to contact them.

Once I find out what has happened, I will get it back. They think they would get away with it. They will not. They cannot.

All my love,

—A

"They haven't gotten away with it," Nicky said quietly.

"No, they haven't," Quinten agreed.

"So how does a letter about the missing mirror end up in a crate that contains the missing mirror?" Nicky asked.

"Good question. We might never know," Quinten replied. "Maybe he wrote it and intended to mail it but didn't get the chance, and figured that if Viv found the treasure, she'd also find the letter."

"I think that's as good as an explanation as we're going to get."

As she put down the letter and looked

up at Quinten, he caught his breath. Her eyes shone in the moonlight as she gazed at him.

For a long moment, neither of them spoke.

"I feel the same way," Quinten finally whispered in response to the look in her eyes. He reached up and stroked a hand down her cheek. He felt his heart beat in his chest when he placed his hand on top of hers and closed his eyes, savoring the sensation.

He opened his eyes, leaned forward, and tucked a strand of hair behind her ear. "I've been suppressing my feelings for you, Nicky," he whispered. "I'm sorry it took me this long to realize that. To voice them aloud."

She swallowed back tears. "And I was so afraid...I didn't have the internal confidence...which made me hold back with you. I didn't want to fully let you in because I thought you were just like my ex. I didn't feel secure in his love for me, so I never let him in all the way. He was never clear. He never came out and told me what he thought and felt about me, about us. And so I thought I had to protect myself from you, too."

"I'm sorry if that's what you thought."

He brushed away her tears with his thumb. "I'd been running away. Putting myself in the way of developing a relationship with you because I was afraid I'd be rejected. Afraid to be seen, afraid to feel and act on the truth in my heart."

"You put yourself through that?" Nicky's breath hitched.

"It's okay," he whispered, "it's okay." He slid his arms around her waist. "How's this for being clear? I'm falling in love with you."

"I'm falling in love with you, too," she whispered, as she slid her arms around his neck.

His heart swooped and he knew, in that moment, that truly, this was real love.

"At last," she whispered, echoing his thoughts as his lips brushed hers, "it's true love."

Don't miss Book 1 and Book 2 of the
Prince Edward Island Love Letters &
Legends trilogy!

Ruby & Nathan's
story

Maggie & Zak's
story

FOR A LIMITED TIME
GET YOUR FREE SWEET ROMANCE HERE!

Get your free copy of the sweet romance *Beside A Moonlit Shore*. Normally, it's $2.99, but this GIFT is yours FREE when you sign up to hear from author Jessica Eissfeldt.

When you sign up, not only will you get this FREE GIFT, but you'll also receive sneak peaks of Jessica's upcoming stories, have the opportunity to win prizes, get exclusive subscriber-only content...and more!

After her sea captain husband dies, schoolteacher Anna Hampton wonders if she'll find the courage to love again...beside a moonlit shore.

Go here to get started:
www.jessicaeissfeldt.com/yourfreegift

FOR A LIMITED TIME

Read on for an excerpt from the first book in Jessica Eissfeldt's Prince Edward Island Love Letters & Legends series.

This Time It's Forever

Available NOW at your favourite online retailer or at your local bookstore!

Chapter One

R UBY ZALONSKI GLANCED out the wide windows at the rain-soaked Simmons College campus lawn. The black umbrellas most students carried intermingled with the occasional pink polka-dot or sunny yellow one, in the heart of downtown Boston's Fenway neighborhood.

Gray clouds scuttled across the August sky. The fat raindrops plopped against the windowpanes of LeFavour Hall, which housed the library at Simmons College.

Ruby sat in an overstuffed chair in the archives room of the library. She took a deep breath and inhaled the cozy and familiar scent of musty paper and waxed hardwood floors. A smile flitted across her face as her eyelids fluttered closed.

For a second, she imagined herself ten years in the future: a nice tenure-track archival position here at Simmons in the library and information science department, living in a historic brownstone, and married to a nice man. She sighed. Then maybe she'd finally feel like she belonged here? Had a real *home*?

She fiddled with the antique heart-shaped locket she wore around her neck.

Never mind that she'd lived in Boston all her life. So it *was* her real home. She let the sterling silver necklace slide through her fingers. But this place, this city, just didn't feel like that.

She didn't quite know why. But she'd always had this vague sense of restlessness. As if she belonged somewhere else. Should *be* somewhere else.

She tapped an unpolished fingernail against her chin as she looked down at the antique love letter fragment. Its edges were torn and what looked like smudges of dirt and gunpowder obscured the neat, curving script.

Though the iron gall ink had faded to a reddish brown, the flourishes of the t's, dots of the i's and flowing lines of the f's remained strong. Defiant.

She broke into a grin.

Even...revolutionary.

Boston   2 Dec. 1775

My darling Edwina.

In the fortnight since I was taken from you, I can but think only of the August night we met, when such horrors of war were furthest from our minds, and I daresay, our hearts, as well.

Though I must confess, I did not think of you as attentive to my affec-tions when I was greeted by dawn gleaming off the blade of your cutlass that November morn. How the com-pass of the heart points in new directions when time and distance have no little significance.

News in Charlotte Town travels at speed, especially among those who frequent Cross Keys Tavern, myself among them. I know you can imagine my state of appal when I, one week prior, learned of your Situation. That General Washington and his Rebel-lious Colonies should treat Callbeck and Wright with such deference and kindness, but leave you to your fate in the hands of those Loyal to the Crown, I do not conceive.

I fear that I may never again see your sweet face—

Ruby sighed. It was too bad Dr. O'Neil hadn't had the other half of the letter fragment like she'd hoped he would. But this couldn't be a dead end. It just couldn't. Her dissertation was riding on Revolutionary War love letters like this one.

Where was the other half of this letter? What did the rest of it say? And, most of all, *who* was writing to Edwina?

Ruby's eyes traced the jagged, ripped edge. Her contact at the rare books store on Cambridge Avenue found this fragment in an old family bible they'd had on display.

Just then, the library clock tower gonged the hour. She scrambled to her feet. How had it gotten to be 5 p.m. already?

She had to hurry or she'd be late for that first date tonight.

After she gathered the rest of the notes she needed, Ruby made her way out of the library and back across the green expanse of lawn to the library sciences department.

She wove her way through the maze of graduate and doctoral students, dropped backpacks and makeshift desks before she finally reached her own desk, shoved into a tiny alcove under the eaves, to transcribe what she'd found.

She lifted the lid of her old, somewhat glitchy silver Macbook. Its edges bristled with bright pink, blue and yellow sticky notes to herself. The ding of an incoming email made her pause.

To. ruby.zalonski@simmons.edu
Sent: Monday, August 12

A note to all current staff and students. The position of special collections & archival librarian, payband 12, has been posted as of this email, with the retirement of long-time employee Marianne Schwartz, who has been with us for 30 years.

There will be a retirement party on Tuesday afternoon for her. So don't forget to stop by the staff lounge for some cake and coffee, and a chance to find out what Marianne will be doing with her retirement!

The position was finally opening up? A little thrill ran through Ruby. She opened up a new outgoing message and attached her resume and cover letter, then hit send. She grinned.

Now, she had to finish transcribing her notes.

She readjusted the No. 2 pencil that secured her messy brunette bun and pushed her cat-eye tortoiseshell glasses further up on her nose. Her fingers stilled on the keyboard as her mind strayed back to the letter fragment.

The bold, sweeping handwriting formed in her mind's eye. No one wrote like that these days.

The way the quill pen had formed each word with a hint of a flourish.

She found herself holding her breath as she recalled the writer's firm belief in Edwina's love. The tender words...

For a second she wished whoever it was had been addressing her. Because she'd never find a love that grand. That sweeping. That, well, legendary...

"Ruby? How's it going?"

She glanced over her shoulder. Dr. Jill Burton, the department head—and Ruby's academic advisor for her doctoral dissertation *In Love & War: A Discourse on Women's Love Letters During The American Revolution*—leaned into the half-open doorway. Dr. Burton crossed one lime-green ballet flat over the other.

"Pretty good, Dr. Burton. Did you know that the special collections position just opened up?" Ruby shuffled the pages of notes on her desk before looking back up at the older woman.

Dr. Burton nodded. "Saw that a minute ago—was about to tell you."

"I just applied." Ruby blurted. "I know I haven't completed my Ph.D. yet. But if I could be considered for that job, it would be a dream come true." She grinned.

The older woman smiled. "While I'm all in favor of your enthusiasm, you do know that a Ph.D. is one of the requirements? They do consider non-Ph.D.'s at a university of this size. But it's rare that someone without a Ph.D.—even someone like you who's almost completed her doctorate—would be chosen. Besides that, competition will be fierce. There hasn't been an opening like this in 30 years."

"I know." Ruby said, and pushed up her glasses.

Dr. Burton smiled again. "Well, if I hear anything about when they want to start interviewing, I'll definitely keep you in the loop. So how's everything coming? Your dissertation is in committee review right now. Which means your defense date is coming up pretty fast. Early next month."

"If I could find more of Edwina's letters, it would definitely support my main theory about women's love letters in the

American Revolution as a vital means of communication and self-expression." She paused. "I'm not prone to conspiracy theories, but whoever was writing to her, I think there was something going on...I know that it doesn't exactly have a direct connection to my original love letter research, but it might be an interesting side note or sub-theory to work in."

"Just make sure there's enough money left in your research grant to go ahead with it. They won't be giving out more funds any time soon." Dr. Burton cocked her head. She tapped a French-tipped fingernail against her chin, a sparkle in her eye. "But you're right—that sounds pretty interesting. It certainly wouldn't hurt to explore that angle. It might even add new evidence you could work into your defense. Make it stand apart."

Ruby laughed. "Thanks! So, what's the latest on those papers of Dr. O'Neil's?"

"It's too bad about his passing away so suddenly." Dr. Burton shook her head. "I just got back from a meeting about the late professor." The older woman crossed her arms, and a frown formed between her perfectly plucked brows. "I don't know how it happened in this economic climate—especially with so much money being re-directed to the sports program."

"But," Dr. Burton continued, "the university lawyers have all been consulted, and the paperwork's all drawn up, so it's been given the go-ahead. Which means our department will finally be able to receive his donated papers. Now we just need someone to go up and catalog them."

Wait a minute. A smile spread across Ruby's lips. Special collections..."You need someone to catalog Dr. O'Neil's papers—why not me?" Ruby's heart thudded. "After all, I initiated contact with Dr. O'Neil in the first place—eight months ago—asking him about that love letter fragment to Edwina."

If she cataloged his papers, then it'd be apparent to all of them here on campus that she was the ideal candidate for that special collections position, Ph.D. or no Ph.D.

"He had so many historical documents," Ruby added. "If I went up there, maybe I could find other love letters written by and to, Edwina, that would help my overall research and add to my supporting documents."

And it would be the perfect opportunity to distinguish herself from the other candidates. She could prove she'd gone above and beyond. Acquired and cataloged this special cache of documents. It'd be easy enough to organize the professor's papers, surely.

"Well, Ruby, you have a good point. All right, the cataloging job's yours. But just remember, you need to be back here by next Thursday so you can prep for your doctoral defense."

"Right," Ruby said. "I'm sure the cataloging won't take long."

Read on for an excerpt from the first sweet historical romance book in Jessica Eissfeldt's Sweethearts & Jazz Nights series, set in 1940s San Francisco.

Dialing Dreams

Available NOW at your favourite online retailer sold separately or at your local bookstore as part of the Sweethearts & Jazz Nights series boxed set!

Chapter One

ELINDA THOMPSON COULDN'T stand one more moment of this. What was she doing here anyway, sitting at a switchboard at midnight, humming jazz melodies to herself? Melodies that she'd practiced through all four years of high school vocal classes. And then sang for hours more in the kitchen at home, with her heart full of hope and dreams. So shouldn't she be enchanting audiences and singing songs, not answering calls and connecting wires?

But the sound of her father's hoarse cough echoed through her mind and tugged at her conscience. She would not abandon him. She straightened up. She was all he had. She might not want to work as a telephone operator at the Hotel Whitcomb but she could still choose how she acted about it. She would do it—for him. Taking comfort in that, she began the jazz tune again. But it faded from her lips when a call came in.

"Operator. How may I transfer your call?" She cringed as a male voice slurred a greeting.

"No...no tra-transfer. Please, can we just...talk?"

Not only drunk, he's desperate, she thought. Yet his velvety baritone intrigued Belinda in spite of herself. "I'm sorry, sir. You have to tell me who you want to connect to."

"Room five oh...five. Yeah, that's it."

Belinda studied the tips of her polished nails. "One moment, please, while I—"

"No, no, no. No. No...need. I don't...*actually* want to talk to her."

"Sir, who *do* you want to be connected to?"

"There isn't a number. I want...to talk to someone like you."

"I need to connect you. Or I really can't continue this conversation."

"Operator, you sound like a nice girl, and I...need to talk to a nice girl. Claire wasn't—"

A little unnerved, she spoke over him. "That's not my job."

"All right. All right. I...won't bother...you."

The line went dead.

Belinda frowned then shrugged. She glanced at the clock. Time to go. She collected her purse and slid on her trench coat before cinching its belt. She pinned her hat in place and pulled on her gloves before locking up the tiny switchboard office on the hotel's main floor. With a sigh of relief, she walked through the marble-floored lobby, waved a goodbye to the doorman and headed up Market Street, her seven-cent fare in hand. The cable car's rumble and screech told her she'd arrived just in time to jump onto the Powell-Hyde line and head for home.

A LIGHT DRIZZLE spattered the phone booth the following Friday night as Nick Hart ducked into it on impulse. Couldn't sleep anyway. And a walk usually cleared his head. He stared out into the darkness enshrouding the Bay Area as the lights of San Francisco winked back at him, as they did every evening across from his place on the waterfront.

Not so long ago, things were going great. His third record was selling well, and he'd gotten his polished shoes onto the crooner stage at last. But this whole thing with Claire had begun to fall apart. He'd put his soul on hold for her. Showed what a fool will do for love. He frowned and shook off the raindrops that clung to his fedora, placed it back on his head, and tugged the brim lower.

Eying the sleek black handset, he ran a finger along it as he pondered last week's drunken call to the Hotel Whitcomb. Was he that desperate that he'd actually tried to get sympathy from the operator? Even though she'd been annoyed with him—he hadn't been too drunk to remember that— he couldn't quite forget her satiny voice.

Read on for an excerpt from the first sweet
historical romance book in Jessica
Eissfeldt's Love By Moonlight series.

Beneath A Venetian Moon

*Available NOW at your favourite online
retailer sold separately or at your local
bookstore as part of the Love By Moonlight
series boxed set!*

Chapter One

HE MOONLIGHT SLIPPED through the partially open window as Alessandra Velocchi smoothed her amethyst gown. If only her own escape could be so easy. But the binding ties of duty wound around her more tightly than the velvet-trimmed silver mask she wore as she stepped out of her chamber, down the stairs, and out into the waiting gondola.

She gasped as the chill waters of the Venetian canal splashed at her hem like greedy fingers trying to reclaim their prize. She shuddered, putting the childhood near-drowning experience from her mind, focusing firmly on the festivities ahead at the Doge's birthday celebration.

"Does the Contessa have an escort?" The doorman addressed Alessandra at the palace entrance.

Lifting her chin, she shook her head. "Tonight, I am a free woman." She felt her heart swell with gladness. No father to watch her, no boring escort to hinder her. Pure, clear freedom. Just the way she liked it.

Candlelight sparkled off cut crystal chandeliers as she took a goblet of wine from a side table. Winding her way amongst mingling revelers, she spotted familiar faces all around. Laughter and accented voices drifted past her as the pull of duty pushed her to the front of the ballroom where the Doge stood.

As she approached, the Doge's ministers bowed, acknowledging her as the daughter of Venice's most powerful palace advisor.

"Before the Doge begins his own speech," stated one of the officials, "he expects to hear the address your father entrusted you with." He nodded toward Alessandra. "You have prepared?"

"Of course." As she brought her goblet to her lips to calm her nerves, a sudden shadow flickered in her peripheral vision. She glanced sideways. Now nothing. Closing her eyes for a brief second to gather her thoughts, she savored the drink's heady sweetness.

Alessandra took another sip of wine, fiddling with the stem of the goblet, watching the carved facets glimmer in the light. And again, the shadow flickered in her vision, this time closer.

She frowned. Looked around. Returned her attention to the Doge, waiting for him to give her the nod. But just then, the shadow appeared again – this time taking on a form – that of a man. With a black silk mask tied around his glossy dark hair and a velvet doublet trimmed in the same midnight shade.

This time, she openly stared at him. Watched while his furtive glances around the room displayed fear. Watched while his fluid movements wound him between guests. Watched while his steps led him closer and closer to her.

She forgot all about her staid speech as she searched the planes of his face. He was not part of the court. Or the Doge's administration. Or even a member of the Venetian aristocratic circles she'd known all her life. Though he certainly was attractive. And certainly not a boring escort. Her lips curved into a smile.

She continued to admire him, noticing that by now he stood only a few paces from her. But protocol and privilege forced her to turn away, forced her to acknowledge the Doge, who now beckoned to her.

She raised her chin and straightened her spine, pivoting to face the assemblage. As the guests' final murmurs died away, she inhaled, about to speak.

But in that brief hesitation, the masked man leapt toward her. As she startled, stepping back, her name tumbled from his lips. "Contessa Velocchi."

His eyes held hers even as he collapsed at her feet, gasping, his hand pressed to his side. And that's when she saw it. Blood. Seeping crimson onto the polished parquet floor.

She knelt, one look into that sea-green gaze telling her she had nothing to fear. Her heart filled with concern at his wound and she pulled out a handkerchief, leaning forward.

His breath warm in her ear, he whispered low, frantic. "Please...I beg of you...help me. They...want me dead."

Author's Note

I've always loved the movie *National Treasure* and the 1940s. So when I found out about U-boats off the shores of Prince Edward Island during the Second World War, I knew I had the perfect piece of history to write the third and final book in the Prince Edward Island Love Letters & Legends trilogy.

When I wrote this novel, I wanted to be as accurate as possible. However, there were some instances where, because of the real historical events' timelines, that wasn't possible.

So I took artistic license to modify some dates, timelines, historical events and such to fit into this plot.

According to Leo Marks' book *Between Silk and Cyanide,* quite a lot of the SOE's codes department records and files were either destroyed after the war or were non-existent in the first place.

As such, it was a bit tricky to track down information about the codes department as so much of the material written about the SOE focuses on the agents in the field.

But with some dogged persistence, I chased down leads. Thanks to the amazing kindness and help of those who I've mentioned on the acknowledgments page, I located several files for a few women who worked in the codes department of the SOE.

I used some of the documentation in those real-life files as a loose guideline for the forms within Vivian's and Andrzej's SOE files that appear in this novel, as I modified some things and omitted others. Also, no Form C.R.2., Form X or Form 6 b) exist—those are all purely a productive of my imagination.

For the sake of the plot, I have given Andrzej dual citizenship—both German and Polish—though I do not know if that was actually possible during World War II.

According to Steven Kippax, the cipher girls were assigned country sections, not specific agents. But, for the sake of this novel's plot, I gave Vivian specific agents who she worked with.

As for the codes themselves, well, I'm

no math whiz. But in order to have Nicky and Quinten decipher Andrzej's secret message, I actually had to reverse engineer the process.

I enciphered it, then worked backwards to figure out how the cipher girls would've deciphered it. I've done everything by hand, as Nicky did in the novel, and, indeed, as the women at SOE would've done, too. So if there are any transposition errors or calculation mistakes, they are entirely my own! (I used the internet liberally to piece together an estimation of how it would've been done, as to my knowledge, Leo Marks in his memoir does not explain the entire process step by step.)

Also in my research, I was not able to discern how the indicator groups for decryption of the agents' messages were, well, indicated, to the person deciphering the message. So I have made my best guesstimation as to how it might have been done.

For the facts I've chosen to use in this novel about the minutiae of the SOE sending and receiving wireless messages to London, I discovered slight differences in my research. In those instances of slight variation, I have chosen the version of details that work best with the plot of this novel.

In addition, the vast majority of the SOE files at the National Archives have not, as of this printing, been digitized. However, for the sake of a streamlined plot, I've made them digital. I've also made some modifications to the National Archives' fee structure for document requests, for the sake of this novel's plot.

The SOE did not begin operations out of the Baker Street location until later in 1940, but in order to fit into this novel's plot timeline of the U-boats around PEI, that date needed to be adjusted.

The legalities described in this novel, while within the (loose) realm of plausibility, aren't considered to be probable. I took liberties with legal realities in order to suit the plot.

In that vein, a hardship discharge for bankruptcy is U.S. law and actually not available as an option for bankruptcy in Canada. However, given Quinten's circumstances, I felt that this U.S.-based solution fit best with that part of the plot. So I have chosen to take artistic license, and give Quinten this option to solve his financial issues by utilizing the hardship discharge.

The U-262's POW rescue attempt is fact. (Of course, Hitler's gold and diamonds aboard that submarine are purely the products of my imagination.)

The Charlottetown's *Guardian* newspaper article I used for research and reference does not specify exactly where in the North Cape area the German U-boat was, so in this novel, the location that the sailor recounts is purely a product of my imagination.

During World War II, German U-boats were spotted in multiple locations around P.E.I. But for the sake of this story, I made the same sub appear on both the north and south sides of the island. That probably wouldn't have been the case in real life, as I imagine the Germans wouldn't have wanted to venture any farther into enemy territory than they had to.

All the shops and restaurants mentioned in this book are real—aside from Leard's Piano Tuning & Restoration. While the house that I've borrowed for Quinten's shop location is real, it is no longer occupied. Island Chocolates is a real chocolate factory and shop in Victoria, P.E.I. (And the chocolate waffles there are definitely delicious! If you ever have a chance, try them.) However, they are only available on Sundays. But, again for the sake of the plot, I've made them available other days.

And yes, the piece of sheet music, "Marsch Impromptu" really does exist. The encoded "lyrics" that Nicky and Quinten solve on that music score are inspired by the fact that real phrases do appear on that piece of sheet music. There are even some people who say the piece does contain clues to the location of a secret cache of Hitler's gold and diamonds.

I first learned about the supposed treasure from the TV show *Expedition Unknown* in an episode called *Deciphering the Last Nazi Code*. My imagination took off after I saw that episode, as I knew that was exactly the treasure hunt angle I could draw inspiration from. I already knew that U-boats had visited the shores of P.E.I. during WWII, so a secret stash of HItler's gold and diamonds somewhere on the island seemed a perfect fit!

And if you happen to find yourself on some sandy stretch of beach on Prince Edward Island, keep your eyes open—who knows what treasures may be beneath your feet...

Acknowledgments

The Special Operations Executive—to all the men and women of the SOE who served their country, and the free world, in so many capacities. Thank you.

The residents of Victoria—everyone's kindness and caring meant a lot, so thank you. I hope that this book, in some small way, honors that.

Dr. Steven Kippax—SOE Society, who very kindly answered my questions and provided me with files of the SOE's "cipher girls," as he called them.

Dr David Abrutat—GCHQ Departmental Historian, who helped point me in the right direction for answers to my historical questions.

Lester Cowden IV—who very kindly took time out of his busy schedule to read through and provide feedback on the legal scenes in the book.

Sabrina Volman—awesome beta reader, who read the story in manuscript form and provided excellent observations that only made this book better.

Shannon Page—line editor, who did a great job with copy editing this book.

Arnetta Jackson—proofreader, whose excellent attention to detail gave this book a final polish.

Jane Dixon Smith—cover designer, who designed the lovely cover on this book.

All the other people, including Lynn Hodgson, who helped me along the way with my research and questions about cipher girls and World War II history. Thank you so much.

Bibliography

Binney, Marcus, *The Women Who Lived For Danger: the agents of the Special Operations Executive* (New York, William Morrow, 2002)

MacKay, Mary. "A Tale of Two Submarines." *The Guardian*, May 5, 2001.

Marks, Leo. *Between Silk and Cyanide: A Codemaker's War 1941-1945* (New York, The Free Press, 1998)

Mundy, Liza. *Code Girls: The Untold Story of the American Women Codebreakers of World War II* (New York, Hachette Books, 2018)

Riols, Noreen. *The Secret Ministry of Ag. & Fish: My Life in Churchill's School for Spies* (London, MacMillian, 2013)